THE HUXIAN FOX

ALSO BY NIKKI BROOKE

Plagued Lands

THE HUXIAN FOX

NIKKI BROOKE

CROW
KNIGHT

CROW
KNIGHT

Published by Crow Knight Film and Publishing Realm
Melbourne, Australia

Second Edition

Copyright © 2025 by Nikki Brooke

ISBN for paperback: 978-1-7635881-2-7
ISBN for ebook: 978-1-7635881-3-4

Cover design and illustration by Matthew Lin: www.matthewlin.com.au

For my sister,
who I would choose as family if she wasn't already.

Chapter 1

Fan

"Don't move ya filthy, cheatin', shinver-stealin', polyps-crusted butt." The dirt grinder points his lava gun at my forehead, and I freeze. "Put ya hands up, girl."

I stare down the large barrel of the weapon and wonder if it's the cheating or the stealing he's most upset with. Surely one small case of shinver isn't worth the trouble, but the woman? She's gorgeous and way out of his league, so it's easy to see why Gussart's angry. He probably didn't even realize she was into girls like me—but seriously, how could she resist?

"Which is it, Gussart?" I ask. "Don't move or put my hands up?"

"Don't mess with me, Sung. I'm not in the mood for ya games. Put ya hands up."

I slowly raise my hands.

Gussart's bald head has turned red, like it's about to explode.

The two goons who had been helping me unload the last cases of shinver take their boss's cue and approach me, flexing their muscles and cracking their knuckles like it makes them look tougher.

It does.

Gussart's young wife stands by the door of the warehouse, keeping several yards between her and potential danger. Her eyes are wide with fear as she wrings her hands; I'm not sure if she's concerned for me or for herself.

"Oh, come on, Gussart. It was just one little kiss. She still loves you."

"Kiss?" He spins to his wife, who hangs her head, unable to hide the truth.

Oh, fiery balls.

Gussart whips back to me, teeth bared. His eyes are bloodshot, the little veins in his eyeballs ready to burst. I run my hand through my short hair and shrug. He doesn't wait for his men to do his dirty work. He leaps over a crate, charging like a bull.

I duck, and he goes sailing right over my head.

Gussart sprawls on the ground behind me, scrambling to get to his feet. As he stands, his two henchmen close in from behind.

"Come on, guys, we can work something out." I show them my open hands, trying to placate them, but they continue their approach.

I can't stick around any longer. I dart to the left, around a chest, and over another. Gussart's large warehouse is filled with hundreds of boxes, crates, barrels, and packages. Not all of them contain drugs; plenty will be filled with weapons, ammunition, and other contraband. I'm grateful the place is full because it gives me loads of stuff to hide behind. My nimble feet take me across the room. All the while, I keep my head low, listening to the fools as they crash along behind.

As I sprint around a large wooden box, a hand makes a grab for me.

"Whoa." I lurch out of the way and jump on top of the nearest crate.

They're right on my tail, rushing through the warehouse, shoving boxes out of the way to get to me.

I dance along the tops of crates, climbing higher and farther away from my pursuers. Stopping on top of a stack of three, I take a breath and look down at the scene below.

The warehouse is a disaster of toppled containers. Some are broken, spilling cigars and bottles of alcohol onto the ground, but most of the mess is white shinver powder.

My assailants spot me and try to climb up. The first crate breaks under their weight, and a cloud of shinver bursts into the air, covering them as they fall in a heap. I try to suppress a smile at the sight of their white-powdered faces. One of them sneezes.

Lucky bastards. That stuff should get them happy.

They stumble to their feet, unholster their weapons, and aim their lava guns right at me.

I raise my hands again. "Come on, I thought we were friends."

Gussart stares up at me, his chest heaving, his skin sizzling with so much anger I can literally see steam rising off it. He looks so stupid with his thick neck and bald head still bright red. He thinks he's tough with all his tats running down his bulging arms, but he's just another fool that can't satisfy his lady. He does have a big gun, though.

"Gussart, let's discuss this like two business partners."

"Ya no partner of mine," he huffs. "No, Sung. This is the end of the road for ya. No one steals from me."

"Don't be so overdramatic. It was just one little case of shinver." I shrug. "I'll give it back."

"I can't trust ya, Sung. And that's a problem for me."

I huff.

"Ya've been foolin' around with my wife—"

"It was only one kiss."

"—and I know it's not just one case a shinver, Sung."

"It is, I swear. Count them."

"One case from this load, but ya've done this before."

Busted. How long has he known?

"Do ya think I'm stupid, Sung?"

I shrug again, which is exactly the wrong thing to do.

"Shoot her." Gussart's face turns so bright it's glowing. "Shoot that smug, redrynch dung smile off her face. NOW!"

My eyes widen. He's seriously going to kill me. I jump from my perch onto the next crate, dodging blasts from their weapons.

I swing from a beam, over more boxes, and sail through the air. Vibrations course up my legs as I land, but I keep on running.

The goons are no match for me. I'm as fast as a fox. I have them chasing me around the room without a chance in hell that they'll catch me. I laugh as they lumber behind.

I head for the exit, turn a corner, and—

Bam! I run smack into Gussart, who is blocking the only way out.

He doesn't hesitate.

He lifts me by my throat, slamming me up against the wall. His fingers press painfully into my neck, and I struggle to breathe, feet dangling.

"Gussart, come on, don't do anything you'll regret." I squeeze the words out.

"The only thing I'll regret is ever trustin' Fan Sung," Gussart growls and presses harder.

I squeak and gurgle. No more words escape. I grasp at his hands. Scratching. But he's too strong. My lungs burn.

I stare wide-eyed into Gussart's dark and determined glare. He's really going to kill me over a little kiss and some shinver.

My vision darkens. I need air.

My arms go limp, giving up the fight. But as they do, my fingers brush my duster pistol in its holster.

I don't want to kill Gussart, but this is my only hope to survive.

With my last ounce of strength, I flip the duster from the holster, hold it to Gussart's leg—

—and shoot.

Gussart shrieks and instantly lets go. I fall to the ground.

Coughing air back into my lungs, I rub my neck; it throbs, and every breath burns. My limbs shake as I pick myself back up and the oxygen starts to circulate once again.

"Ya shot me!" Gussart howls, clutching his leg.

"Yeah, but only in the leg." My voice comes out in a croak, but I still grin as I holster my duster.

His eyes grow dark again, and he reaches out with his bloody hands. I quickly step out of range. As he moves to follow, he groans in pain, and his hands promptly return to the hole in his leg.

"I'm just saying, I could have killed you. But I didn't. Drop a Y chromosome and walk it off. It's just a graze. Remember that next time we meet."

I give Gussart a casual salute and dash out of the warehouse door.

"After her!" Gussart's pained roar fades as I run past his wife, winking as I go. Her eyes go wide as she lets me pass.

The pavement outside is slick from rain, and the lights of the city reflect in the puddles. The rain has stopped, but there's still plenty of water dripping from the overpasses and skyways that weave around the grid of skyscrapers.

It's past midnight, but the streets are still crowded with people. They're out for a good time—drinking, eating, getting high on shinver, looking for love or just a shag.

Instead of washing away the scents of the streets, the wetness enhances the stench of street vendors cooking meat, alcohol spilled from drunken fingers, the sickly sweet perfume of a prostitute, and the acrid odor of human excrement.

Kep City. Such a lovely place to retire.

I sprint past it all while my pursuers lumber behind. There are more than just two of them now—Gussart has called in reinforcements.

When I skirt around a woman in six-inch heels, she stumbles and almost breaks her ankle.

"Sorry, milady," I call while I speed on, pushing past a group of men. They yell obscenities at me but are cut short when the goons crash into them, causing a bigger commotion.

My assailants disentangle themselves quickly, spot me, and take aim with their lava guns.

Oh no.

I shelter behind a street vendor serving roasted sangue nuts that smell like they've been burned.

Bam!

The cart explodes, and smoke billows around me. If the sangue nuts weren't burned before, they are now, and my cover is gone. I look up into the eyes of one of Gussart's men taking aim again.

I run.

Sliding on the slick streets, I slip as I turn a corner into a dark alley, but catch myself before I hit the ground. It's lucky because they're right behind me.

But they won't catch me. Because—right where it should be—my squito awaits, gleaming red in the night with Luchlon astride it and the motors running. It hovers a few feet above the ground.

I leap onto the back, straddling the vehicle and gripping Luchlon around the waist. He guns the engines and takes off with a roar.

"I see it didn't go too well," Luchlon calls over his shoulder.

"He accused me of fooling around with his wife and stealing shinver," I say over the roar of the engines.

"You *did* fool around with his wife and steal shinver."

"Semantics."

He chuckles as he spins the squito out of the alley and onto the street, swerving around other vehicles and pedestrians.

"They're following us," I say when I see more pursuers, one on a black squito—not as pretty as mine—and two more in a hovercar with the top down. Both of them are gaining on us.

Luchlon isn't going fast enough. He's not the skilled pilot that I am. Lava blasts shoot past our heads.

"Let me drive," I say, rising to stand on the back of the squito with one hand holding onto Luchlon's shoulder for balance. Another blast flies past my nose, and I bob my head.

"I can't stop now," Luchlon says, refusing my command.

"You don't need to."

I slide one leg over his shoulder and then the other until I'm precariously perched on his right shoulder.

"This is crazy, Fan," Luchlon complains.

The squito wobbles as he tries to keep control of it. With one foot between the squito's handles and Luchlon's crotch, I slip my other foot down the side of the bike, my bum sliding down his chest until he's forced to move back on the seat, allowing me to take hold of the handles and the pilot's position.

"See? Easy."

Ba-bash-bash!

The squito is hit from behind and jolts with a squealing judder. I glance back as a shot almost takes off my head. The guy on the black squito has caught up and is ramming us. Luchlon shoots over his shoulder, buying us a moment.

I lower my eyes, concentrating on the street ahead.

Let's see them catch us now.

I gun the engines, and the squito takes off at a speed so fast the two of us will be obliterated if we crash. But we won't. Not with me piloting.

The neon signs blur together as I speed past. Luchlon's one-handed grip tightens around my waist while he points his lava gun behind us.

Whomp! Whomp!

He lets off two shots, and a crash behind tells me he hit his mark.

Bam!

Luchlon and I duck as a shot rings out over our heads. It hits a mega-rig instead, creating a crater in the side of the hood. The motor sizzles to its death, and the truck crashes five feet to the ground. The driver jumps from the cabin, running for his life.

The rig is so big it blocks our way, and we're charging toward it at a deadly speed. I pull back on the handles, and the squito rises higher.

"Stop, Fan. We won't make it."

I don't listen. I gun the engines harder. Luchlon grips me with both hands so tightly I'm scared I'll lose my dinner.

"Feet up," I call. I feel him lift his legs just in time. The bottom of the squito clips the top of the mega-rig as it scrapes over it.

I hope that didn't damage the paintwork.

We sail above the street, but we can't stay at this height for long. The overpass is as much of a hazard as the rig was, so I lower the squito back to ground level before we lose our heads.

Bam! Bam!

Those two shots were too close for comfort; the reverberations echo in my ears. The black squito has cleared the truck and is still gaining on us. They must have some crazy spectacular mods if they can keep up with me.

Whomp!

Luchlon is shooting again, but he keeps missing. He's a good shot most of the time, but the pilot of the black squito is better at evasive maneuvers. We duck as more blasts shoot past us.

Do I have to do everything?

I reach down my leg and pull out my duster. A quick glance behind tells me where the dirt grinder is. I point, shoot, and—

Crunch! The bullet hits the black squito's motor, and it goes into a spin as it crashes to the ground.

With a flick of my wrist, I holster my duster.

That's how it's done.

The hovercar is nowhere to be seen, and I think we've got away clean.

Bam! Bam! Bam!

Where the hell is that coming from?

I look up to see a hovercar bearing down on me from the overhead street. It charges right off the overpass, the driver apparently unconcerned that the hovercar isn't designed for heights.

Gussart is at the wheel, the crazy crud dweller. He's got a dirty big hole in his leg, but instead of getting patched up, he's coming after me.

The hovercar falls fast.

All the while, Gussart is shooting at me. I take evasive action to avoid his shots. One sizzles past my ear, singeing the ends of my hair.

"Luchlon," I growl.

"I've got 'em," he shouts back.

"You'd better."

Whomp! His shot takes off the hovercar's mirror. *Whomp!* The next hits the hood.

Gussart's eyes go wide before his face disappears in the smoke swirling from the engine. His hovercar plummets. It was never designed to descend from such a height, and with the primary engine busted, there's no hope for it.

I watch the scene play out in the squito's mirrors.

Gussart stands. Just before the hovercar hits the street, he jumps free from the crash. I lose sight of him in the hustle and bustle on the street, but no matter if he lives or dies, that has gotta hurt.

I give the street ahead my full attention again. Everything seems normal. The people are still going about their business, and the havoc Gussart and I caused hasn't impacted the traffic ahead. It should put my mind at ease, but it doesn't. There should be sirens, flashing lights, maybe even a blockade. But there's none of that.

"It seems a bit quiet," Luchlon says, echoing my thoughts.

"Yeah," I say. "Where are the royal guards?"

Chapter 2

Eshan'ya

THE PALACE IS IN chaos. Royal guards charge down the corridors—they look frightened but ready to do their duty.

I shelter behind pillars, statues, curtains, doors, potted plants—anything—hiding whenever I hear them marching toward me. They're too focused on their mission of protecting the palace and the king to notice me.

I'm glad for the distraction. Hopefully, they won't notice me missing for some time.

Peeking around the curve of a massive vase, I watch the backs of five royal guards as they hurry out of the palace. My heart beats rapidly, but I'm determined to get out of here. I'm no longer safe. None of us are.

If they find me, if they realize I'm escaping the palace, the royal guards won't hesitate. They'll take me back. They'll restrain me. And I'll be doomed.

Once the guards have disappeared outside, I follow them. My delicate heels aren't the stealthiest footwear, but they're all I have, and I'm going to need something to protect my feet once I reach the city streets. I keep on my toes as much as possible, grateful for all the dance lessons that trained me to stay light on my feet and the plush red carpets that stifle my footsteps.

The long halls I creep through are bedecked in a soft wall fabric gilded with gold stitching on fields of dark red that matches the carpet. I reach the exit the guards used. Heavy wooden doors—carved with flowers and depictions of battles—hang open, and I peer around the doorframe into the rainy night. The grounds should be dark at this time of night, but instead, the stately gardens are lit up by fire bursts coming from ships overhead.

The Quain.

They don't target the palace directly because they won't risk destroying what they came for. Instead, they target the royal guards on the walls and battlements.

Whoosh!

A fire burst hurtles through the night—*Boom!*—and part of the wall shatters into pieces. Brick, mortar, bodies, and weapons all fly through the air.

The royal guards scatter.

They weren't prepared for a battle tonight; no one expected the negotiations to come to this.

I'm not surprised, though. Not after I was dragged in front of the lieutenant, leader of the Quain army, Kriinal Braxt's right-hand woman. She doesn't look so different from me: blond, young, a determination in her blue eyes. But that determination scared me. As soon as I was dismissed, I packed my knapsack with a few meager supplies I stole from the kitchens and hoped to leave this life before the fighting started.

But the lieutenant isn't stupid, and she won't rely on negotiations. The Quain are ruthless. They're not taking any chances.

Some of the royal guards have gained their wits and are shooting back at the Quain ships. The guns on the battlements pack enough power to shoot ships down.

One gunner has good aim. He shoots through the rain at the closest ship, two, three, four times, all direct shots. The ship's shields flash green each time.

Then the ship turns, targeting the gunner.

The gunner doesn't leap from the wall in time. The fire blast hits its target on the first attempt, and everything is obliterated.

I turn from the sight, and my eyes fall on the silhouette of a person standing in the hall with me. I straighten my back.

The figure steps into the light. Madame Aphelion.

I inhale sharply.

Aphelion is the last person I wanted to see.

I could run, but in my heels Aphelion will catch me quickly. Talking my way out isn't an option—my knapsack gives me away. Stand and fight is the only choice.

"Eshan'ya, you shouldn't be out here," Madame Aphelion says in her fake kind voice. She's holding something in her hands. "It's not safe for you."

The madame isn't dressed in her bedclothes. No, she's dressed as she always is in her simple white habit that hangs like a sack off her body, complete with a veil and an angry scowl that overshadows her smile.

"I'm not going back." My voice is firm, authoritative.

Aphelion steps closer, and now I can see what she holds.

A taser.

I lift my chin, and with even more conviction, I say, "I'm not going back."

"You don't have a choice," Madame Aphelion sneers and then darts forward with the taser extended.

I narrowly avoid it by twisting to the side. Aphelion recovers quickly and tries again. I swing my knapsack at her. It's a poor weapon, but Aphelion has to back away or risk losing her taser.

"Stop this, child. You'll do yourself harm," she says, as if she has any genuine concern for me.

"Get away from me. You're no better than a crusty old jailer."

I leap, swinging my bag over my head. The madame takes two more steps back. The bag misses her completely, but now I'm within reach of a stone statue depicting our king that's about the size of a watermelon. I snatch it up and throw.

Aphelion ducks, though not quick enough. The statue clips her ear and thuds onto the carpet behind her. She cries out, gripping her ear. Satisfaction floods through me at the sight of blood glistening on her skin.

All hints of Madame Aphelion's smile have been wiped from her face. Her eyes are deep sockets of rage. She bares her perfect white teeth.

She charges.

I can't move fast enough, not in these stupid shoes. I stumble backward, trying to avoid Aphelion's attack, but she barrels right into me, knocking me to the ground.

Pain runs up my back.

The king won't be happy if I'm bruised.

The moronic, self-centered King Vald.

But why should I care what he thinks? I've just got to get this monster off me and get away from here. Then it won't matter at all what makes the king happy.

Aphelion sprawls on top of me, making ridiculous little grunts as she tries to swing her arm around to taser me. I grab her wrist before she gets the chance, holding on with both hands.

It's a battle of strength: Aphelion pushing the taser toward my chest and me pushing back.

I let go with one hand, pull back, and punch her in the face as hard as I can.

The madame cries out again as she falls away.

I jump to my feet, and with my bag clutched to my chest, I run.

I make it all the way to the end of the hall before Aphelion tackles me from behind. The taser slides across the carpet.

Aphelion has the upper hand this time now that she's perched on my back, pressing my face into the soft carpet. I inhale the dust while my heart tries to pound its way through the floor.

The madame reaches for the taser, fumbling after it and trying to keep me under her as she does.

My bag is sprawled on the ground only a few feet in front of me. I squirm under Aphelion's weight, crawling, reaching, stretching for it. I rip it open and rummage through the contents. My dresses, food, jewels...

Where is it?

There. My fingers wrap around the hilt of my multitool, and I flick open the blade. I awkwardly stab backward, flailing wildly as I try to dislodge Aphelion. Finally, the knife connects, and she screams as she tumbles off my back.

I crawl away, dragging my bag with me and holding the blade high. Blood stains Madame Aphelion's white habit, spreading from her side and slowly covering her stomach.

Between cries of pain, Aphelion pants heavily, her chest rising and falling like the tide in a storm. I scramble up from the ground, finding it difficult to balance in my heels with such wobbly legs, but somehow I manage it. I sling my knapsack back over my shoulder, keeping the blade at the ready as I point it at Aphelion.

"You can't leave me like this," Madame Aphelion gasps between breaths.

I back away.

"Eshan'ya, you wouldn't leave me like this, would you? You kind-hearted girl. Please don't leave."

"You're only getting what you deserve," I spit back.

Then I turn and hurry down the corridor again, ignoring her cries and pleas. I feel no guilt for leaving her. Whether or not she survives, Madame Aphelion chose her fate.

As I approach the exit again, Aphelion is drowned out by the sounds of war outside. The royal guards scream and shout, blasts from the Quain ships rock the foundations, and shots from the palace battlements ring out over the roar of fire.

The rain has stopped, but the ground is still wet. I dash out, taking cover behind manicured trees and hedges to hide from the royal guards and the Quain. The guards have had some success while I did battle with Aphelion; they have managed to bring down one of the Quain ships. It burns where it crashed just beyond the palace walls, filling the air with smoke and the stench of melted steel.

Two other ships are still in the air.

Does the Quain Lord, Kriinal Braxt, look down from one of them? Or did he just send his lieutenant to do his dirty work? I hope I never find out.

Unseen, I sprint from tree to tree until I reach the palace walls.

I look up at the brick wall, which would be unclimbable if it weren't for the thick gershy vines growing over this section. The vines are periodically eradicated, but I found this new growth a week ago.

The aggressive vine grows quickly and strongly. Left long enough, it will pull down the entire wall. This pocket is only young but still strong enough to bear a human—at least a seventeen-year-old girl.

I look over my shoulder. The view of the garden is mainly blocked by a large tree and a few smaller ones. From what I can see, no one is interested in this part of the wall; the fighting is concentrated near the front gates. Still, the occasional guard runs atop the wall, and I'll need to time my climb over the battlements to avoid them.

I tuck the blade back into the multitool and put it in my bag—I need both hands to climb—and I reach for the vine, tugging to make sure it will hold my weight. It does.

As I ascend, my fingers grip the coarse branches, holding on for dear life as my toes rest on whatever can give me purchase, either vine or brick. I'm halfway up the wall when the heel of my shoe gets hooked in the vine. I wish I'd thought to take them off for the climb. I could have put them back on after I got over the wall, but it's too late for that now.

The whole vine shudders when I shake my foot, and I'm scared it might pull away from the wall. Even if I survive the fall, it would be impossible for me to try the climb again.

With heavy and labored breaths, I take a moment to calm myself. Once my heart rate is back under control, I slowly let go with one hand and reach down to my foot. The vine creaks and starts to pull away from the wall, but I don't stop. This is my only chance.

My fingers graze my heel and tug at the vine wrapped around it.

A snap and a creak warn me the vine is coming loose. My heart pounds harder, but I have no more time to spare to calm it again.

Slowly, slowly, I peel the vine from my shoe. With a soft pop, it releases my foot. Phew.

Returning to my climb, I'm extra careful which branch I reach for. Some have come away from the bricks and will break off if I try to use them for leverage. My arms are shaking from terror and exhaustion when I finally make it to the top.

I stay there, listening for movement. When I hear none, I roll over the top of the wall and land with a thump on the battlements.

"What the broken hearts are you doing?"

I jump up from where I've fallen to see a guard growling at me from a few yards away. He's dressed in the standard red blazer with gold lapels that mark him as a common foot soldier in the king's army—but he'll get a promotion for capturing me.

I gawk at him.

"You're from the palace," the guard says, his eyes widening as he realizes what's happening, that I'm trying to escape. "You need to come with me," he says, reaching for his lava gun.

"You should focus on the battle," I say, and I'm rewarded by him glancing over his shoulder. It's enough of a distraction for me to make a run for it.

I take four long strides, then leap right over the battlement—"Stop," the guard yells—but instead of falling to my death, I crash into a tall sycamoria tree growing on the opposite side. The branches scratch and snap before I grab hold of one to stop my fall.

I shuffle around to the other side of the tree so I'm not in the guard's line of fire, then resume climbing down.

The guard is shouting. I hope no one can hear him over the other noises raging through the night.

By the time I reach the ground, my arms and legs are trembling, the scratches from the branches are stinging, and my back is tender from when Aphelion knocked me down. There's no time to tend to my injuries, though. I need to get as far away from the royals and the Quain as I can. I need to get off this planet.

I take two deep breaths and then sprint.

I thought I'd stand out in my long, flowing dress in Kep City, especially now that it's torn and wet. But no one looks at me twice. There are plenty of other women and some men wearing dresses of a similar style, if not the same quality as mine.

No one looks close enough to see the fine stitching and intricate details of my gown, nor the royal crest that decorates the gold cuff on my left upper arm. They don't seem to care that my skin is scraped or splattered with dirt and blood. There are others in the street who look worse than me.

An old crippled woman sitting at the curb shakes her fist as people splash through the puddles, spraying water all over her. A young boy, his clothing torn, shivers as he huddles in the dark doorway of a boarded-up shop. A shinver addict, so thin his skin looks stretched over his skeleton, hobbles toward me, his eyes glassy with oblivion and bliss.

I hurry past them all, careful not to slip on the wet street. I wish I could help them, but the best way for me to do that is to run away. No one can afford for me to be captured by the Quain. These people don't know the danger they're in. They can't even see the battle going on at the palace from here. The streets are too built up, the buildings too high, and the air is already filled with noise. If I didn't know better, I would think it was a normal evening on Keplerane.

I continue glancing over my shoulder, wondering when the royal guards will come after me. Or maybe the Quain will come looking first. I scan the faces of those walking toward me on the sidewalk, my muscles tense and ready to run if I need to.

Soon the buildings, the neon signs, and people start to thin out as I approach the docking bays. This area of the city is quieter than the rest, but I can still hear the sounds of revelers partying inside a nearby tavern. It seems surreal that they're having so much fun while a war rages only a few miles away and I'm running for my life.

A group of drunken men bursts out of the tavern and heads toward Kep City. There are five of them dressed in scruffy pants and shirts; they're probably dock workers if their large boots are anything to go by. Talking loudly, their footsteps swerve from the drink. They spot me and make a beeline to where I'm walking.

"Well hello, pretty lady," one of them calls, looking me up and down.

I tense. There was always a risk of apprehension from the guards or the Quain, but I hadn't considered the danger from locals.

My steps hasten, but they soon surround me anyway.

"Why ya in such a hurry?"

"You're out here all alone. Don't you want some company?"

"Check her out. She's a real looker."

I stop, straighten my spine, and pull my shoulders back, looking each of them in the eye. My confidence seems to unnerve them because their smiles falter and they glance at each other. One even takes a step back.

"I'd like to be left alone, gentlemen." My voice doesn't waver.

One man opens his eyes wide. "Are you...are you from the palace?" he asks, then turns to his friends. "Do ya hear how she speaks? She must be royal."

There is nodding and some shaking of heads between them.

"Is she one o' the princesses?"

"Nah, I've seen 'em before. She ain't one of 'em." He's lying, of course. King Vald never allows any of his daughters out of the palace or to be seen in public—he's very possessive of his women.

It spurs the others into an argument as they call him "phony" and "full of it," providing me a moment to slide through their little group and hurry to the moored spaceships.

"Hey!" Footsteps run after me, and I hurry up.

"Let her go," one of the friends calls.

The footsteps fade, and I'm alone once more, running among the spaceships and hoping the men don't change their minds. I keep my head low in case they do.

I tiptoe along the gravel among the large and small spaceships, skirting around the wood of broken pallets and other abandoned rubbish waiting for the junkyard. Most of the ships sit dark and silent like giant statues bearing down on me, judging me. I hope no eyes look out from their windows.

Ahead, a ship glows brightly. It's a large freighter, and its outer hull is ugly and unpainted other than the name of the shipping company printed on the side: UUPS. It's long but bulging with several rectangle containers protruding from its belly where people swarm in and out, loading cargo.

From the shadows, I consider it, trying to work out if I can sneak aboard somehow, maybe in one of their crates. But there are so many people. I can't see a way to get to the crates without being seen, and what if they stack them on top of each other? I could be stuck in there for weeks and die before I'm found.

There's got to be another way.

I wrap my arms around my shoulders, rubbing them quickly. The adrenaline of my flight has worn off, and the air feels suddenly very cold. Even though I avoid the puddles, my feet and pretty heels are covered in mud. My toes are ice.

The glint of lights alerts me to another potential ship ahead. I hurry to the end of the spaceship that hides me, peeking around its hull to spy.

It's a much smaller ship than the freighter, but still big enough to dwarf me. There are four main engines at the rear, five smaller engines, plus the hatch and airlock. The front tapers slightly, like a long hood, and gives an impression of a snout. The cockpit sits behind dual windscreens, making them look like eyes. Its sides jut out, and bulky engine intakes raise above the roof. The whole vehicle looks like an odd-shaped animal's head. A fox, I realize. A fox with boxy cheek bones.

It might once have been a people transporter—a bus—but it's been converted. Gun turrets have been added to the underside in addition to sensors on the roof and sides.

The outside is mainly gray but decorated with orange-and-red wavy stripes, making it appear even more like a fox's head. And written in faded red paint down one side is Chinese lettering that I can't read.

The hatch that sits between the four rear engines is wide open, spilling light onto the gravel of the docking yard. A ramp is extended to the ground. From this angle, I can't see everything inside, but it looks like the reception has been gutted. There are no chairs like there would be in a space bus, and it's not decorated in those awful colorful fabrics public transport always seems to have. Instead, the walls are bare, just metal and steel, and a few wooden boxes and containers pushed against the walls. The ship must be used as a courier.

There's no one around, but I know better than to think an open ship is unmanned. I stay where I am, watching.

After a time, my fingers and toes ache from the cold, and my teeth chatter. When still no one has gone in or out of the hatch, I maneuver to a different shadow to get a better view.

There. Inside, a tall black girl with short curls stalks back and forth. She's dressed in worn olive-green overalls that are cinched tight at her tiny waist with a belt. I can't hear what is being said, but she's keeping up a constant stream of chatter, hazardously waving her hands as she paces. A droid stands farther into the hold, not paying any attention to the girl. It's humanoid and has pearl-white limbs, chest, and head, and coiled bronze joints. Its eyes are two square sensor pads with round green lights for irises. I recognize it as a Renker Android Nomad model, and the eight on its chest shows the design type: RAN-8.

There are just the two of them in the hold. If they can be distracted for one moment, maybe I can sneak inside. I look for something that will create a diversion. The rubbish and broken wooden pallets will do.

A memory from my childhood flashes across my mind: Declan teaching me how to make fire. He was always teaching me something like a father would—gentle, but firm. All that time ago, he kneeled so our faces were level as he showed me how to strike rocks together to create a spark. Then he handed me the rocks so I could try it myself. He was patient while I tried and continuously failed, but he never gave up on me, and eventually, I made those rocks spark, and a fire leaped into life.

I quietly back away from my hiding spot and start collecting rubbish and wood into a pile, seeking to find dry items sheltered from the rain by ships or other trash. I don't need rocks this time; instead, I fish the multitool out of my bag. Before, I was unsure how useful it would be because I don't know how to use half the tools, but it's been handy. I use it now to set the rubbish on fire.

Once there's a small flicker of flame, I back away, hurrying around spaceships before the fire gets larger and the shadows smaller.

I approach the modified bus, waiting for my chance.

I can't see inside the hatch from this vantage point, but I can see the glow of the fire burning between the two ships opposite.

A muffled discussion breaks out inside the ship, but I can't make out the words.

The droid rushes out first, the *clunk clunk* of his metal feet on the gangway ringing out as it rushes straight toward the fire. The girl follows but stops halfway between the ship and the fire, looking at the droid and then back at the ship. Eventually, she says, "Oh, oh, oh, you'll get lost if I don't come with you," and she runs into the night with the droid.

With my back against the modified bus, I edge around to the hatch. Before stepping into the light that spills out from it, I take a deep breath. Then I tiptoe up the ramp as quickly and quietly as I can.

Thank the broken hearts, I'm alone. No one stands in the gutted reception of the bus. There's only me and a handful of wooden crates. I waste no time finding a hiding place among them where I curl into a ball, my arms tight around my knees, hoping beyond hope I'll soon be off this forsaken planet.

Chapter 3

Fan

"PEDDERS, TIKA, PREPARE FOR launch. We could be coming in hot," I speak into my tech point. I'm worried that if Gussart survived his crash, he and his shinver goons will still be chasing us. Without the royal guards around to stop them, they could gain some serious ground. No telling when they might be right on top of us again.

The squito weaves through traffic, still traveling well above the speed limit. A drizzle of rain starts up again, making the streetlights bleed into the night. I keep my eyes peeled, looking for Gussart or the royals.

Finally, we reach the docking bay. Rounding a corner between spaceships, I behold the *Huxian Fox*, my beautiful spaceship, ready and waiting with the hatch lowered. I steer the squito straight up the ramp and cut the motors. Tika sprints over as I dismount and shake the droplets from my hair.

"Oh, Captain Sung, you're all right," Tika says. "We were so worried when we hadn't heard from you—"

I ignore her as she fusses and instead glance back out the hatch. No one there.

Yet.

"—and I tried calling your tech point several times, but you didn't answer. And then with everything going on at the palace, and then the fire, we thought something might have—"

"What's going on at the palace?" I ask, paying attention again.

"Oh, it's a terrible business, Captain," Tika says. "Just terrible. I couldn't keep my eyes off my tech point. It's on all the feeds."

"Tika, cut the dramatics and just spit it out," I say.

Luchlon secures the squito in the hold so it won't hover across the room when we take off, then comes to listen to Tika as well.

"Why, the palace has been attacked, Captain." Tika's dark eyes go as wide as saucers. "It's the Quain. They've gone mad and are invading. They've already gotten over the walls, despite all the royal guards fighting back from the battlements."

"The Quain were always mad," I mumble.

"Why are they attacking the palace, though?" Luchlon ponders.

"Well, that's the question, isn't it?" Tika says conspiratorially. "They were having their peaceful negotiations, and then all of a sudden, it's war. Such a nasty business."

Luchlon turns to me. "Is there anything we should be worried about?"

I wonder if the Quain are finally going to take over Keplerane like they have so many other worlds. I know the Quain Lord, Kriinal Braxt, has had his eyes on the planet for some time. He also runs Vegasin—I think he has a headquarters there—but that hasn't stopped the shinver lord Shikha from running her business out of the planet. And it hasn't stopped us from doing business with her.

I respond, "Only that Gussart's crew will have no opposition from the royals if they want to rip up the streets or muster their own army. And they'll be on their way here." I charge out of the gutted reception that I use as the main hold and toward the cockpit. "Pedders? Are you ready for launch?" I call as I stalk down the corridor.

"Yeah," comes the gruff reply.

Entering the cockpit, I take the pilot's seat beside my trusty copilot, strapping in while Pedders flicks several switches and buttons. I hear the clunk of the hatch closing, the whir of the airlock cycling, and the roar of the engines readying themselves. The ship vibrates, ready to launch.

Before we take off, I see headlights shimmering through the rain, coming straight at us.

Gussart.

"Take your seats," I call over the ship's intercom. "This could get a little bumpy."

Not waiting for a response from the crew, I pull back on the flight lever, and the *Fox* soars into the air.

"Whoa!" Tika calls from somewhere within the ship, followed by the sound of her crashing into something.

The rapid *ting ting ting* of bullets on the outside of the ship tells me I took off just in time.

Gussart's crew pulls up to where we were docked and takes aim with a collection of bazookas.

"We need more air," I say. "Pump the thrusters, give us a boost."

Pedders carries out my orders, and the ship picks up speed. Just because it was a bus once upon a time doesn't mean it's a slow cow nowadays—it's called a *Fox* for a reason.

A shot rings out through the night, then another and another, and Gussart's missiles are in the air.

The dashboard screens monitor the rockets and their attack on the *Huxian Fox*.

I pull hard to the left, spinning the *Fox* and narrowly avoiding the first rocket. Through the rain-streaked windows of the cockpit, I see a trail of red smoke streaming behind the projectile as it harmlessly flies past us.

But two more are advancing quickly.

I continue with evasive maneuvers, turning the *Fox* left and right, swirling through the air like a dance—*and it's just as sexy*.

The second rocket skims underneath the *Fox* within a miurtle's hair of the hull.

"That was close. Wasn't there a third one?" I say, searching for it on the scanners.

"There!" Pedders shouts, pointing out the window.

It's dead ahead and directed right at the cockpit, the red smoke from its tail glowing menacingly.

"What the...?" I mumble as I push on the lever, dipping the *Fox*, trying to get below the rocket. But I'm not quick enough.

The ship shudders with the impact.

Alarms blare.

Lights flash on the console: *Outer hull damage. Sensor III damage.*

Nothing that will stop the *Huxian Fox*. The shields will have absorbed most of the impact. I pull back on the lever again, and the *Fox* pushes toward space.

"Shut those alarms off," I bark.

The alarms disappear and so does any threat from the ground. They're out of range now.

Pedders turns in his chair to face me. "So I guess Gussart found out about the missing shinver?"

"And his wife," I admit with a raised eyebrow.

As the *Huxian Fox* enters space, I put the ship on autopilot with navigation set to Vegasin. There, I can rendezvous with my other shinver buyer, Shikha.

Pedders groans and shakes his head. "She's a fine woman, Fan. We're lucky to be alive right now."

"Tell me about it." I run my hand through my short mop of hair. Gussart might be a buffoon, but he's got a nasty streak, and he won't tolerate being humiliated. I'm gonna have to watch my backside. I climb out of my chair and leave the cockpit. "Tika, Ranate," I call as I stalk the corridors. "Do a quick patch on the repairs and get us out of here."

When neither my mechanic nor droid can be heard clunking down the halls, I stop. "Tika? Ranate?" When there's still no response, I call, "Luchlon?"

"Oh, Captain, we're in the main hold," Tika responds on comms. "We don't understand how...we just don't understand..."

"What is it?" My skin tingles like I've been stunned by a pulse gun on high. I'm worried the ship is damaged more than I thought.

"You'd better get down here," comes Luchlon's gruff voice.

I jog the rest of the way down the corridor to the ship's rear and barrel into the hold to find Luchlon, Tika, and RAN-8 staring dumbly at the crates stacked there.

"What...?" I start, but as I step forward, I see what has them transfixed. "Whaaaat?"

Between the crates stands a young woman.

I notice her bright blue eyes first. They're wide with shock, but there's determination behind them and something that demands respect. The same goes for her posture; she stands tall with her head high as if she's poised in a ballroom, not hiding in the hold of a smuggling ship.

She wears a dress made from a silky material in an unusual shade of silvery-blue that matches her eyes. Beautiful stitching and lacing show it's finely made, but it's been torn in several places.

Her blond hair, which looks as though it had been styled fashionably, is now a bird's nest of a mess. Several strands have come loose and now fly around her face. Her pale, exposed skin is scratched and dirty, but even in her disarray, she is stunning.

I have joined my crew as a statue, staring at this girl, wondering how she got on my ship. Eventually, I ask, "Tika? Why is there a Keplerane royal on my ship?"

The crew gasps. "A royal?"

The girl's chin lifts higher, and the look she gives me is nothing less than regal. A heat flushes through me in some unexpected places—mainly my knees.

I ignore the feeling and explain. "The emblem on her cuff is the crest of King Vald. And peasants don't dress in such expensive custom made dresses."

There's another collective gasp as the crew realizes I'm right.

"Your Majesty," Tika says with a bow from the waist. "Or is it Your Royal Highness?" She switches to a curtsy. "To be in the presence of royalty...such an honor. I never thought we would be so luck—"

"I'll repeat my question. What is a *princess* doing on my ship?"

The princess steps out from behind the crates, straightens so she's somehow even taller, and says in a commanding voice, "I require safe passage off Keplerane."

Chapter 4

Eshan'ya

"You must provide transport to Shadé."

Four figures stand before me: the girl with dark-brown skin and the RAN-8 droid I saw earlier, a broad-chested white guy, and a girl of East Asian heritage. None of them look older than twenty, and half are carrying weapons. I keep my eyes on their faces rather than focusing on the guns in their holsters or any potentially twitchy fingers. I need to appear calm and totally in control.

"Sorry, princess. But you have no authority here."

It's the Asian girl who speaks. She's very attractive, even if she is rough around the edges. She's dressed in a gray synth leather jacket and a sturdy pair of trousers with a pistol in a holster strapped to her leg. Her damp brown hair is cut short, just long enough to hang over one eye, and the other side is almost as short as a buzz cut. A black spike pierces the top of her right ear, and her large eyes are rimmed in kohl. She stands with her head tilted, eyes roaming up and down, assessing me. I purse my lips while I endure her insubordination.

The girl doesn't seem at all perturbed by my commanding tone; the one I use with the servants in the royal household, which has never failed me before. Instead, her stance is relaxed, her fingers hooked into her belt and legs planted wide. She raises one eyebrow quizzically.

Heat rises from the pit of my stomach as I watch her.

"Captain Sung," says one of the crew, "don't you think we should—"

"Not now, Tika," the Asian girl interrupts.

"Captain Sung." I address her, suppressing my feelings and turning to reason instead. "My name is Eshan'ya. And I'm sure you understand that if you ever want to be welcomed back to Keplerane, you'll do as I command."

"Listen, lady...Princess Eshan'ya," Sung responds with a sly smile, "we just got hit by a missile getting chased off this rock, so I don't think we'll be visiting anytime soon."

Despite the captain's distressing story, her voice is husky and completely at ease.

"Very well then. Since you're leaving anyway, you can take me with you," I say decidedly.

Sung's jaw drops open. She blinks several times while I try not to smile at her reaction, and then she says, "Well...yes. OK then. But we're dropping you off on the nearest planet. The *Huxian Fox* isn't a taxi."

"On the contrary," says the crew member who spoke before, "the vessel was once a bus to taxi people—"

"Tika," Sung growls.

I can't hold back my smirk this time, which doesn't seem to help Sung's mood.

Crash!

The ship is rocked sideways, and the hold quakes. The crew and I are sent hurtling across the floor, stumbling and battling to stay upright.

"What in the grand hurrah?" Sung exclaims. "Pedders? Report!" she calls into the tech point on her finger while she runs from the hold.

"Three, no four, hostiles on our tail," comes the reply.

The crew follows Sung down the unadorned metal corridor, now more interested in what's going on outside than with me. I trail behind them and into the cockpit where a large East Asian guy sits in the copilot's chair. He's just as young as the rest of the crew, and I wonder if they're all too young to get me out of this mess.

The guy glances at me and utters, "Who?"

"She's a Keplerane princess," Sung says dismissively.

"How—?"

"Pedders! Priorities! What the fiery balls is going on?"

The guy drags his eyes away from me, glances at the captain questioningly, and then focuses on the screens in front of him. Warnings brightly flash across the dashboard, which looks stuck together with tape and bubblegum. Wires hang underneath, twisting around each other like tinsel on a Christmas tree. I wonder how this ship even flies.

"One sensor is down, so we didn't pick them up until now," Pedders says.

"How did Gussart get four spaceships off the ground so quick?" the white guy asks. "I didn't even think he had that many vessels."

"I don't think it's Gussart's crew," Pedders says.

"He's right," Sung says as she monitors the screen on the dash. "They're bigger than anything Gussart can get his hands on. They look like royal battleships to me."

The captain looks back at me.

Crash!

The crew brace themselves against the walls and chairs fixed in the cockpit as the ship rocks from another direct hit. I stumble backward, my already tender back painfully slamming against the wall. To avoid crying out in pain, I grit my teeth. I can't show any weakness in front of these people.

"They're firing on us," Pedders reports.

"Really? I couldn't tell," Sung says. "Why the hell is the royal fleet shooting at my beautiful ship?" She sneers at me.

I shake my head. I can't trust this crew. They're obviously criminals, smugglers of some sort. If they know why the royals are after me, they'll probably hand me over and ask for a reward.

I shrug. "Don't look at me," I say. "What crimes have you committed?"

The captain doesn't answer, looking back at the scanners instead. Taking the pilot's seat, she says, "Let's get the hell out of here."

"That would be a good idea," I agree.

Captain Sung flicks three switches and pulls on the central lever. There's a whirring noise, but nothing happens. The captain repeats the process of flicking switches and pulling the lever, but again, nothing happens.

"Now would be a good time for you to leave the Kepler-X system," I warn.

"What do you think I'm trying to do?"

"Playing with your joystick."

Pedders grunts with humor, but a quick glance from his captain silences him.

"Ranate, what the hell is wrong with my hyperdrive engines?" Sung asks.

The droid has his finger hooked into a port in the cockpit's wall, running analysis on the ship. "The diagnosis is that they are *royally* screwed," the droid reports in its metallic voice, "if you don't mind the pun." When no one laughs, the machine continues. "Seems the external power coupling has been damaged, preventing power from reaching the hyperdrive."

The ship shudders as it takes another hit, but it must have some decent deflector shields because it hasn't blown up yet.

"Right." The captain gives out orders, saying, "Pedders, evasive maneuvers. Luchlon, on weapons. Tika, Ranate, work on those repairs. Princess, strap in. Now."

Her crew responds immediately, racing out of the cockpit.

"I'm not a pawn for you to command," I protest.

"Sit down. Now." She glares. She pulls on the flight controls, and we enter a barrel roll. The ship's inertial dampeners stop me from spinning with it, but I get her point.

I sit down in one of the passenger seats behind Pedders and strap in like I was told. I don't go to the trouble of hoping this motley crew and beat-up old bus can defend themselves against the royal armada. I just hope it's not blasted into oblivion before the royals board and drag me back to Keplerane.

The ship shudders again.

In front of Pedders and the captain, I see two oranges rolling back and forth on the dashboard between the screens and the outer window. *Strange.* The inertial dampeners are good, but they can't counteract every movement as the ship spirals, so the oranges keep on rolling.

The view out the front windows is empty other than a sprinkling of stars in the darkness of space until the ship veers to avoid more blasts from the royal fleet. As it does, the attacking ships come into view.

My blood runs cold.

There's three royal battleships out there—that's bad enough—but the fourth ship isn't part of the royal fleet. It's the Quain. It has a shiny black exterior with a silver sigil of three stars.

If it had been attacking the royal ships, I could think they're only here to continue the battle that started below on the planet. But they're not. Their weapons are locked onto the bus.

"What the hell are the Quain doing out here?" Sung mumbles.

The Quain ship shoots, and the bus quakes.

"And why the grand hurrah are they shooting at us?"

A series of red pulse shots hurl through the air as the bus finally starts shooting back. The white guy, Luchlon, must be on weapons now.

Some shots go wide, but two hit the closest ship in the royal fleet, causing a small burst of fire on its hull but nothing else. It sweeps forward.

"Ranate! Where is my hyperdrive?"

Through the comms, RAN-8 responds, "The hyperdrive engine is located left of middle at the rear of the ship."

"You know what I mean, Ranate."

"I'm diverting the power through the secondary circuits and via the sublight engines. Please allow a few minutes for me to finalize the adjustments."

"We might not have a few minutes," Sung growls while she pulls a lever above her head that gives the bus a burst of speed, and we shoot over and away from the attacking vessels. But it's not far enough to take us out of range.

Shots spray out from the four ships as they turn to follow us. All I can do is stare out the window while the young crew fights their way out of this mess. I wish I could do more. I wish I could help them. I wish I didn't have to put them in this situation.

The captain continues to give orders. "Pedders, jam their scanners. It'll mess with their targeting systems."

Pedders grunts his compliance and flicks several buttons.

"You can't block scanners. It's impossible," I say.

"I beg to differ." Sung smirks back at me. "Watch."

As the bus swerves and ducks, it's clear that fewer shots are landing. The ship isn't shuddering under fire as it had been, and more blasts fly over our heads, fading into the distance—all indicating that Captain Sung is correct and the bus is outfitted with something that can block scanners on other ships.

It must be some illegal modification.

As I continue to watch, something like awe comes over me. I hide my admiration as Captain Sung and her crew continue to evade not only the royal fleet but also the Quain's lethal ship. If it weren't for the obviously state-of-the-art inertial dampeners, I would have retched by now from the constant twirling of the bus as we avoid shots from all four battleships.

"Hyperdrive is functional," RAN-8 announces over comms.

Sung doesn't hesitate. She pulls the central lever, the ship lurches, and the space out of the front windows turns from black to a shimmering silver as the bus travels faster than the speed of light.

Our attackers disappear from all sensors.

Relief turns my muscles to jelly, and I relax into my chair. I watch the empty screen, amazed it shows no rival ships.

When the captain turns in her pilot's chair to face me, I sit up straight again.

"Not a bad bit of flying, hey?" she says, grinning. "It's times like this that even *I* am impressed."

"I'm impressed this hunk of junk didn't fall apart, too." I roll my eyes.

"Watch your mouth, princess." Sung points her finger in my face. "This ship is the sturdiest, most trustworthy ship in the 'laxy. It's withstood more than that little scuffle."

Pedders nods in agreement with his captain.

I humph.

As the captain leaves the cockpit, Tika enters.

"Your Highness." She bows low.

"There's no need for that." I wave my hand in dismissal.

"Your Majesty, my name is Tika and my pronouns are she her. May I show you around?"

I incline my head in gratitude.

"Firstly," Tika says with enthusiasm, "please let me introduce Qiqiang." She gestures to the large Asian guy who spins in his chair to salute me. "He's our copilot and goes by the call sign Pedders."

He doesn't say anything but looks at me with kind eyes and a quiet smile hidden beneath a scruffy mustache. His black hair looks like he cuts it himself, and it falls unevenly across his forehead. He wears oil-smeared blue trousers and a blue-checkered shirt with a fraying red bandana looped around his neck.

I smile. "A pleasure."

"Follow me," Tika says.

We walk out of the cockpit and down the corridor.

Now the danger seems to be behind us, I'm once again aware of how cold I am in my wet dress. But I walk with my head high and my arms at my side as if I'm perfectly comfortable.

Unlike the homey adornments I've seen in the corridors of royal ships, the walls are bare metal. It's only wide enough to allow two people to pass each other if they both turn sideways, so I walk behind Tika as she continues to talk.

"The *Huxian Fox* is a converted QM-Z66 people transporter, otherwise known as a space bus. However, the *Huxian Fox* has been modified—*I* was instrumental in its conversion. It now accommodates many different tasks beyond the bus's original purpose."

"Like smuggling?"

"I cannot comment on that." Tika quickly continues. "It's named the *Huxian Fox* after the Chinese shapeshifting deity, which often appeared in the form of a nine-tailed fox and was known as a trickster."

"So the deity was evil?"

"Not precisely," Tika says cryptically.

The white guy clunks through an opening and joins us in the corridor. He glances at me with gray eyes, but doesn't slow his stride as he squeezes past.

"Luchlon, may I introduce you to the royal princess? Princess Eshan'ya, this—"

"We met," he says gruffly as he stalks away down the corridor, which is not quite the warm welcome a royal member would hope for. He's dressed like the captain, yet his synth leather jacket is longer, reaching past his knees. He has dark hair, which matches the stubble on his chin, and quite a handsome face—if you're into rugged males.

Tika turns to me. "Luchlon Blustroll is our weapons expert. He's been with the crew for six months now and has been very valuable."

"I'm sure he has."

My sarcasm falls flat, and Tika continues into the engineering station where the RAN-8 droid is connected to the ship through an adaption within his finger. The room is the size of a small cupboard, just enough space for the droid to sit inside, so Tika and I stand in the doorway. The walls are lined with circuit boards and wires—the exposed computer system of the ship.

"This is our systems analytics droid, an R-A-N-8 model, commonly referred to on the ship as Ranate. The number eight is supposed to be very lucky, but I'm yet to see it."

The droid looks up from the circuits and says, "If you ever get bored of this fool, come sit with me. I'm much more interesting." Although the droid's eyes are only a set of pale green lights, one turns off and on, briefly giving the impression of winking.

My eyebrows rise in surprise.

"Have some respect for a member of the royal family," Tika chides.

"Yeah, yeah." The droid waves Tika off with his free hand and turns back to the circuits.

"I have to apologize for my artificial colleague. He's suffered a few blown circuits over time."

"Speak for yourself," the droid replies.

I can't help but grin at their bickering. A stab of guilt strikes me when I'm reminded of the girls I left behind in the palace. But I had to.

As we head to the rear of the ship, we run into Captain Sung barreling out of what looks like the engine room.

"Ah, our fearless leader, Captain Fan Sung."

The captain runs her hand through her hair, her rich brown eyes glancing at me before she turns to Tika with a scowl.

"Shouldn't you be repairing the ship like I commanded?"

"Of course, Captain. Right after I finish showing Her Highness around the ship. Fan Sung was the youngest pilot ever to win the Earth-168mk obstacle race. Two years ago and at only sixteen years old! That's how she got this ship; she bought it with the prize money and has been the captain of the *Huxian Fox* and its crew ever sin—"

"Tika," Fan growls. "Priorities! Repair the ship, then play out your fantasies of serving royalty."

She storms away. Her tight pants briefly draw my eyes to her behind before I turn back to Tika.

"So, Tika, are you the ship's mechanic?" I ask.

Fan turns back and snaps, "She's the ship's accountant. And it shouldn't matter to you since you'll be parting ways at the next opportunity."

45

Chapter 5

Fan

The *Huxian Fox* has a bumpy landing on a remote planet designated GRN-801, or Gerangan, according to the ship's navigational system.

The ship needs repairs but, more importantly, I want to say farewell to our stowaway before we reach Vegasin. I don't understand why the Quain showed up in the Kepler-X system, but I suspect it has something to do with the princess, and I want her gone before they show up again.

I don't need any more trouble chasing my sexy behind.

The hatch opens, and beyond it stretches a large plain of pink dirt and sand that's contrasted by the occasional blue shrub and the clear blue sky. In the distance, I glimpse some rocky mountains that are the same shade of pink. There might be some lakes out there, but more likely, they're just a mirage. A nearby sun glows coral-pink through the atmosphere. The air is so hot and dry I feel the fieriness of it as it travels down to my lungs.

What a wasteland.

Sensors show there's a settlement only a few klicks to the west from where we've touched down. I didn't want to get closer, not when the *Fox* needs so many repairs. Plus, the smoke coming from engine two might scare the locals.

I stroll down the gangway, my crew behind me, and turn to look at the offending engine. It's gonna need some work, but it's probably best we get it fixed before landing on Vegasin. I don't want to appear the slightest bit vulnerable when dealing with Shikha.

"All right, princess," I call back up the ramp to where Princess Eshan'ya stands, appearing forlorn as she looks out on the pink desert. "This is your stop."

"You're despicable, Captain Sung," she snarls. "I don't know how you can sleep at night."

I flick my hair out of my eyes and grin. "Usually not alone."

The princess huffs and stomps down the exit.

She's changed clothes, but what she's wearing now is no more practical than her last outfit. It's a pink dress with a beautiful lace bodice that's going to blend in with the scenery here—although I can't imagine this girl ever blending in. She still wears the gold cuff with the royal crest on her upper arm, but she has turned it so the crest is no longer visible. Her long blond hair has been brushed out and cascades down the length of her back. When she gets to the bottom of the ramp, she gives me a look of contempt—her eyes are calculating and judging.

"Can I at least beg you for some more sensible shoes?" The princess lifts her skirts to reveal a pair of strappy high-heels that are already scuffed and covered in grime. I look out at the sandy pink desert. Yeah, that's gonna be hell.

I nod and call to Tika. "Do you have shoes that will fit the princess?"

"I would be honored if she would wear my shoes."

Tika runs back onto the ship and soon returns holding a pair of sturdy dark brown boots that match the ones she's wearing and will reach up the princess's calves.

The princess visibly relaxes when she sees them, evidently grateful.

I wonder, not for the first time, if I'm doing the right thing by leaving her behind, but I can't change my mind now. What would that say about me? That I'm weak, that's what.

Tika rambles on about the pleasure of lending her boots to royalty while the princess sits in the pink dirt to replace her shoes. She smiles up at Tika with a brief thank you, unconcerned that her dress might be ruined by the dirt. She doesn't act how I'd expect a princess to act. The boots completely clash with her pretty dress, but she doesn't care at all. She just stashes her strappy heels into her knapsack and stands up, brushing the dirt from her nicely-shaped bottom.

I shake away that thought and say, "Just keep heading west and you'll reach a settlement."

"Thank you all for your assistance." The princess nods to each crew member, then walks into the west with her head held high.

I sigh, watching her go. I turn to my crew. "OK, get to work."

"Sensors?"

"Fully functional."

"Navigation?"

"Fully functional."

RAN-8 and I finalize the checks after the repairs on the *Huxian Fox* have been completed. Tika is worth her words in gold; no other mechanic could repair engine two within a few hours without completely replacing it—especially with only minimal supplies. The rest of the crew help where they can, but Tika is the genius.

"Right, then we're ready for launch," I call into my tech point to the rest of the crew. "Let's get off this silly planet, people."

"It's such a shame Princess Eshan'ya couldn't stay with us," Tika says from the seat behind mine in the cockpit. "It was nice to be in the presence of royalty, and she is oh so pretty. Don't you think?"

"Mm-hmm." Pedders nods as he rearranges his oranges on the dash.

"Yes, very pretty," I mumble, "but we can't afford...distractions like that. We gotta offload the rest of this shinver, and we can't do it with the Keplerane royals on our backsides."

Pedders huffs again, but it doesn't sound like an agreement this time.

I don't care what Pedders thinks. King Vald has a larger military than many of the indie planets—it's probably the only reason the Quain haven't attacked sooner. I'm not scared. I'd go up against Sultan Bayezid IX, Queen Anyaugo of Sabon Gida, and Emperor Hiroaki all at once—well, maybe not *all* at once.

They each have an *armada* protecting their planets. My point is that we'd have a better chance of survival without getting on King Vald's bad side.

Luchlon's voice comes through the tech point. "The hatch is closed, Sung."

Both Pedders and I reach forward, flicking switches and pulling levers, and the *Fox* roars to life. It lifts off the ground, but as it does, a tremor runs through the ship.

"What was that?" Tika asks, her voice an octave higher than her normal pitch.

The ship continues to ascend toward space, and I can't see any warnings on the controls. "You're the genius mechanic," I say. "You tell me."

"I promise you, Captain, if I knew, I would tell you."

As the *Fox* gets higher, still within the atmosphere of Gerangan, it's clear that everything is not OK. The ship shudders, starting with just a small shaking, but then great big jolting rattles take over.

"Fan?" Pedders asks, his voice low with worry.

The ship tilts, and suddenly we're free falling.

I desperately pump levers. Flick switches. The display shows no warnings, no indications of what's wrong or how to fix it.

"Tika, check engines."

She leaps from her seat and runs from the cockpit.

"Ranate, systems diagnostics."

But I know we don't have time for any of that. The *Fox* is descending rapidly.

We're going to crash.

I clench my teeth and take a firm grip on the ship's control wheel.

"Switch to manual navigation," I bark at Pedders, and he reacts instantly.

Control switches to my wheel, and I turn it gently, maximizing any atmospheric resistance I can, catching air where possible to slow the fall and pushing the engines as much as I can—which isn't as much as they should be able to handle.

We're falling:

8,000 feet.

6,000 feet.

4,000 feet.

Out the front window, clouds swirl around and around, but it's the *Fox* that's spinning. The oranges on the dash roll up and down the length of the console until one bounces off and hits me in the forehead.

I blink twice as it falls to the floor, but then my eyes return to the view outside.

"Brace yourselves," I call over the comms.

Outside, the pink ground is getting closer and closer, rushing up to meet us. The scenery is no longer a barren desert. Ahead, there's a lake or inland sea in the same hue of pink as the desert that might cushion our landing. I direct the *Fox* toward it.

2,000 feet.

1,000 feet.

We reach the edge of the pink lake just as the *Fox* hits the surface.

Shouts of alarm burst from each of the crew.

The *Fox* bounces once, twice, jolting everyone inside—inertial dampeners can't help with an impact like that—and then we skim across the top of the pink lake,

shuddering,

rocking,

until finally, the *Huxian Fox* slides to a stop with a final bump.

I take a breath, then speak into the comms. "Is everybody OK?"

"Fine," comes Luchlon's gravelly voice.

"No, I am not fine," comes Tika's whine. "I tripped and fell, and now my knee is bleeding, and my hands are a bit grazed and—"

"I am undamaged," RAN-8's metallic response cuts Tika off.

I look over to Pedders.

He nods, but the tightness around his mouth tells me he's not impressed by the situation.

I turn from the dash and spot the orange that hit me in the head. I collect it from the floor and lob it across to Pedders, who catches it easily. "Maybe you should find a way to secure these somehow?" I say, grinning.

Pedders laughs.

"Let's figure out what went wrong."

I leave my chair and head to the back of the ship. Tika is hunched over in the hold, grumbling to herself as she inspects her knee, which barely has a scrape on it.

"Will you survive, Tika?" I ask, patting her on the back.

"I just might," she mumbles, but she gives me a small smile.

When the hatch opens, I'm already at the top of the gangway, more than ready to figure out what the grand hurrah is wrong with my ship. The rest of the crew is with me, but before we reach the bottom of the ramp, I freeze. And so does the crew.

The end of the ramp has sunk into the pink lake. I now notice it's more like a swamp than a lake—a thick, sludgy, pink mess we'll have to walk through to get to dry land.

But that's not what makes me freeze.

Standing at the edge of the swamp, pointing spears, arrows, and large knives at the crew of the *Huxian Fox*, is a large group of...well, I'm not sure what they are. They're human shape, but their skin is bright pink, just like the land around them.

Are they aliens?

I've never heard of humanoid aliens, only animal-like creatures. Of course, I know they must have once existed—there have been plenty of discoveries of ancient Protogenoi art that depict the ancient race very similar to humans.

But the Protogenoi seemed to be an advanced race based on their ancient architecture, the superior artifacts discovered, and strange technologies no one knows how to use now. These pink people appear quite the opposite. They wear almost no clothes, only loincloths—also pink—and some shells, furs, and carved ornaments that hang from their necks all in different shades of pink. They all look strong, their arms bulging—warriors. I don't doubt they can skewer me through the heart before I can reach my pistol.

One of them barks a string of words I can't understand, but I *do* understand the shaking of weapons, so I slowly raise my hands. The rest of my crew follows my lead.

How many times can I be attacked in one day?

First Gussart and his thugs, then the royal fleet and the random Quain ship, and now a bunch of primitive pink aliens. And what is wrong with the *Huxian Fox*? Can this day get any worse?

"Ranate, do you know what this species is?" I ask, speaking quietly out of the corner of my mouth.

A brief whir comes from RAN-8, and some of the pink people flinch as a green light beams out from RAN-8's eyes, scanning their physiques. Besides this, none of the pink people move as it scans them up and down.

RAN-8 finishes his scan and says, "It appears they are human."

"I didn't know humans came in *pink*," Luchlon says.

"Usually, they only have pink bits," RAN-8 says, and the rest of the crew groans.

"It seems their skin has been thoroughly stained by the terrain on this planet," Tika says.

Another bark from the leader of the pink people silences me and my crew again. The tribe step into the pink sludge, approaching the *Huxian Fox* until they eventually surround us.

Tika's voice is almost a screech. "What are they doing? They're coming closer! What do we do? Captain?"

"Stay calm, Tika," I say. "We'll get out of this. We've been through worse."

"Like that time we were captured by the Farnth crew? Or that time we fell into that trap set by the Juanties? Or what about—"

"Yes! Just like all those times, we'll find a way out of this."

The pink people prod us in the back with their spears and knives, prompting the crew forward and away from the *Huxian Fox*.

I glance back at my beautiful ship sinking into the pink mud. I hope I'm right and we'll all see it again soon.

Chapter 6

Eshan'ya

THE SUN OF THIS planet, Gerangan, is still high in the sky, beating down on my nose and cheeks and probably turning them as pink as the desert. My nostrils are filled with a sweet scent instead of the earthy smell I'd expect from a desert. The skirt of my dress keeps clinging uncomfortably to my sweaty legs, making it even harder to walk. I stop and use my multitool to cut it into a mini-skirt instead. To my relief, cool air brushes my knees. I wrap the extra fabric around my head to create a hood and shield my face from the sun.

Taking a large sip from my canister of water, I hope I find more soon. Or the settlement Fan mentioned.

At the thought of Fan Sung, it's not only my skin that burns; I feel the fury throughout my veins. Her contempt, her arrogance, the way she runs her hand through her hair, those smoldering eyes. I'm glad to be rid of her. If she wasn't so stubborn, the *Huxian Fox* could have delivered me all the way to Shadé. The crew have the skills required to get me there if it weren't for their bullheaded leader.

To others, my predicament might seem like a disaster—abandoned in a desert with only a small sack of supplies. But it's better than where I came from. Those stifling palace halls, the threatening stare of Madame Aphelion, curtsying to King Vald. I'll never miss that.

I will miss some of the other girls though—Lina, Charlotte, and even Aubrey, who was haughty and self-centered but had a great sense of humor. They were part of my life for the past five years, and as much as I tried to keep my distance, they became like sisters. Sometimes we laughed and danced together, sometimes we fought, and sometimes we held each other close while we cried. Not everyone cried; some were happy to be there, and some were honored to be part of the royal household. Not me. I always missed Declan and the other Protectors from my childhood.

It seems I'm always destined to miss someone.

I push down thoughts of the girls from the palace. I can't go back, so there's no point in dwelling on it. Still, my heart aches, and I wish I could help them.

You are helping them, I remind myself. This mission will help. Just not in *all* the ways I want.

Ahead of me, rock formations jut up from the pink desert floor, reaching high into the sky like a city of natural pink stones. They stand tall like trees in a forest. Their height makes me think of the obelisks that stood out front of the city I grew up in. But those were white, not pink, and they certainly weren't naturally formed the way these monoliths were.

Once I'm among them, I find some shade from the sun at last. I take another sip of water as I walk, wiping sweat from my brow.

Suddenly my skin crawls, like I'm being watched. I look over my shoulder, but I see only the rocky monuments I've passed and the pink desert beyond. Facing forward again, I stop.

Three figures stand before me.

They look human, albeit quite primitive and completely stained pink.

A sound attracts my attention, and I find three more have moved behind me. They're all crouching to some extent and holding rudimentary weapons, mainly spears and knives. I hold out my hands, palms up, and give them a wide smile to show that I'm not a threat.

At first, they skitter away while I wait patiently in the same position, not moving a muscle, still smiling. Eventually, they come toward me again. They lower their weapons but keep them at the ready. I'm careful not to make any sudden movements, although blood is speeding through my veins, readying me for fight or flight. They creep closer, and then, with hesitant, outstretched hands, they touch my pink dress, which is a paler shade of their stained skin but an obvious source of fascination to them.

One reaches for my hair, and I steel myself against the sting when the pink female pulls a handful to her nose and sniffs it.

Once they're satisfied, they step away, and I'm relieved when they smile back at me.

Softly, I ask, "I need to get to Shadé. Can you help?"

The pink warriors look at each other; they frown and shake their heads. They don't understand. A niggle of doubt tingles along my spine. If this settlement is as primitive as these six, I'm never getting off this pink planet.

Slowly, I drag my knapsack off my shoulder and rummage inside. The tribal people watch cautiously, but they make no move to stop me. I find the wrapped hessian package I'm looking for and open it to reveal my small stash of food.

I hold some grapes out to my new companions. None of them move. So I take one grape and bite into it. The sweet flavor fills my mouth.

"Mmm, mmm," I murmur, holding the grapes out again.

Hesitantly, the female from before steps forward. The others keep looking at her, so it's clear she's the leader. Her eyes stare into mine as she moves. She snatches the small bunch from me and then quickly backs up again. The others surround the brave one, each of them plucking a grape for themselves. As each takes a bite or pops the whole grape in their mouth, their eyes go wide with delight.

All six of them take another grape from the branch and quickly consume them. Before long, all the grapes have disappeared, and the tribal people hold out their hands for more.

"I'm sorry. Those were all my grapes," I say. I'm hesitant to give them all my supplies, but I need to gain their trust. I pull out an individually wrapped protein ration and break off a piece of the square bar for each of the outstretched hands.

They pop the food into their mouths eagerly, but as they chew, their excitement wanes, and one female even spits it out again.

I laugh. "Yeah, that's not quite as delicious, is it?"

The leader looks at me for a moment, not comprehending, and then she laughs with me, encouraging the others to join in.

When they gesture for me to follow them, I do; I've got nowhere else to go. On the stars above, I hope someone on this planet can help me.

It doesn't take long to walk through the valley of pink monuments, and I'm sorry to leave the shade behind. The terrain returns to sandy-pink desert, but to my right lies a swamp of pink mud.

If I never see the color pink again, it'll be too soon.

My heart sinks when the settlement finally comes into view—if *settlement* is even the right word for it. It's a collection of thirty or forty pink mud pyramids so small that I can see over the tops of them without standing on my toes. The pyramid houses have been built among several trees, their bluish leaves creating some shade. It's a relief to finally see a color other than pink.

But it's obvious these people are not technologically advanced enough to be of assistance to me.

Between the trees and pyramids are many more villagers, all stained pink too. When they see their comrades approach with a stranger in their midst, they come out to meet us.

My new friends speak animatedly in a language I don't know, gesturing back at me in excitement, their fingers forming an *o* like the shape of a grape. All those in the village get excited as well, pantomiming eating with their hands. I think they're asking me to share more food. At this rate, I'll run through my supplies quickly.

One holds out a crude bowl with some blue substance inside. I realize they're not asking me for food but offering some of theirs.

I accept the bowl with a smile and look into it. It's a sticky-looking, earthy-smelling mash of something the same shade as the trees. The leader gestures, picking up imaginary food with her fingers and putting it into her mouth. I mimic her by scooping a small amount between my fingers and popping it into my mouth.

It's disgusting.

I imagine this is how moldy grass tastes. It's a struggle to keep my face neutral and smiling. I nod in thanks, and the Gerangans seem pleased, beaming so all their pink-stained teeth show.

Excited, they chatter among themselves. Two pull on my hand, and I'm dragged around the village with them. They talk as they walk, pointing out this and that. Others follow behind. It's obvious they're proud to show me their home.

The little pyramids look like they've been created from mud bricks hardened by fire or the sun. They look sturdy and big enough to sleep a few people at a time, despite being so low to the ground. Inside are simple beds or crude cooking utensils. In one, a man sits cross-legged among a pile of blue leaves as he mashes food like the mush I just ate.

We round a corner at the edge of the village, and I'm shocked by what I find: Captain Fan Sung and her crew tied to the blue trees. Fan's face is a mask of rage as she pulls against her restraints, trying to free herself. All she manages to achieve is making the restraints tighter for her whole crew. They bicker among themselves, each shouting directions and tactics that are unlikely to be successful.

"Pull here."

"Yank that rope."

"You're squishing me."

The Gerangans point at them and laugh.

When Fan hears, she stops struggling, and her head flicks up. Her eyes go wide when she sees me standing there, watching.

"Oh, princess, Your Highness!" Tika calls. "Please help us."

"Eshan'ya, you have to help us," Fan says and starts struggling again. It's the first time she's used my name instead of just calling me princess—she must really be desperate.

"We're not on your ship anymore, Fan. You have no command here," I say evenly as I slowly walk toward them. My new pink friends hold my hands and scowl at Fan's crew, showing exactly whose side they're on.

Tika continues to beg for her freedom, pleading with me and the Gerangans. Pedders looks up with eyes like a puppy dog's. Luchlon scowls. RAN-8 sits still and quiet. He's been powered down so he can't help them escape.

Fan looks at me with those large eyes that show no fear. She might be tied up and need my help, but there isn't an ounce of panic in her. I can't help but respect that. However, I get some pleasure from seeing Fan sitting there helpless, tied up, and less cocky than usual, especially with pink mud streaked across her forehead and down her cheek. I grin.

"Oh, come on," Fan says, rolling her eyes.

"Now, why should I help you when you wouldn't help me?"

"Because...then I *could* help you?" Fan raises one eyebrow.

I pretend to think about it for a moment, not wanting to appear desperate, but it's obvious Fan knows the score.

She says, "You've surely realized by now that these pinkies can't help you. You still need us."

My lips are pressed tight, but finally, I nod. "Fine. I'll help you, and then you take me to Shadé."

"Deal." Fan grins. "Now untie us."

Fan twists to give me better access to her restraints, but when I move, the villagers step in front of me, shaking their heads.

"Why not?" I ask, but all I receive in response is more head shaking.

Then they usher me away. The crew shout, demanding to be released. The Gerangans make quick work of shutting them up by stuffing their mouths with cloth, and their protests are reduced to incomprehensible mumbles.

"What about a trade?" I ask as I'm dragged along. They don't understand, so I pull my small provisions from my knapsack once again. I select a green apple and hold it out. When one of them goes to take it, I pull it back to my chest.

They look at me curiously, waiting for my next move.

I point to the apple, the villagers, and then the crew of the *Huxian Fox*.

The villagers start chattering with each other. Once they have conversed, the leader holds up one finger and points to the apple. Then she holds up five fingers and points to the five tied to the tree.

"One apple, one person?" I ask.

There's only one more apple in my provisions, but there are several protein bars. I hold them up to the villagers, but they shake their heads. Some even pull away, sticking their tongues out in disgust. No, they want fruit. I also have a tomato, and I wonder if they'll know the difference.

I walk in the opposite direction of the crew, my brain ticking hard, trying to come up with a solution. I could bargain for two, maybe three, but what would Fan do then? Would she attack these people to free the rest of her friends? I don't want the Gerangans to get hurt.

As I look up from my pondering, my eyes fall on the *Huxian Fox*, lying damaged on the edge of the swamp that's a short distance from the village. The hatch is still open.

That's it!

The two oranges bouncing on the dash of the cockpit as we escaped Keplerane.

I take off toward the ship. A few of the Gerangans follow at a distance—I'm not sure whether they're guarding me or just curious. Either way, they let me go.

The *Fox* is wide open, and although some compartments are sealed, I have no problem navigating to the cockpit. I grin at the two oranges lined up on the dash right in front of the copilot's chair.

Thank the breaking hearts.

I return to the pink settlement and hold out the two oranges along with the two apples and the tomato. I hold my breath.

They scrutinize my offering and, after a moment, nod eagerly. They take the fruit, and all of them crowd around to see their treasures, sniffing and licking the skins.

"So I can free my friends?" I ask, pointing to the crew.

The leader raises her head, interprets my meaning, and nods.

I hurry over to the *Fox's* crew, pulling my multitool from my bag. I remove Fan's gag. "You promise to take me to Shadé?" I ask before cutting her bonds.

"Yes, I promised, didn't I?" she snaps.

"I'm not sure if I can trust your word."

"What choice do you have?" She grins. She knows she has me over a barrel.

I huff and swiftly cut through their bonds with the blade from my multitool. Sighs and mumbled thank-yous come from the crew as they remove their gags and rub their chafed wrists.

"Where'd you get those oranges?" Pedders asks, his dark brows pulling together in worry. "Those were my oranges, weren't they?" He covers his face with his hands.

"That was clever." Fan's still grinning as she climbs to her feet and hooks her fingers into her belt. "Don't worry about Pedders here. He'll get over it."

"Why are you so concerned about those oranges anyway?" I ask.

"It's a Chinese New Year tradition to bring luck and fortune," Tika explains.

I blink with disbelief at Pedders' reaction. "Take heart, man," I say. "They *did* bring you luck. If it weren't for them, you'd still be tied up."

Pedders snaps his eyes to mine, his mouth gaping. I think he's about to rage at me, but instead, he bursts into laughter, a massive guffaw that makes his belly jiggle.

The others join in.

I smile. Maybe there is hope.

Chapter 7

Fan

From the roof of the *Fox*, I watch the princess negotiate further with the pink tribe. They flock around her like she's a queen, and she is royalty, but she's not *their* princess. Still, she inspires such devotion in them. They follow her around, fussing and trying to please her. It's not just because she gave them fruit, and it's not because of her looks—although her pink dress probably helps. There's just something about Eshan'ya. Maybe it's her easy smile or the kindness of her tone, even when she's being bossy.

Though her pink skirt is torn above her knees, revealing her long, *long* legs, she still looks regal. Her makeshift hood is like a headdress, and she is poised, her head held high, her every movement as graceful as a dance.

She hands the pink people more fruit from the *Fox's* stores in exchange for their help. I wonder if they actually understand what Eshan'ya is asking of them. I doubt they do, and I start to regret giving her access to those supplies.

Fool! But I'm not sure if Eshan'ya is the fool or if I am.

"She's extremely pretty, isn't she?" Luchlon says, coming alongside me on the roof.

Quickly, I return to my repairs. "Well, yeah." I shrug. "And she's a princess, so she's rich too."

"Hmm." Luchlon is looking at Eshan'ya like he'd eat her for dinner. I wonder if that's how I looked a moment ago.

"Why do you think she was hiding in our hold?"

"*My* hold," I stress and then glance back at the princess, trying to work her out. "Must have something to do with the attack on the palace. It was pretty weird that Quain ship pursued us over Keplerane. Maybe they were after the princess."

Luchlon's brow furrows. "Weird that they weren't attacking the royal fleet. On the surface, they were at war, but they seemed kinda friendly with each other when they attacked us."

I nod. "And if they were at war, why did the royal fleet bother with us?"

"Something doesn't add up."

We both assess Eshan'ya.

"So she's coming with us?" Luchlon raises an eyebrow.

"A deal is a deal."

"Better watch your hide then." He slaps my behind.

I wink at him. "That's what I keep you around for."

Luchlon jumps off the roof, and I return to my work on the *Fox*.

I'm so engrossed in my repairs and constantly wiping sweat from my brow that I don't notice the pink people on the ground and in the swamp. It's not until the ship lurches and almost topples me off the roof that I look down to see they've surrounded the ship.

The tribespeople have wedged the trunks of felled trees under the *Huxian Fox* and are using them as leverage to shift the ship out of the swamp.

"Hey, boss," Luchlon calls from the safety of the ground. "You might want to get down from there."

His warning is too late. The pink warriors pull on their tree trunks again, grunting and shouting, and the ship tilts. I stumble. Then, planting my feet wide, I ride the movement like a surfboard.

"Whoa, all right then." I manage to stay upright as they lower the ship, but I decide it'd be best to get down before they try that again. Running across the metal roof, my boots echoing below, I leap off the edge onto the dry banks of the swamp.

I land with a grunt and turn to see if the princess saw. She rolls her eyes and turns away, watching the tribe rescue my ship.

The pink people are ripped with toned, lean, hard bodies. Their muscles bulge as they heave, pull, and push, grunting and shouting as they do, moving the spaceship inch by inch out of the swamp. From here, I can see the damage that caused our crash. One of the propulsion engines is bent, and there is no way the ship can fly straight like that. It must have happened when the *Fox* was hit by the royals. But why didn't anyone see it before we tried to leave Gerangan?

"Well, at least we know the cause of the crash," I say to the crew, eyeing each of them. "Who worked on that engine?"

"Tika!" Luchlon growls.

"It wasn't me." Tika shakes her head emphatically. "I worked on engine two and then the sensors."

Lips pursed, Luchlon shakes his head at her.

"Tika," I say, "why do I bother keeping a mechanic if you can't guarantee my ship will stay in the air? I want that fixed now."

"But...but..."

I glower at her.

"Yes, Captain." Tika swallows. She pulls out her multitool and heads over to the engine, waiting for the ship to be lowered into place, all the while mumbling to herself about how she didn't even know that engine was damaged.

Slowly, slowly, the tribespeople maneuver the ship out of the swampy water. Sludge oozes down its side, and the smell of spicy mud fills the air. I should be happy that my ship is getting saved, but I'm not. There's something wrong. The more mud falls off, the more apparent the problem is—

—the whole bottom half of the ship is pink.

My ship is stained pink.

Pink!

My crew sniggers behind me. I whirl on them, and they instantly shut up, but they can't completely hide their smiles.

My face drops as the tribespeople drag the ship the last few yards to the sand. They lower it, and the *Fox* rocks slightly before coming to a complete stop.

Pink covers the landing gear, the underbelly, and some of the nose. Luckily, none of the Chinese writing with the ship's name is covered, but the pink hides many of the orange and red stripes.

The *Huxian Fox* looks like it's dressed for Mardi Gras.

I groan.

Pedders pats me on the back, a grin splitting his face. "Guess those oranges really were lucky."

"Oh, shut up."

✳ ✳ ✳

I've got a stiff bristle brush and a bucket of soapy water—what little I could spare from our supplies—and I furiously scrub at the underside of the *Fox*. But the pink isn't budging. Still, I run the brush to-and-fro, to-and-fro, my muscles working hard at the stain. I've got RAN-8, Luchlon, and Pedders scouring with me while Tika works on the engine.

Father's fist, I'm never getting this pink off. Where's Eshan'ya? She should be helping.

Just as I think of her, my ears pick up her voice at the back of the ship.

"Can you repair it?" she asks.

At first, I think she's talking to me, but then Tika responds, "Of course I can. If I knew it was damaged earlier, I would have already fixed it. There's no way I would have let the captain take off with the engine the way it is..."

As Tika keeps talking, I realize she's right, and I was wrong. Tika is a wonderful mechanic. I should apologize, but I scrub harder at the pink instead.

"You're obviously an excellent mechanic," the princess says—trust her to be the one to say it. Now I'm coming off even worse.

"Well, yes, I am, and it's kind of you to notice. I'm not always appreciated around here and—"

"How did you join this crew?"

"I was on a rival crew when Captain Sung competed in the Earth-168mk obstacle course. She just had Pedders as a mechanic, and he's not really that good."

I grin at her description of Pedders' skills.

"You should have seen the crappy ship she had then. It was a mess."

"Then how did she win?" the princess asks.

"The captain is the best pilot I've ever seen."

I slow my scrubbing so I can hear better.

"She can get the best out of any ship. She pushed that hunk of junk to its limit, burned the engines out, and it practically limped over the finishing line. But she did it."

Yeah, I did it. I flip my hair as I scrub harder.

"But you were on the rival team?"

"The guy I was working for—Conte was his name—well, he wasn't happy he lost. He blamed me. He backhanded me."

The princess gasps, but Tika doesn't stop.

"Knocked me to the ground in front of everyone in the pits. It was embarrassing and hurt like hell. And it wasn't the first time. Captain Sung leaped from her crappy ship and ran straight over to help me. Conte got right in *her* face, accused her of cheating, and even tried to hit her. But the captain is quicker than that old brute. She dodged his punch and had him in a headlock before you could say the *Huxian Fox*. Captain Sung offered me a job, and I quit Conte then and there. She pays me more, got me away from the Earth slums, and I get to work with a fantastic pilot. I know she's gruff at times, but she has a good heart."

I feel a glow swell through me, and I resolve to be more patient with Tika in the future.

However, as she continues to ramble on and on, I think, *Or maybe I'll just invest in some earplugs.*

I'm still fuming about my ship stained pink even after it's finally repaired and takes off from the planet. I'm not sorry to say goodbye to Gerangan or the pink people. At least there's no hitch to the launch. It seems the ship has genuinely been repaired this time.

All my scrubbing did no good; the pink isn't going anywhere without a repaint or some heavy-duty cleaners, which I don't have.

Now I stand in the main hold, surveying the mess around me. Seems the tribespeople didn't think to close the hatch after catching me and the crew, and when the *Fox* sank further into the swamp, the pink water rushed up the ramp and into the hold, which now has a pink floor.

And not only that, the crates of shinver are drenched in it; the bottoms of each are now a dusty rose.

I groan with apprehension as I pry a crate open and look inside.

"No, no, no, no, no." My hands run down my face.

"Captain?" Tika's voice echoes down the corridor as she runs to the hold. "What's happened?"

Luchlon enters a step before her. "What's wrong?" And the rest of the crew pile in behind with the princess poking her head around Pedders.

By way of explanation, I thrust my hands at the crate before me. Pink jam—the crate is filled with it. The swamp water eroded the individually wrapped parcels and contaminated the entire crate of shinver, spreading itself into the fine white powder.

"It's all ruined," I moan.

"Maybe we can salvage it?" Luchlon suggests.

"It's pink." I thrust my hands in the direction of the shinver again. "Nobody is gonna want pink shinver." I poke at it but quickly wipe off the pink paste-like substance before my finger is stained like the Gerangans. "Plus, it's gluggy. We can't sell this."

"What is it?" the princess asks.

"Don't you worry about that."

I cover up the shinver. If she's naive enough not to know, then it's not my job to educate her. Better that she doesn't know. It's *highly* addictive and *highly* illegal in the Union of Worlds. And since we're going to Shadé, a UoW planet, it's something I would rather keep quiet. And dump at the first opportunity.

What a waste.

"All right, let's flush them out the airlock," I say as I leave the hold.

Everyone follows me, and I lock the internal door. When I modified the QM-Z66 bus into the beautiful ship it is today, I made sure we could equalize the pressure within the hold so it could be used as an airlock and flush anything in there out into space. It's handy if we're about to be boarded by UoW officials.

I hit the release button, and the hatch opens. Through the window into the hold, I watch the crates get sucked out, the wood breaking apart and the pink paste spilling into space. I think about the lost income—that shinver was worth a lot of money. What am I going to tell Shikha Jhirl? She's gonna blow her top. And I'll have both her and Gussart after my head.

But a deal is a deal. I have to take the princess to Shadé as promised, even if the planet is in the same asteroid belt as Vegasin, right where I do *not* want to go—the same neighborhood where Shikha keeps her operations.

"Set a course for Shadé," I call over comms, committed to my deal. I'll work it out somehow. I always manage to.

On my way to the sleeping quarters, I find Tika showing the princess to her room. Tika carries a pile of blankets and pillows that towers over her head.

"I don't think the princess is going to get that cold," I say.

"I didn't know which one she would like," says Tika's muffled voice behind the bed linen.

"Anything will be fine. Thank you, Tika," the princess says kindly.

Tika sets the linen down and starts to lay it out on the bed, but a grunt from me has her scuttling out of the room.

The princess turns her eyes to me, her head tilted slightly as she patiently waits for me to say something. She's still dressed in her cut-off pink dress, but she's lost her makeshift hood, and her blond hair flows down her shoulders.

"So..." I begin. "We've gotta bit of talking to do, don't you think?"

The princess huffs but nods. "I suppose we do." She takes a seat on the edge of the bed, and I lean against the opposite wall.

Both of us are quiet for a moment as I assess her. She sure is savvy. I can tell by the way she handled the pink people, even making it to their settlement in the first place, and doing whatever she had to do to get off Keplerane.

"Why did you need to leave Keplerane in such a hurry?" I ask, crossing my arms.

"Because the Quain attacked the palace, of course."

It's a smooth lie, but I've played enough poker to know her answer isn't the whole truth. The twitch in her cheek gives her away.

"Why did the Quain attack the palace?"

"I don't know. I'm not privy to the king's strategies and dealings."

"There's more to this that you're not telling me," I say, squinting to scrutinize her more thoroughly, but she just purses her lips. "If you won't tell me that, maybe you'll explain what's on Shadé and why you want to go there." I uncross my arms and let them flop at my sides.

The princess looks down to her lap, and at first, I don't think she'll tell me, but then a blush creeps across her cheeks.

"About that..." She takes a deep breath. "I actually don't want to go to Shadé."

"What? You don't?"

She chews on her lower lip before admitting, "I need to get to Vegasin."

"No! No way." I push off from the wall, shaking my head emphatically. "I'm not taking you there."

"It's not so far from Shadé. They're in the same asteroid belt."
I continue to shake my head.

"You have to," the princess says in her commanding voice. No pretend bashfulness here. "The fate of the world depends on it."

"The fate of my butt depends on *not* going to Vegasin right now." I pace. "Why in the stars would you want to go there?"

She huffs. "Now that is a long story."

"I'm listening." I lean back against the wall, waiting.

The princess sits quietly for a moment. "The truth is, I *do* know what the Quain are after." She stands up to tell her story, pacing just like I did moments earlier. She's taller than me, so I look up into her face as she walks back and forth. "You've heard of the Protogenoi?"

I nod, though I'm shocked to hear mention of the ancient race—what could the Protogenoi have to do with the Quain?

"Legend has it that the Protogenoi built something that could bring the galaxy to its knees. They called it the Device."

"What does the Device do?"

"No one knows. Of course, it's suspected that it's a weapon. It's believed it will cause mass destruction, blow up planets, or poison atmospheres. Legend says that whoever commands the Device will have absolute power."

"What superstitious nonsense." I cross my arms again.

"Maybe." Eshan'ya nods. "But Kriinal Braxt believes it."

"The Quain Lord?"

"Yes. And he's determined to get it."

"And he believes King Vald has it? That's ridiculous. If King Vald had it, surely he would have used it."

"No, King Vald doesn't have it, but he did have a precious jewel in his possession. Something that would help Braxt and the Quain to find the Device...if it's real. According to legend, there are three *keys*, special Shadé diamonds. Get one, and it will lead you to the next until all three will finally lead you to the Device. Braxt believes in the legend because the first key was found exactly where the legend said—in the ancient city on the second planet of a six-planet system, orbiting a red dwarf, adjacent to a three-star system. Keplerane."

I frown. "But there isn't an ancient city on Keplerane."

"Not anymore. Kep City was built on top of it, but not before King Vald's grandfather excavated the area and removed all the priceless artifacts. That's how he bought a kingdom—by selling off his collection of Protogenoi relics. Of course, he kept several pieces for himself. They're located throughout the palace, and among them was the first key. It's a red Shadé diamond roughly the size of your palm."

I gulp at the idea of a diamond the size of my palm—the money something like that would fetch would get both Shikha and Gussart off my tail. I stop my daydreaming and focus on the princess again. "So the negotiations were actually the Quain trying to buy the piece from King Vald?"

"Exactly. But King Vald and the Quain have never seen eye to eye. Of course, King Vald has been watching the Quain closely since they've been invading several planets outside the Union of Worlds, taking them over. King Vald knew he was in their line of sight since Keplerane isn't part of the Union," the princess says as she busies herself with making her bed.

I already knew that Braxt and the Quain controlled several planets, *including* Vegasin, and I'm starting to suspect that's why the princess wants to go there. The Quain have been causing some concern throughout the galaxy recently, their armies getting bigger with each world they take control of. If the army grows big enough, they could take on the Union. If Braxt gets a hold of a device like the one the princess is describing...but that's ridiculous. Any technology the Protogenoi left behind is always completely unusable. No modern scientists have been able to work them, and they sit useless in museums. Even if the Quain get hold of this Device, they won't be able to use it.

She tucks the sheets into her mattress, then flicks the blanket out and lets it settle on the bed. "King Vald tried to buy his continued independence with the key. He doesn't believe in the Protogenoi legend anyway, so he thought it was an easy way to keep the Quain at bay."

"What went wrong?"

"Braxt sent his lieutenant to do the negotiations, but once she confirmed the key was in King Vald's possession, she ordered the attack. There were no negotiations. They wanted the planet and the key."

She turns to unpack her knapsack and hang her clothes in the tiny slit of a wardrobe. First, she hangs the ruined silvery-blue dress she wore as a stowaway. Next is a flowing lilac dress, then an impressive aqua blue dress that looks like it's made from Saturn silk, which would cost about the same as a crate of shinver. All of them are completely inappropriate attire for someone on the run.

"That doesn't surprise me," I say. I've seen how ruthless the Quain are. The crew and I narrowly escaped from the planet Urfaria where I had been doing some peaceful—if not legal—business. Then the Quain attacked the planet. They were ruthless. Cities were felled within hours, their empress killed, and the entire planet succumbed to their rule before their sun had set on the same day. It didn't help that Urfaria didn't have any organized government and therefore no collective army to protect them, but still. It was fast. Yet King Vald won't fall as easily since his military is large and capable. That's why the Quain's attack is so outrageous.

"Why did they come after you when we left Keplerane's atmo?"

"I'm not sure." There's that look again, a tension in her cheek that betrays her. "I guess they don't want anyone alive that knows about the Device."

I decide not to push it. Accusing the princess of lying won't get me answers, and I don't want her to shut down completely. Instead, I nod like I believe her.

The princess relaxes slightly and that tension in her cheek goes slack. Her relief tells me more about the princess than her lies or half-truths—it tells me she fears whatever it is she's hiding.

"So why the hell do you want to go to Vegasin? I'd think you'd want to get as far away from the Quain as possible."

The princess lifts her chin, standing tall, and turns those bright blue eyes on me. "I want to retrieve the key, and I want you to help me."

Chapter 8

Eshan'ya

"No, no, no, no. No!" Fan starts to pace again and shakes her head. Her usually husky voice has a high-pitched twinge as she says, "Are you crazy?" Then she whirls on me, eyes wide in disbelief.

It's exactly the reaction I expected from Fan. Of course she's going to say no. She's not going to risk herself or her ship for my mission. But there is something that may convince her.

"There will be a reward in it for you," I say, catching Fan's attention. Our eyes lock, but it only lasts a moment. Her gaze quickly lowers.

Her cream linen shirt hangs loosely over her slight form. The buttons at the neck are unfastened, and I glimpse the curve of her breasts. I flick my eyes back to her face and push down the heat rising to my cheeks.

Focus.

Fan continues to shake her head. "No money in the 'laxy is worth a crazy mission like that."

I lean my body toward hers. "And here I was thinking you were brave. You fought off those royal ships without much trouble. But I guess I was wrong. You're afraid."

"I am not! It's a suicide mission. You'll get us all killed." Her face is inches from mine, and even though her eyes flash with anger, she glances at my lips.

"OK." I step back with as much nonchalance as I can muster, slowly turning away and pretending to focus on tucking in a blanket. "I guess I'll just have to find someone braver to give my riches to."

"No one is braver than this crew," she says in a deep, quiet voice. "And no one is that mad."

"There's always someone crazy enough for the right amount." I wait. 3...2...1...

"How much money are we talking about, princess?"

I stop making my bed. "More than you could dream of." I smirk internally. I know I've got Fan on the hook, even if she doesn't realize it yet.

"My dreams are quite ambitious, Your Highness," Fan growls, and strangely, my heart skips a beat at the sound.

"It'll be worth more than the little shipment you just flushed out the airlock. You can pay off your debts and then live a life of luxury. You'll never have to work again. I can't do it without help. It's just one little job and you'll be set for life."

Fan doesn't face me while she thinks. She takes a few moments and then finally turns to me. "Oh, blazin' rockets!" she says and storms out of my quarters.

I slump onto the bed. Thank the stars. I might not fully trust Fan, but I can trust that she'll do what she can to get that money.

✳ ✳ ✳

RAN-8 informs me it's a two-day trip from Gerangan to Vegasin traveling via hyperspace, so once my quarters are settled, I go in search of the communal bathroom.

It's a relief to use the steam shower and clean all the pink dust off, not to mention the dirt and grime that's still clinging to me from Keplerane. For the first time in a long time, I feel refreshed and full of hope.

Wrapping a towel around me, I exit the bathroom. As the door clunks shut, I look up to find Luchlon, the handsome weapons specialist, standing in the corridor and blocking my way.

His gray eyes roam my body all the way down to my bare feet. I feel vulnerable with nothing but a towel.

His eyes come back up, and I realize too late what he's about to see. Still, my hand flies to my upper arm, trying to cover the tattoo stenciled there.

It's no good. He's already seen it, and his eyes go wide with recognition.

"So...you're not really a princess." He gets straight to the point. His lips curl into a smirk. I don't respond, but I don't have to.

I give up trying to hide my tattoo and pull my towel tighter with both hands.

"Well, this could be a problem." He leans against the corridor wall. "What will Sung say? She believes she's getting a big payout after this job. It's the only reason she's agreed to do it. She doesn't know you're a whore."

I flinch at the term.

"What's your deal, Eshan'ya? If that's your real name." His eyes bore into mine.

"I have money," I say, because a man like him is only concerned with money. He's afraid he won't get paid. "I can still deliver what I promised."

His voice lowers further. "How could a girl like you get the kind of money you've promised?"

He won't believe the truth, not when I've already been caught in a lie, so I say, "I assume all of your dealings are above board and legal then? You've never heard of stealing?"

He tilts his head. "I didn't think you were the type."

"*You* thought I was a princess."

"Touché." He grins.

"Like I said, I can deliver."

He looks over his shoulder toward the cockpit, then back at me. "OK, let's say I believe you. What do I get for keeping my mouth shut?" He reaches out and trails a finger down my arm over my tattoo. My skin tingles under his touch. I want to flinch away, but I hold my ground and my stare.

My voice is a steely whisper. "Remove your hand, and I'll give you a down payment now for your silence and an additional payment when the job is done. You'll be richer than Fan Sung."

He pulls his hand away. "What's the down payment?"

I answer by stepping around him. He follows me down the corridor to my quarters. When he steps inside my room, my heart crashes into my chest, sending warning signals throughout my body. It's an effort to sustain my calm countenance.

Images of another man crossing the threshold flash through my mind—vivid colors, a blur of robes, skin. I shove down the image and my rising panic.

But Luchlon doesn't come any closer; he stands just inside the doorway, watching me closely. Still, I can't trust those eyes. My hands tremble as I collect my knapsack. Gratefully, I find what I'm searching for without trouble: a leather drawstring pouch.

I don't bother opening it. I hand the whole pouch over to Luchlon, stretching out my arm so I don't need to get any closer to him.

He weighs it in his hand. His eyebrows raise in question, but before waiting for an answer, he pulls on the strings and pours the contents onto his palm.

Four jewels spill out, each about the size of a blueberry—one red and three clear Shadé diamonds, distinguished by their particular glow when the light hits them. Though many counterfeit artists have tried, no one has ever been able to fake that glow, so Shadé diamonds remain one of the most sought-after jewels in the galaxy.

Luchlon licks his lips as he lifts one up to the light and peers at it. A silver light glows on his high cheekbones. When he picks up the red diamond, a vibrant crimson glows on his fingers. He looks at them the way he looked at me in the corridor.

"So do we have a deal?" I ask.

"Yeah, we have a deal." He reseals the jewels in the pouch and walks toward the door. "A pleasure, Your Highness." He winks as he steps outside. My stomach churns.

Going to close the door behind him, I spot Fan coming around the bend in the corridor. She sees Luchlon exiting, looks from him to me and back at him, but she says nothing.

Neither does Luchlon. He gives her a casual salute and carries on down the corridor.

I close my door and slump against it.

Chapter 9

Fan

Pedders is leaning back in his chair with his feet on the dash when I enter the cockpit. I can't be angry. It's a good footrest. I put my feet on the dash all the time too.

"How's she sailing?" I ask.

"Smooth enough," he grunts, and I take the pilot's seat next to him.

"It better be. We don't need any more engine problems."

We both sit silently, watching pinpricks of stars streak past the window as we travel through hyperspace. It's comfortable. It always is with Pedders. We've known each other so long we don't need to fill the quiet, and I don't need to admit to him that I'm here to take comfort from his easy peace. So we go on for several long minutes just watching those stars.

"Vegasin ain't gonna be fun," Pedders eventually says.

"Yeah. I'm crazy, aren't I?"

"Ya always did like a pretty face."

My eyes bulge. But he's probably right, so I shut my mouth before I make a fool of myself by denying it.

"Remember that time in the orphanage?" Pedders asks.

"Yeah," I reply, but neither of us elaborate further.

We fall back into effortless silence until Pedders says, "Do you think it could be true?"

Classic Pedders. He doesn't linger on a single subject. He says what he thinks and moves on.

"About the Device?"

He nods.

I shrug. "Sounds like a load of mumbo jumbo to me."

He grunts.

Some might think that was a grunt of agreement, but I know Pedders better. That grunt said, "*You don't legitimately think that. You're worried there might be a Device, and it's got you scared.*"

I grunt back at him. My grunt says, "*You're right, but I don't want to talk about it. Let's keep pretending it's not real.*"

We keep watching the stars.

After another period of tranquil quiet, Pedders lowers his legs from the console and stretches out his large frame, arms reaching up over his head.

"Well, she's all set for Vegasin. Imma get some sleep."

I nod my goodnight as he leaves the cockpit. My feet replace his on the dash, and I lean back, closing my eyes. Maybe I can get a minute or so of sleep.

Eshan'ya's striking blue eyes float across my mind. She *is* pretty.

But she's a pain in the neck. She's smart—that's the problem. She can read me like a book, which means she keeps catching me off guard. She completely played me to take this mission, even if it's true that we need the money.

If it wasn't for Her Majesty, the *Fox* wouldn't have space scum shooting at her beautiful hull. The Quain wouldn't have shown up, and I doubt the royals would have either. We'd have gotten away from Keplerane with barely a scratch and still have all the shinver. But she had to show up on *my* ship. Hide in *my* hold. And for some reason, they're after her. Why?

And now the *Huxian Fox* is pink. Pink! Of all the damned colors, it has to be pink.

I open my eyes. The dash looks empty without Pedders' oranges, but they sure came in handy. Might not have been luck, but that was some smart thinking by Her Highness. I've gotta give her credit for that. Quick, clever, beautiful, rich...if only she wasn't so stubborn.

What was Luchlon doing at her door? She was only in a towel. There's no doubt he's keen on her—he'd be crazy not to be—but is she into him too? If she isn't, why would she stand around talking to him in a towel?

Oh fiery balls, I've gotta be nuts just thinking about her. She's royalty! And I'm a scoundrel. A girl like that with a girl like me? Nah...it just doesn't happen.

Stop kidding yourself, Sung.

I should be thinking about this grand hurrah upcoming mission and what I've gotten us all into. We're taking on the Quain. We need to break into their headquarters, sneak right under their noses, and take something their leader, Kriinal Braxt, is desperate to keep. It's going to be heavily guarded, locked up tight.

And don't even get me started on Shikha.

If she figures out we're on Vegasin and I don't have her shinver or her money, then we'll have a lot more to worry about than just the Quain. She's gonna go nuts.

I groan, running my hands down my face.

So much for sleeping.

I take out my personal tin of shinver and the eyedropper from the top pocket of my favorite jacket. Scooping a pinch of the powder into the liquid of the eyedropper, I shake it until it's dissolved.

I tilt my head back, and the dropper hovers above my eye. Just as I squeeze—the droplet connecting with my eyeball—there's a noise behind me.

I spin to find the princess standing in the cockpit's doorway, staring at me with those stunning blue eyes that I was just thinking about.

"I...I..." she stutters. "I was looking for Tika."

My stomach does a somersault, but it lands heavy, like when you try to dive but end up doing a belly flop.

Her lips press together. I'm not sure if that's disgust or pity in her expression.

Hadn't she gone to bed? Didn't think she'd ever see me doing this crap. My hand runs through my hair as I slouch lower in my seat.

I can't answer her. I don't know what to say, and my throat feels thick and tight.

But the drug is already taking effect, and I feel my muscles relaxing, my feelings of shame, or disgust, or embarrassment fade away. And I don't care. I don't feel anything.

Slowly, I shake my head.

She continues to stare. All blue, blue eyes. And then she's gone.

I rest my head back against the pilot's seat and let the drug wash over me, reveling in the pliability of my muscles—even my bones—and all my troubles washing away.

Once it has fully taken effect, a spike of adrenaline hits me. I climb out of my seat. Every movement seems to be in slow motion, but faster than the speed of light.

Just like the *Fox* right now.

I make my way to the main hold on rubbery legs.

He's there. I thought he might be. His shirt is off, and he's doing one-handed push-ups.

I marvel at the shape of the muscles bulging from his arms, his lean physique, the V of his back, until he feels my eyes on him.

"Fan." Luchlon stops his push-ups and climbs to his feet, grabbing a towel to pat his sweaty chest.

He comes over to where I stand, towering over me, his damp hair falling down into those eyes. Gray eyes, not blue.

His chest is heaving.

"I saw you talking to the princess earlier," I say, now watching his chest, not his eyes.

In my peripheral vision, I see him smile. "Just getting to know her."

"Without any clothes on?"

He shrugs. "She was wearing a towel." His voice is deep and low. "What, Fan? You know I only have eyes for you."

I scoff. "We both know that isn't true."

His chuckle is a deep rumble. "It's not like you save yourself for me either, Fan."

My eyes snap to his, and I give him a crooked grin. "You like it that way."

"I do," he growls, his gaze lowering to my mouth.

I tug on his towel. "Why don't you finish your workout in my quarters?"

Chapter 10

Eshan'ya

THE WHOLE OF FAN's crew is gathered in the main hold with me. Due to all the cases being spaced, there is almost nothing in here besides plenty of room for everyone.

Luchlon leans against a wall, looking completely at ease, although his eyes fell on me when he entered. I sit against the opposite wall, keeping my distance. Tika sits cross-legged and straight-backed. Pedders is beside her, leaning on his hands with his legs splayed comfortably in front of him. Fan leans casually against the doorframe. Her eyes are clear and alert—not like last night when I found her in the cockpit. She doesn't look any worse off from taking the drug, but looks can be deceiving.

The way they casually lounge around, obviously at ease with each other, reminds me of times around the fire with Declan and the other Protectors. They're like a family.

RAN-8 stands to attention in front of us. His green-lit eyes survey all of us as he speaks.

"There is a *lot* of information about the Quain on the 'laxy-net. They've done some pretty wild stuff. Did you know they already have six planets under their rule? All of them are planets outside the UoW. They even invaded Bradbury, that elitist planet with the super high-tech defenses—how'd they manage that?"

"What did you find out that can help us?" Fan asks, prompting RAN-8 to get to the point.

"Rumor has it that Kriinal Braxt keeps a vault full of valuable junk at the Quain headquarters on Vegasin, like Neil Armstrong's original space suit, the tooth of a higrasaur from Shadé, and even the original *Mona Lisa*. That's likely where we'll find the key."

"Great. How do we crack the vault?" Luchlon asks.

"Well, when it comes to sensors, this vault has got them all: motion, heat, pressure plates, humidity, biometric. I'm brilliant, but I can't crack all of that, not without triggering the firewall sensors. This place is impossible to sneak into."

"So you found nothing? No way to get in?"

"I didn't say that. Did I say that? No, we just need to trick security into letting us in."

There's a stir of movement from everyone around the hold as they lean in to hear more. If RAN-8 has found a way, then this mission is going ahead.

"I can't hack the vault, but I can hack the personnel files." When no one says anything, RAN-8's eyes dull. "Nobody get too excited. I'm just a genius, is all."

"Yep, you're great," says Fan. "Now can you tell us how hacking the personnel files is going to help?"

"How many people at headquarters do you think have ever laid their eyes on Kriinal Braxt's lieutenant in the flesh?"

Fan shrugs. "Given that she was trained on Earth and is always off world on missions, probably very few."

"They probably know she's a young female with blond hair and blue eyes. They may have even seen a picture of her before. But who remembers pictures? Especially if the personnel files are updated with a new headshot. A headshot of someone who fits the description, even if she doesn't look exactly like the lieutenant."

All eyes turn to me.

"What? Me?" I sit up straighter. "No." I shake my head. "No one will believe I'm the lieutenant. We look nothing alike." I think back to her angry face as she inspected me in the palace, her lips pressed into a straight line and her posture rigid. She's completely different from me.

"You *are* blond, blue-eyed, female, and young," Fan says, a crooked smile forming. "And you're just as bossy."

"I'm assertive, not bossy."

"Exactly." Fan grins, and a bolt of anger runs through me. She turns to RAN-8. "OK, so that's the plan. What do we need to make it work?"

I jump to my feet. "The deal was that *you* will get the key for me. I never said I would take part in this." I point my finger at Fan.

"The *deal* was that we would *help* you get the key, actually. And if you want it, Your Highness, then you will be posing as the lieutenant." Fan stands with her hands on her hips, with *that* smug smile.

She likes this idea.

"I won't do it."

"You will."

✳ ✳ ✳

Pedders navigates the ship to a secluded area in a large botanical garden that lies at the heart of Vegasin's capital city, Zhinü. It's a short distance from the Quain headquarters and well away from where the shinver lord, Shikha, has her base, so I'm told.

Vegasin is a humid, tropical planet, and as soon as the hatch opens, heat runs throughout the ship, causing me to sweat—*it's got nothing to do with this stupid plan.*

My arguing got me nowhere with Fan. We went around in exhausting circles until RAN-8 made it clear we had no other options. We go with this plan or cancel the mission. I finally conceded.

As soon as we land, Fan, Luchlon, and Tika depart the *Fox* to get the supplies required to make this plan work, leaving me to prepare with RAN-8.

"I need to update the files with your biometrics, not just your photo," he explains. "Open your eyes wide."

I do as he says, and a beam of green light shoots from his eyes, making me squint as the laser scans my irises.

"Your eyes are an unusual shade of blue," RAN-8 comments. "I doubt anyone will notice the difference from the lieutenant's, especially if they've never met her. We will update the photos anyway, so if they check, they'll all have your shade of blue."

He scans my fingerprints as well and even pricks my finger to take a sample of my blood, drawing it into an adaption on his little finger.

"Hmm, that's strange," he murmurs.

"What?"

His green-lit eyes blink a couple of times, but then he says, "No time for that. I have now cataloged all your biometrics. I just need your headshots."

As RAN-8 finishes taking photos for my security headshots, the others charge up the ramp.

"Step one of the mission is successful," Fan says, holding up the uniform of a Quain soldier.

"Oh, very successful." RAN-8's eyes glow brighter. "I love a hotty in uniform."

"How did you get those?" I ask.

"Let's just say some soldiers are going to have sore heads tomorrow."

I don't know if that means they were knocked out or if they got them drunk before stealing their uniforms. Either way, it worked, and Fan thrusts a set into my hands with a wink. "Here you go, lieutenant."

I snatch the uniform away and go to my quarters to change. I still can't believe I'm doing this. But if the alternative is Braxt gets the ancient Device, then we're all doomed anyway, so I might as well risk my neck trying to stop him.

The uniform is a pair of trousers, a short-sleeved shirt, a jacket, a cap, and big sturdy boots—all black, except for the three silver stars that adorn the pocket of the jacket. I dress in everything but the jacket and the cap because even though it's nighttime, it's boiling hot. I'll put them on before we leave. Thankfully, the shirt sleeves are just long enough to cover the spiraling tattoo and stars printed on my upper arm. As I leave my quarters, I tug on the sleeve anyway, just to be sure.

RAN-8 lets out a low whistle when I enter the hold. "Looking good, princess. I mean, lieutenant."

A nervous laugh escapes my lips, not just because of RAN-8's inappropriate behavior—which is particularly humorous because he's a droid with no sexual instincts—but because this mission is terrifying.

Luchlon and Tika are also dressed in soldiers' uniforms, complete with hats and jackets. They're ready for this mission.

Fan strolls into the hold with Pedders behind her. Neither of them are in uniforms; Pedders will stay with the ship, and Fan doesn't need a uniform for the plan. Instead, she wears her usual casual gear, a loose cream shirt over her tight brown trousers, her guns strapped to her legs. "I hate black," Fan says, "but I must admit it looks good on you."

Heat rises to my cheeks.

"Are you guys all set?" she asks, surveying us, and we each nod. "OK, keep comms to a minimum, but don't enter until Ranate has time to upload the doctored personnel files and I give the signal."

We nod again.

"At this moment," Tika says, "I'd just like to point out that the chances of mission success are one thousand to one."

"Actually, they're one thousand and twenty-one to one," RAN-8 corrects her and then says cheerfully, "Good luck."

I exhale slowly, then pull the black cap over my head, my blond ponytail poking out underneath. I feel eyes on me and turn to see Fan staring. She'd been loading her duster pistol, but now she's looking at my upper arm. My tattoo. The sleeve moved when I put the cap on. My stomach lurches.

Her eyes flick to mine, back to my arm, and then away to her duster pistol. She continues to load the pistol and then slides it into her holster while I throw on the soldier's jacket with shaking fingers, hiding any incriminating evidence.

If she knows what the tattoo means, she doesn't say so. All she says is, "All right, let's go."

Chapter 11

Fan

Vegasin is a stinking hot planet. I never did like it much. Too humid, too full of scoundrels, too many wannabe overlords. It's bad enough that Shikha's base is here, but it's got the Quain as well—this planet must attract crazy people.

I must be crazy too.

A one thousand and twenty-one chance of success. RAN-8's statistics run around in my head.

I'm definitely worried for my sanity.

RAN-8 runs along beside me. We've split from the others. They're heading to the side entrance while we're heading to the tech hole. By the stars, Eshan'ya did look cute in that uniform. I wonder what the deal is with her tattoo. I can tell she's ashamed of it because she always keeps it hidden. Maybe she regrets getting it? But it's quite pretty—a swirling geometric design all in black ink, and I think there were stars in the middle. It looks familiar, but I can't put my finger on what it reminds me of right now.

And I should be paying attention to the mission.

We've left the gardens far behind, but this planet is overrun with plant life, even in Zhinü. The city streets are lined with trees, large thick leaves, and vines. It gives us lots of cover as we approach the tech hole, the security system RAN-8 needs to hack in order for this plan to work.

The tropical climate is a perfect habitat for an array of bug life, and I feel them creeping on my skin no matter how often I swat at them. Plus, the tickle of the foliage on bare skin as I pass makes me itch all over.

We're still a hundred yards away when I start to see soldiers. Some are out in the open on patrol, their lava guns at the ready. Others are only silhouettes within the foliage.

"Dim your lights," I order RAN-8, and he does so immediately. His eyes go completely dull, so the only light that can be seen is the reflection of the moons on his white steel body. There's nothing we can do about that but keep to the shadows, which we intend to do anyway.

I signal to RAN-8 to wait before creeping ahead.

Silently, I sneak up on one silhouette. I'm little and I'm stealthy, so the soldier doesn't see me coming. Before he knows it, I've stunned him with my pulsar gun, just like we did to the other soldiers to get their uniforms. He'll be out for at least thirty minutes. Plenty of time for RAN-8 to load the files and for us to get out of here.

A quick wave to RAN-8, and he joins me in the foliage. He's got his stealth programing running, so he steps lightly on the ground and slides around the leaves with careful movements. We pause while a soldier on patrol walks past, and then start moving again.

I take out two more soldiers as we approach—just putting them down for a little evening nap. Such a shame they won't wake up feeling any better.

There's no foliage around the entrance to the tech hole—even if I can still feel it on my skin, *urgh*—but I've taken out all the hidden soldiers watching this side of the complex, so it's just the soldiers on patrol we have to worry about.

This one particular crud dweller is taking his time, walking slowly, not even paying that much attention—must be daydreaming. I wouldn't mind taking him out, but if he stops passing the main entrance regularly, that'll probably attract attention.

Nah, better to time our approach between their rounds.

After several minutes of me breathing as shallowly as possible to keep from alerting him to our presence, finally—*finally*—he passes around the corner of the complex.

We creep forward. My heart pounds, and I'm sweating buckets, but, of course, RAN-8 is completely at ease. He doesn't really have emotions, even if he pretends to sometimes. And he can't feel this stifling heat. I slap at my arm—damned bugs—and RAN-8's head spins at the sound.

"Sorry," I whisper.

We duck under the little arch that leads to the tech hole, and my heart drops.

"What the stars is that?" RAN-8 whispers.

The way is locked—and not with a security pad like we expected. No, it's locked with a grand hurrah old-fashioned padlock! I haven't seen one of them in years. And I've never seen anyone use them beyond Earth.

I did *not* prepare for this.

I had bet on RAN-8 being able to hack past the system silently and quickly. But this? Didn't think I'd need bolt cutters—so primitive!

RAN-8 has a blowtorch adaption so he can cut through it, but it's going to take longer than I anticipated. The tip of his finger flips backward, and a blue flame jets out of it. He gets to work on the lock while I keep a lookout.

I know I always look cool on the outside, but waiting for RAN-8 to burn through the lock is giving me the heebie-jeebies. I can hear all sorts of stuff in the darkness—footsteps, animal calls, mosquitos buzzing, the click of a gun as the safety switch is turned off. But there is no sign of movement out there. The next sentry hasn't approached this side of the complex yet, but I have no doubt they will get here soon.

Finally, I hear the lock clang as RAN-8 cuts through the last of it—the sound echoes through the quiet. I pull my head back under the arch and yank the lock from the door, burning my fingers as I do, and dragging the door open.

The room inside looks like a mini city of towers with blinking blue and green lights and wires crossing above and behind. We enter quickly.

RAN-8 goes straight to a tower, pops the tip off of a different finger, and shoves the connector into one of the many available ports.

I'm still near the door when I hear the unmistakable crack of a tech point with its comms on. It's still some distance away for now, but it's definitely not my imagination anymore. RAN-8 hears it too, and turns to look at me, awaiting my orders.

"Stay here," I whisper. "Get those personnel files uploaded and confirm with the others as soon as you do." I peer back out the door. "I'll draw them away." With that, I slip into the night.

Chapter 12

Eshan'ya

RAN-8's voice comes over the comms. "The personnel files have been successfully uploaded. You can proceed with the mission."

Luchlon, Tika, and I are among the shadows just outside the side entrance to the complex. The foliage has kept us hidden from the sentries and soldiers walking past.

But now we step out onto the path.

I take the lead, Luchlon and Tika posing as my subordinates. I hold my head high like I know where I'm going and what I'm doing.

My heart beats harder as we approach the entrance and the two guards finally see us. If they know what the lieutenant looks like—

"Halt."

The female guard blocks our way. She looks me up and down. I narrow my eyes at her in my best imitation of the stern, angry way the lieutenant did it.

We mustn't look out of place because the next thing she asks is, "Rank and business?" Then she holds out the portable biometric scanner.

"Lieutenant. And my business is classified." I use my most commanding, powerful tone with a little added contempt.

Her eyes flick up to mine in shock. "Oh, oh, lieutenant...it's an honor." She hastily salutes me, as does the other guard.

I salute back. I hope that's what I'm meant to do. Neither of them says anything, but the female blinks, and I wonder if she has realized something is wrong.

The guard blocks me when I try to walk past.

"My apologies, ma'am." She looks down at her scanner and back up to me hesitantly. "You know protocol. I must scan you."

I tut in annoyance as I hold out my hand, palm up, hoping the slight tremble isn't visible.

My face pops up in a hologram that displays the photo RAN-8 took only an hour earlier, and underneath is the rank: lieutenant.

"Thank you, ma'am." She salutes me and steps aside.

I don't let out my breath until all three of us have entered the complex, and the door is closed behind us.

Luchlon grins. "Nice going, lieutenant."

"Very well done, Your Highness." Tika does a small bow.

"Shh, none of that in here," I say. "We don't know who might be watching. Treat me like the lieutenant at all times."

Tika gulps and nods solemnly. No wonder she's been quiet. It's obvious she's scared and trying to hide it as much as possible.

We carry on into the building.

It's so much cooler in here, and it's a relief to get out of the suffocating humidity outside. The place is state-of-the-art. We only came through the side entrance, and it is beautiful here. I imagine the front entrance is quite spectacular. Shiny gray tiles adorn the floors, walls, and ceiling, which makes it seem cold but sleek. Silver lights run down the walls from a gap in the ceiling, highlighting the red leaves of several trees growing in even intervals, incorporating the beautiful part of the jungle outside.

"It's this way," Tika says, checking the schematics on her tech point.

She leads us through three sections, each adorned with a different species of plant. After the red-leafed trees are green shrubs with six-pointed leaves. Then we come across tall pale blue trees that have branches that droop all the way to the ground like Ra'punzelle's hair.

On the way, we pass two other Quain guards, but they don't look at us, so none of us look at them.

In the room of pale blue trees, there's a spot of darkness on the other side. No silver light shines down on that section. I glimpse stairs leading down into the darkness.

"What's that?" I ask, nodding at the shadows.

"Braxt keeps a prison, and that's the entrance," Tika says.

The back of my neck prickles. The entrance is so foreboding that I'm glad we're not heading down those steps.

Tika rounds another corner, and we enter a space with purple flowers the size of my head. Just like in the other rooms, they're highlighted by the silver light shining down from a crevice in the roof. Halfway into the room stand two guards, and beyond them are ornately decorated doors. Instead of door handles, there is an unadorned square—the security point.

I straighten my back and press my lips into a hard line before charging right up to the two guards.

"Move aside," I say.

"My apologies, ma'am. We cannot allow entrance to this area of the complex," the one on the left says.

"Not even to Braxt's lieutenant?" Luchlon growls.

I give him a look that says, *"Shut the stars up,"* and turn back to the guards, who are saluting me now.

"Ma'am," they say with respect.

I salute back, though I'm still not sure that's what I'm meant to do. "Please stand aside," I say, my heart pounding like a gorilla in a cage.

"Ma'am," she says, resolute. "My apologies, but our orders are to keep everyone out. No one can be let through. Not even you."

"I will not ask you again," I say in my most commanding voice. "By order of Kriinal Braxt himself, you will move aside and provide me access."

Neither guard moves.

The left guard goes to speak again, but before she has the chance, she's shot with a pulsar stun. Luchlon quickly aims again, and the second guard drops before he can get out a warning.

"We don't have time to negotiate," he growls. "They were never going to let you in anyway. Open the door and let's drag them inside."

My lips purse again, but I do as Luchlon says.

I hope this works. It won't matter that RAN-8 could swap my biometrics if the lieutenant never had access in the first place.

I stand before the square in the middle of the doors and press my finger to the access point. It scans my fingerprint, and a soft beep sounds. One scan down. A portal pops open, and I lower my left eye for it to be scanned too.

There's another soft beep, and then the whole square clunks as it automatically slides to the right, unlocking. I exhale.

It takes a bit of strength to push the large doors open, but they're unlocked, which is a miracle.

Inside, the silver light continues to glow around the edges of the room, but there are no illuminated trees this time. Instead, the light shines upon art hung on the walls, statues standing in the center, and glass cabinets containing an array of artifacts.

I stand in the entrance, staring for a moment.

Luchlon knocks me out of the way as he drags one guard and then the other into the space. He leaves them in a heap by the door.

Tika pokes her head inside. "Oh wow, this is beautiful. I see the famous *Starry Night* painting by Van Gogh. And oh my, is that the bust of Colonel Wang from the battle of Pernicus? And look there—"

"Where is it?" Luchlon whispers.

"It's got to be in here somewhere," I say.

"Oh my, and there is the *Mona Lisa*, just like the rumors said."

"Well, find it," Luchlon scowls. "Tika and I will pose as the guards. But find it quick."

I swallow. I don't like the idea of leaving them outside, but it makes sense. They might be unknown to the other guards here, but it's far more likely we'll be discovered if no guards are at the post at all.

Luchlon closes me inside Braxt's personal museum, and I take off to explore this large room.

I could spend a lifetime in here. Some of the artifacts haven't been seen in centuries, and I wonder how Braxt got his hands on them. There are a lot of relics from Earth, some of them as old as the pyramids of Egypt. But there are also Protogenoi relics, which are a *lot* older.

An ornamental axe with blue glass within its head and swirls engraved into the hilt is clearly ancient Protogenoi. A necklace inlaid with dark blue Shadé diamonds, which emit that strange glow those jewels are known for, is undeniably from a Protogenoi dig.

Rushing through the room, I try to ignore the beautiful treasures surrounding me. I had expected the key to be in a prominent position in the middle of the room, but it's not there. I circle outward from the center, but I can't find it.

It's not here.

I'm starting to sweat, and my steps get more hurried and frantic.

"What are you doing?" Luchlon whispers from the door. He has it propped open, and I can only see his head. "Have you got it? Let's go."

"I can't find it," I hiss.

He disappears for a moment to whisper at Tika before he slips inside.

"What do you mean you can't find it?" His brow is drawn low as he looms over me.

"It's not here," I say.

"You *do* know what it looks like, right?"

"Yes." *Somewhat.* I huff, "Like I said on the ship, it's a red Shadé diamond the size of your palm. And within is printed a map."

That's all I know.

He grumbles as he storms through the room. After several minutes, we still haven't found it, and it's getting dangerous to stay here.

"Princess," he calls in a loud whisper, even though he knows now that I'm not one. I rush over. He's staring into an empty glass cabinet that stands in the middle of the back wall. I hadn't noticed it before because it's empty. But now that I'm closer, I see that there are three indents in the cabinet's base, each big enough to fit a palm-sized diamond. And engraved on the glass at the back of the container is the Protogenoi sigil—the symbol my tattoo is inspired by. Three silver stars surrounded by three half circles which overlap. Three spaces for three keys.

"It's not here." Luchlon's whisper is more of a snarl.

I feel like I'm falling through the floor. "Braxt must have it with him right now. He must already be searching for the second key."

It's the only explanation. Suddenly, I'm finding it hard to swallow.

Luchlon spins on me, his face so close I feel his hot breath on my neck, and I try not to cringe. "We came all this way on your word. You risked us all, and the key isn't even here."

"There's no way I could have known that. We had to try. Braxt can't get his hands on the Device." Anger burns in my veins, but the truth is, I'm just as angry with myself as I am with

Luchlon—he's right, but he doesn't need to be such a jerk about it.

Luchlon's face has gone red, and he looks like he might hit me, but I stand my ground. I stare into his eyes as he scowls into mine.

Finally, I say, "We need to get out of here."

He huffs and turns away, clomping to the exit.

"What happened? Where is it?" Tika asks, urgently looking for the key in our hands.

Luchlon's eyes slide to mine, but he simply rumbles, "Let's go."

We hurry away from the museum, leaving the guards inside. Their absence will soon be noticed, so we don't have a lot of time to get back to the *Huxian Fox* and leave the planet. I hope Fan and RAN-8 have already returned and are ready to leave when we get there.

Chapter 13

Fan

WHEN I SLIPPED AWAY, leaving RAN-8 to upload his files, I got the attention of the sentry and led him away from RAN-8.

Problem is, he's *still* following me. And so are two of his friends.

I've considered shooting them with my duster, but it's loud and will attract more trouble. I've still got my pulsar gun, but I need to be in closer proximity to use it. And since there are three of them, getting closer is a whole lot harder. I might be able to knock out one of them or even two, but at least one will have the opportunity to disarm me.

If this mission wasn't so reliant on stealth, I could take all three of them out, no problem. Instead, I find myself running and hiding in bushes, bugs running across my arms, sweat pouring off my brow, not to mention the sweat in my cleavage. Stars, I hate this planet.

At this point, I don't think I'll be able to get back to RAN-8. I just hope he calculates the necessity to head back to the *Fox* without me. I'm going to have to go into the center of Zhinü to lose these guys. Usually, using the city's twists and turns would be a great idea, but we're on freaking Vegasin, and the city is crawling with Shikha's crew—*and* Shikha herself.

I've gotta take the chance and hope I don't run into any of them. There's no way I'm going to lose the Quain guards in this garden, and I can't risk leading them to the *Fox*.

I make a dash from the cover of a bush and head in the direction of the streets. There's a shout and the thumping of three sets of boots making chase.

The city is almost as overgrown with plants as the gardens are. The only difference is that the vines climb up the sides of buildings and, of course, more people.

Zhinü isn't as crowded as Kep City, but it's a city, so it's busy enough. The place stinks of moss and rotting plants, not to mention the stench coming off the water in the canals. The squawks of several large birds are loud enough to be heard over the hover traffic, and they fly among the cars and plant-covered buildings.

People go about their evening activities while I duck around them and under the overhang of giant leaves. At one point, I don't move quick enough, and a branch slaps me in the face.

The guards are still on my tail. They're staring right at me! They push people out of the way and hack away at leaves, all with the single purpose of catching me.

Geez, they are persistent. I didn't even *do* anything...well, nothing they know about anyway.

I wish I had my squito.

As I lope around a corner, I crash into a cart, tipping it over and spilling a thousand buttons onto the street.

"Sorry," I yell to the button vendor as I keep running. What the hell are they doing selling buttons at this time of night anyway—are they expecting a sewing emergency?

One of my pursuers slips on the buttons and crashes to the ground. The two others jump over him and keep coming. I skip across the street, causing cars to rear up on their propulsion engines. Some skid to a stop; others zoom overhead.

Around another bend, I see a train up ahead.

My legs are pushed to their limits, and the two remaining guards are close. If I can just get to the other side of the magnetic tracks, I could lose them. The train is a huge freighter, barreling at deadly speeds through the city. No one would be crazy enough to run in front of it. But as I've already mentioned, I *am* crazy.

I reach the tracks.

I dive—

—right in front of the train.

The horn blares.

And then I'm rolling in the dirt on the other side, pain jarring in my wrists, gravel slicing into my skin.

With a heavy grunt, one of the Quain guards falls on top of me. The other is trapped on the other side of the tracks, the train between him and us.

"Who are you?" the guard shouts, grabbing my collar and slamming me into the ground. My head rattles. "What were you doing at the Quain complex?"

My hand reaches down to where my trusty duster pistol sits in its holster. I whip it out and press it against the guard's head.

"Please get off me," I say, raising an eyebrow.

He moves slowly, inching back and off, getting to his feet. I stand up too, keeping my pistol trained on him. Then I pull the pulsar gun out of my other holster, and before he can beg me not to, I shoot him. Lucky for him, it's still set to stun.

The guard crumples to the ground, and I run off. I don't need to be around when that other guard gets past the train. I'm in a train yard with resting engines, shipping containers, and shunters, so I put a few of them between me and the tracks before I slow down. My breath rages as I try to replenish my oxygen. I've finally lost all three guards. Now I've just got to get back to the *Huxian Fox*.

I speed around another shipping container and run headfirst into an enormous stomach so hard that I bounce off.

"Captain Fan Sung." My arms are gripped so hard I can't get away.

I look up into their face and think, *Father's fist, now I'm done for*.

Chapter 14

Eshan'ya

THE *HUXIAN FOX* IS waiting where it's supposed to be, the glow from the open hatch a beacon of sanctuary in the night. Pedders stands inside holding a lava gun, peering into the dark with a frown. I'm comforted to see him.

I charge up the ramp with Tika and Luchlon in stride with me.

After everything we did, we failed anyway. Braxt will find the Device, and then he'll rule the galaxy.

"No luck?" Pedders asks.

I shake my head.

"It wasn't there," Luchlon growls.

"They've taken it to find the second key," I say. "It's the only explanation. But without knowing what information it contained, we can't know where." I shake my head again. "I truly thought they would keep it locked up here rather than risk taking it with them. This place is more secure."

"Well, you were wrong."

"Yes, I was wrong. Thank you, Luchlon, for pointing that out. I didn't know that before."

Pedders grunts, and somehow I understand that he's on my side.

Luchlon approaches me menacingly. "I want the riches you promised me, girl."

"The task isn't over yet," I spit. "We can still retrieve the key from Braxt. We just need to figure out where he is."

"Don't expect us to be a part of that."

"The deal I made with Captain Sung was to get the key. Do we have the key? No. So the mission isn't over."

Luchlon bares his teeth. His chest expands like he's about to explode...or hit me. I lift my chin higher.

"Where is the captain anyway?" Tika asks, breaking the tension between us.

I blink and glance around. There's only me, Luchlon, Tika, and Pedders in the hold. We all look to Pedders, but he only shrugs, an expression of worry on his face.

"Shouldn't she and Ranate have returned by now?" I ask.

Pedders nods, his eyes returning to the dark gardens outside.

"Have you called her?" Tika asks.

"Her tech point is off," Pedders says without taking his eyes off the garden.

We all turn to follow his gaze.

As the minutes drag on, the skin on the back of my neck prickles. What if she was captured by the Quain? Will they kill her on the spot or take her to their prison? And what will it mean for me if she doesn't return? My eyes slide to Luchlon. He stares out of the hold like the rest of us, a scowl on his face—although I'm not sure it's from concern for Fan, or anger at me.

My spine tingles as if icy water were dripping down it.

I remember him entering my quarters, his eyes dark and menacing. The way he looked me up and down when I wore nothing but a towel. The fury in his eyes just now. I shiver.

My eyes return to the darkness. But as they do, they fall on a distant light...in fact, two lights. Green lights that could be RAN-8.

My hand flies to my mouth. It *is* RAN-8. He moves closer and closer, his form coming fully into view. He's unharmed. He blazes up the ramp, and even though he doesn't need oxygen, he feigns the sound of being out of breath.

"Thank god you're still here," he says while wheezing.

"Where's Fan?" Pedders asks.

His wheezing stops instantly, and he looks around quizzically. "She's not back?" RAN-8's eyes shine a brighter green, and he appears shocked.

Luchlon growls at RAN-8.

"There were guards. She took off to deal with them," RAN-8 says.

"And you left without her?" Luchlon's face twists into a vicious scowl.

"*Ò tiān ā,*" Pedders says under his breath.

"She was supposed to come back, but it was past our rendezvous time, and I was still waiting. It was logical that she would return to the ship. And it wasn't wise for me to wait any longer where I was."

"You did the right thing, Ranate," I say. If he had waited any longer, he would have been at risk of capture too. No, something must have happened to Fan. She would have returned to RAN-8 otherwise.

Tika moans. "I knew this mission was doomed. And now we don't have our captain or the key. Where is she?"

"You didn't get the key?" RAN-8 asks.

"No. The mission is a failure," Luchlon snarls, and I brace for his anger to turn on me again. RAN-8 speaks before he can do anything.

"Well, it might not be a complete failure. We might not have the key, but I did find this." His eyes shine brightly again, but this time, an image is projected out of them. In the green hue is a solar system. There are three sister stars and eight planets orbiting the smallest star. The fifth planet flashes brighter, flickering every second like a signal.

I recognize the collection of celestial objects.

"That's the Farnth system," says Luchlon, which surprises me. I wouldn't expect celestial cartography to be something many smugglers learn. He must see the shock on my face because he continues, saying, "They mine a key ingredient of shinver there."

"Ah."

"Remember that time the Farnth crew almost killed us?" Tika interrupts. "We weren't even near Farnth. We ran into them in orbit around Urfaria."

"Why are you showing us this?" I ask. I already have an inkling, but it's too much to hope for.

"It's where the second key is hidden," RAN-8 replies, confirming my suspicions. My heart does a little leap. "I found it on the Quain database when I hacked into their system."

"Ranate, how do you know that's real? You can't trust a strange computer," Tika objects. "We need to be careful this isn't a trap."

RAN-8's eyes flash red. "It's not a trap. The intel is good. I'm sure of it because my processing skills are much better than Tika's."

"We can still stop him," I whisper, my hand on my heart.

"We're not going anywhere without Fan," Pedders says. His brow furrows, and I know there will be no changing his mind. Even if it *is* more important to get the key than to save Fan—even though we risk the galaxy—he won't leave this planet with his captain in the Quain's custody.

I swallow my objections and say instead, "She must have been captured. They'd take her to the prison cells in the basement of the main complex." Better to get this done quickly so we can find the second key, I tell myself. My compliance has nothing to do with my feelings for Fan. I barely *have* any feelings for Fan. I just know there isn't any point arguing with Pedders.

"Do you know the way?" he asks.

I nod. Within the complex, I remember the darkening stairs. I shiver at the thought of them.

"We'll need night-vision goggles. The prison is kept in complete darkness," Tika says and goes to retrieve them.

"Luchlon, you go with the princess. Do you need Ranate?"

"Yes, he might be needed to unlock the prison cells."

"I can do many things with my fingers." RAN-8 waves at me, the gesture somehow sleazy, though there's no change to his metallic face.

Tika returns with the goggles and hands a pair to Luchlon and me. RAN-8's laser eyes can see in the dark without them.

"We need to be quick. Those guards are going to be missed any second now," Luchlon says.

As we head back down the ramp, I pause to look at Pedders and Tika, who are staying behind. Pedders' hands are clenched together.

"We'll bring her back," I say with more confidence than I truly have. I need to believe we can do this. I need this team to help me get that second key.

We make good time returning to the Quain complex; we've already traveled these paths twice, so they're becoming familiar.

The same two guards are still standing at the side entrance.

"Lieutenant." They nod to me, and I hold out my hand to be scanned once again. If they're suspicious of my reentry—this time with an unknown droid—they say nothing. They probably don't want to risk offending the right-hand woman to the Quain lord, but I wonder what the guards will say after we're inside. The urgency of this rescue isn't lost on me.

We hurry through the complex, past the red highlighted trees, and the green, and into the corridor of pale blue trees. We find the entrance, stairs running down into pitch black.

My skin prickles as we approach.

I gingerly place my foot on the first step. It's so dark down there. I can see three steps clearly, but then they fade, getting darker and darker until the seventh step is in complete darkness.

I take out my night-vision goggles and flick them to my eyes. The darkness takes on a green hue, but all of a sudden, I can see every narrow step below me.

My muscles are still tense. I don't want to go down there, but I force my legs into action and hurry to the lower level. Luchlon and RAN-8 are right behind me.

The stairs end in a small room no bigger than a modest pantry, but a secure, thick metal door stands in front of us. The door to the prison.

I step up to the access pad to the left of the door, scan my finger, and remove my goggles to scan my left eye. After a few seconds that seem to stretch on forever, the door makes a small click and opens.

The smell hits me before anything else—the smell of unwashed humans kept in a small space—sweat, feces, urine, blood, and vomit. It hangs in the air like a humid summer day. I can feel it soaking in and wonder if any quantity of the palace soaps would ever be enough to wash it from my skin. I try to breathe through my mouth instead of my nose, but the taste of it is just as bad and I almost gag.

Luchlon's face is also drawn with disgust. RAN-8 can't smell anything, and I find myself wishing I was him.

The walls are solid brick—large gray stones washed in the green hue from the night-vision goggles. There are six cells on either side. Each cell is barricaded with electrified bars that barely glint, the only light in the darkness, but they're not bright enough to illuminate anything but the bars.

We can't leave Fan in one of these cells. *I* can't leave her here. It's so horrible, and she doesn't deserve this.

I approach the first cell. Inside, a frail old body is curled up in the corner. Only skin and rags cover the torso. Any distinguishing features have long wasted away. The eyes flicker open as I approach, but otherwise there's no movement.

The prisoner is alone. Fan isn't in there.

While I move to the next cell, Luchlon inspects the cells on the opposite side.

A large man sits in the middle of the next cell. Shockingly, I recognize him. He was hunted throughout the galaxy for the countless murders he committed. If I remember correctly, he carved words into his victim's flesh while they still lived, keeping them alive for days while he tortured them. He stares straight ahead with his dark murderous eyes. It seems like he's staring right at me, but I realize in the dark and without night-vision goggles there is no way he can see me. Still, I'm unnerved and move on quickly.

The next cell holds two women.

"Who's there?" one asks, searching desperately through the dark, her eyes darting around. I peer closer at her companion; her frame is slight and her hair short, but it's not Fan.

"Is someone there?"

I don't recognize either of these women, but I do remember a story of two sisters kidnapping children to work their mines digging krast, a substance often used in the reactor cores for hyperdrive engines. Even through the green hue, I can see their fingers are darker than the rest of their skin—stained black, just like many krast miners.

My stomach lurches when I see the next prisoner curled on the ground. It's a man I've seen before, a man I despise. A rapist and human trafficker. I remember his slimy smile as he shook hands with King Vald. He doesn't move as I hurry past, and I wonder if he's dead. I hope not; I'd rather he suffer in this prison.

The next cell is empty.

There's only one cell left on my side. I glance at Luchlon, but he continues searching the cells.

I reach the last one and look at the prisoner inside.

It's not Fan.

It's just another scruffy-looking man with tattoos on his knuckles that spell 'Kill' on one hand and 'King' on the other. I turn away in revulsion.

Luchlon looks at me with his eyebrows raised. I shake my head.

"Not here either," he says.

"You're sure?" I ask. I don't trust him. What if he's just saying that so he can steal Fan's ship and crew? "Fan? Fan, are you here?" My voice echoes through the prison, bouncing off the stone walls.

Luchlon scowls at me. "She's not here."

"She's got to be. Fan?"

"Fan? Fan's here?" A gravelly voice comes from a cell on Luchlon's side. Slowly, the man approaches the bars. He's terribly thin, and his teeth have turned black with rot. "She's come for me?" The old man peers into the darkness. He's clearly lost his sanity.

"Ain't hear of no Fan in these cells, girly," Kill King says in a low rumble.

He's come close to the bars without me realizing, and I gasp even though I know he can't get through them. He snickers at my fear.

"Where is she then?" I ask Luchlon.

"Who knows?" He shrugs. "But we gotta get outta here."

"Do you need me to let these prisoners out?" RAN-8 asks.

"Yeah, let us out," Kill King barks.

"Let us out," cries one of the sisters. A few others echo her demand.

"Fan?" calls the man with rotted teeth, and his howl causes the hair on my arms to stand on end.

It is disgusting in here, and it's not right to keep people in these conditions. But these are rapists, murderers, slavers—what would we do with them if they were released?

"Let them rot," I say and stalk out. They've made others suffer worse than what they will experience in here. They already chose their fate.

I take the stairs two at a time, lowering my night-vision goggles as I reach the lit room with the pale blue trees. Before I can head to the exit, I'm pulled up short by a voice.

"Lieutenant?"

It's the guard from the side entrance who scanned me into the complex. Something told me she was suspicious the second time we entered, and there's no doubt now. Her hand rests on the top of her lava gun, her eyes slanted into a squint.

"Yes?" I ask, stopping and turning to face her.

Luchlon and RAN-8 also stop.

"It seems there's a problem—"

Shwoom!

The blast from Luchlon's pulsar hits her in the chest, and she tumbles to the ground. It's not on stun anymore, and smoke rises from the deadly wound.

"Go!" he says.

I don't need to be told twice. All three of us take off at a run.

I pull out my own borrowed pulsar, ready to take aim.

We run through the room of green plants and then into the one with the red trees. More guards are waiting, which I discover when a shot misses my head by mere inches. I duck behind a red tree.

The other two retreat to the green room where Luchlon uses the entrance as cover.

He's an excellent shot. He takes two guards out within seconds.

I'm not as good, but my shots let him dart out from the entrance and get off more rounds.

I peek around the tree. Six against three—not great odds.

"OK, OK." I hold up my hands in surrender. "Let's talk."

The shooting stops, and I slowly rise, my hands over my head. The guards step out from their cover, but it's not a smart move. Luchlon jumps out from his hiding spot and zaps three of them before the others have a chance to react.

It's not moral. It's against the unspoken rules of a gunfight to feign a surrender, but it is effective. And I can't let politeness impede this mission. Too much is riding on it.

I duck back behind the tree when the remaining three guards start shooting again.

But Luchlon is like a storm, raging and unstoppable. He keeps approaching the guards, his gun blazing. He snatches up a guard's weapon and shoots that as well, alternating between the pulsar in his right hand and a lava gun in his left. The pulsar's electronic shots sizzle when they hit skin while the lava gun blasts ungainly balls of fire through anything and everything. The barrage forces the remaining guards to dive for cover. Luchlon is unrelenting. Determined. I may not like him, but I can't deny he's useful.

One of the remaining guards dares to pop his head up, trying to get a shot off, but he's rewarded with a zap to the head.

The other two have had enough. They run from their cover and away from Luchlon. He catches one in the back during her retreat, and she falls. The last guard rounds the corner, but Luchlon follows and gets them too.

There's carnage everywhere—bodies lying throughout the red room, smears of blood across the floor, the stench of burned flesh. The walls are riddled with smoking holes from all the blasts. My tree is wilted from being hit so many times.

RAN-8 runs with me, and we catch up to Luchlon. He doesn't frown or glare like I expect. Instead, his face is a mask of concentration—all business. And despite myself, I am grateful to him. He opens the side door, shoots a guard standing there, and holds the door open for us to dash out into the night.

Pedders paces up and down the main hold, muttering and rumbling, shaking his head.

"What do you want us to do? She's not there," Luchlon snaps.

When we returned to the *Huxian Fox* without Fan, Pedders wasn't happy. He hasn't stopped growling since.

"Let's think about this logically," I propose. "If the Quain haven't locked her in the prison, then they must have taken her with them."

"Or they killed her instantly," RAN-8 supplies helpfully.

I purse my lips as I give him a sidelong glance. He's got a point, but not one that needed speaking aloud.

"If they *have* taken her," I continue, "then our best chance of saving her is by following them. We need to get to the second key before Braxt does anyway. It'll be two for the price of one."

We're currently in orbit around Vegasin. In case the Quain tracked us to the *Fox*, we moved, but the crew can't decide what to do next. Not one of them wants to leave Fan behind. I don't either, but since we don't know where she is, I want to get on with my original mission: stop Kriinal Braxt and save the galaxy.

"What if Shikha somehow captured her?" Tika asks. "If she got a hold of Fan and Fan couldn't produce the drugs she owes her, she'd skin her alive."

"Surely that's an exaggeration," I say.

"Not necessarily," Luchlon says, and Pedders grunts his agreement. "If Fan had to lead guards away from the tech hole like Ranate says, she might have ended up in the city. That place is riddled with Shikha's crew. You can't swing a hurball in Zhinü without hitting one of Shikha's minions."

"Hurballs are such sweet, fluffy creatures," Tika says. "You shouldn't swing them around. But otherwise, I agree."

"So we need to go back down to the planet?" I ask. It's the last thing I want to do, but it touches me how much Fan's crew cares about her. We have the Quain chasing us, and they're willing to risk adding another foe to their long list of would-be killers. I wish I still had such loyal friends. I did once—Declan's gentle smile and the faces of the other Protectors cross my mind—but it's been a long time since then, and Declan never came back for me. The memory of the loss makes my chest feel empty, as if my heart is missing.

Pedders grunts, and my memories fade. It's clear his grunt means, "*I'm not taking this ship anywhere until we get Fan.*"

I stand up. "OK, so what's the plan?"

Chapter 15

Fan

THEY DISARM ME FIRST, taking my duster and pulsar, my multitool, and my tech point. I feel naked without them. Then they bind my wrists and ankles with magnetic shackles—impossible to get out of—and I'm slung onto the back of a goon like a bag of rice. I grunt as my gut slams into his shoulder.

No one says anything until the procession of tough guys carries me onto their freighter and dumps me unceremoniously onto the floor of their dirty hold.

"Well, well, well, if it isn't Fan Sung."

Gussart strolls toward me, his thumbs hooked into the band at his waist so his beer belly sticks out.

"In the flesh," I mutter, flicking my hair out of my eyes, but it falls back where it was. With my hands bound behind my back, it's hard to look dignified. I shimmy around so I'm sitting up properly with my bound legs in front of me.

"I want my shinver back," he says.

"Well, I'm a little tied up at the moment." I wiggle my ankles pointedly.

"Yeah, but even if ya weren't, ya can't get me that shinver, can ya, Sung?"

"Just give me a little time, that's all I ask." I try to bargain.

"Ya time is up, Sung. Ya've had more chances than ya deserve. Now ya hide is mine."

"And what do you plan to do with my nicely shaped hide?"

He grins so wide he bares his shinver-rotted teeth. I cringe at the sight. That's why I don't chew the stuff. "You and ya nicely shaped hide are not gonna enjoy what I have in store for ya." He then turns to his men. "Make sure she's secure for the trip back to Keplerane. Feed her, keep her in good shape for now. She'll work it off when we get there."

For two days, they keep me bound and sprawled on the floor of the hold of their freighter. The only reprieve I receive is during my brief visits to the bathroom, which I drag out as long as possible, because *broken hearts*, my arms are aching. Plus, my backside has gone numb from the cold, hard floor. I long for my bunk on the *Huxian Fox*.

I wonder how my crew are. Did the princess find the key? Have they set off to find the second key? Or are they looking for me? I hope so.

But where would they even start to look?

None of us could have predicted that Gussart would be on Vegasin. His relations with Shikha usually keep him away from that planet. The crew won't know I've been trapped by the stupid dirt grinder and that he's taking me back to that bum-smear planet, Keplerane. Why in the stars would they look for me there?

I'm in trouble.

By the second day, not only has my butt gone completely numb and my arms burn like crazy, but I'm also getting the shakes.

It's been three days since my last hit of shinver.

That's why my head is pounding. And it's only going to get worse. I've heard how bad it can be—heads feeling like they've been hit by a lava gun, and sweating followed by intense cold, cramps, vomiting, and, worst of all, diarrhea.

I groan at the thought of shitting myself around these goons. Oh, Gussart would have a good laugh—that grand hurrah guffaw of his. I groan again.

My guards give me food, but I can't stomach it. My guts are twisting like an Urfarian snake with four tails. Just the thought of food makes me curl into a ball.

"Ya gotta eat," one of them grunts. "Boss's orders."

"I need shinver," I croak.

"Fat chance," he says and dumps the platter of food next to me. It's a steaming bowl of meat stew with a thick green gravy, but don't ask me what kind of meat. It could be beef, but it's more likely hurball. *Gross.* Even if it was Pedders' famous dumplings with real pork, I couldn't stomach it. The stench wafts under my nose, and I retch, my body convulsing.

The goons back away, probably worried I'll hurl on them—and I might. It's the smartest thing they've done so far.

They get blurry as they step farther and farther away—which is when I realize I'm going to black out.

Chapter 16

Eshan'ya

I'M ON THE BACK of Fan's squito with a pulsar gun strapped to my leg, gripping Pedders' waist as he speeds through Zhinü. The squito isn't patched together like the *Fox* is. Fan put down a large amount of money to get a hover bike of this caliber. The ride is smooth with a fast takeoff and speeds greater than the legal limits.

Pedders is loaded up with weapons on both legs, another strapped under his arm, and a fourth attached to his back. I don't doubt he has more hidden out of sight. He's ready for war.

And it might actually come to that.

It's a wonder how I've gotten myself tangled up in this mess. I'm supposed to be stopping Kriinal Braxt from taking over the galaxy, not stuck in the middle of a drug war. But I dragged Fan into my mission. She didn't want anything to do with it, so it's the right thing to do to get her back. I need to suck up my fears and get this job done.

Luchlon and Tika were dropped off closer to Shikha's complex, rappelling out of the ship directly to the ground. Now the *Huxian Fox* rests in the shipyard. It was a risky place to leave it given the circumstances, but it was the closest Pedders could get it to Shikha's complex. He decided it was worth the risk.

I hope he's right because only RAN-8 is 'manning' it now.

The squito swerves around the traffic, up a ramp to the higher roads, back down to the ground level, and up again, not waiting for lights to turn green. We need to hurry to get to the complex and cause a distraction so Luchlon and Tika can sneak inside.

Pedders' muscles are taut, his back hunched over the handlebars. He's like a runaway hover train—nothing is stopping him.

This is a crazy mission, but these people are the best chance I have at stopping Braxt and the Quain. They might be a bit scruffy, a melting pot of unusual personalities, but they've got some useful skills, especially Fan. She's a brilliant pilot, she's highly intelligent, and she's very good loo—

She's an asset.

I mentally shake my head and refocus.

If we can get Fan back, then we can return to the more important mission. So, of course, this rescue will be worth it.

Pedders skids around a corner and into an alleyway, bringing the squito to a halt. We both dismount. Vines cascade down the walls of the alley, and Pedders tucks the squito behind them.

I follow him out of the alley and creep along the street toward a dark, squat building with trees growing all over it. We take a moment to monitor Shikha's building, both of us huddling behind a large leaf. Pedders is silent as a stone, all of his attention on that building.

There are ten or so people milling around the front, men and women tattooed from head to toe who lounge on modified squitos and laugh loudly, beer cans in hand. It's our job to distract them and then get away without them knowing Luchlon and Tika have entered their complex.

Pedders takes a step toward them just as I see something out of the corner of my eye. Instincts kick in, and I stop Pedders. He frowns in question. I point to where three other men stand, a little farther down the street. They look like they're just casually talking, but there's something about them, something that makes them appear on edge—a stiffness to their muscles, like they're ready to pounce.

"Do they look suspicious to you?" I whisper.

Pedders squints at them, then grunts his agreement. "They're Gussart's men."

When I look around the area a little more closely, I see even more to the left and right who are trying to look like they're just hanging around, but they're waiting for something.

"We need to find out what they're doing before we go ahead with this plan."

Pedders doesn't look happy. He grunts again but clicks on his tech point. "Luchlon, hold position."

"Why? Is there something wrong?" Tika's voice comes through in a loud whisper, but Pedders quickly switches the tech point off.

He nods to indicate I should follow him, and we move farther down the street. Trying to look casual, Pedders takes my hand as if we're a couple out for a romantic stroll. His hands are so big they devour mine.

We stop a couple of yards away from the first group of Gussart's men. Pedders turns to me, taking both of my hands in his, and looks into my eyes like we're about to kiss. I feel a little uncomfortable, but I know what he's doing, so I play along, staring back longingly and trying not to laugh at the strangeness of what I'm doing.

From this location, we can hear what they're saying.

"...Such a crazy plan. I don't know if we can pull it off."

"It's insane, but this is the best time to do it."

"Yeah, if we're ever going to overthrow Shikha, now's the time."

"Do you legit think capturing Sung will have any effect?"

Pedders' hands tighten on mine. His eyes glimmer with emotion, hope, and fear. He must be relieved to hear Fan's name, but he'll be worried about her safety. She could be in grave danger, and his grip on my fingers tells me how much that pains him.

"With Fan in Gussart's hands, Shikha has lost another smuggler. She's barely got anyone to carry for her..."

They continue talking, but Pedders abruptly pulls away. One man gives us a suspicious glance, so I gently pull Pedders back and lean in as if giving him a kiss. Instead, I whisper in his ear, "Don't worry, we'll get her back." I give him a loving, adoring smile and hold his hand as we walk back to the squito.

Gussart's men continue their conversation, unconcerned with us.

Pedders grunts into his tech point, "Abandon mission."

"What?" Tika exclaims.

"Why?" Luchlon asks at the same time.

"Withdraw to the *Fox* immediately."

"Why?" Tika repeats.

"Copy that," Luchlon says.

To me, Pedders says, "Let's go get Fan."

Now that the moment has passed, and the adrenaline has worn off some, my stomach drops as I seat myself behind Pedders again. If Gussart has Fan, he'll take her to Keplerane—the one place in this universe I don't want to be. The pudgy, sweaty face of King Vald, red with exertion, pops into my mind as we speed back to the *Huxian Fox*. I almost gag. I can't let the royal guards capture me. I won't go back to the palace.

I'm in a haze the entire return trip to the *Fox*, trying to think of ways to avoid Keplerane. Maybe I can convince the crew to go to Farnth first and *then* go rescue Fan? Unlikely.

Maybe I should get them to leave me here. I could try to find someone else to help. But that seems impossible, especially with the Quain after me. Sooner or later, I'll be recognized as the fake lieutenant, or worse, the Keplerane royal that both the Quain and King Vald are searching for.

What if the crew drops me off at a different planet, just a minor detour? Maybe Shadé—but is there anyone left there who can help me? The Protectors aren't there anymore.

We arrive at the *Huxian Fox* before I have a solution.

Pedders calls Luchlon and Tika to get their location, and when the *Fox* reaches them, he doesn't land. Instead, he swings the *Fox* low, opening the back hatch, and Luchlon and Tika run straight up the ramp before Pedders closes it again and takes off.

Pedders doesn't consult any of us. He immediately sets a course for Keplerane.

Chapter 17

Fan

I'VE SPENT TWENTY-FOUR HOURS in and out of consciousness, hating every moment I'm awake. All energy has been leeched from my veins. I'm weak, hot, and cold. I can barely stand on my shaking legs.

Did I mention how much I stink?

The stench is a new form of torture, though my spirits lift briefly at the thought of what Gussart's goons are having to endure as they haul me out of the ship—a small amount of karma for what they've put me through. My feet keep stumbling, so they drag me out and let my feet dangle along behind.

We're back on Keplerane. And surprise—it's raining. Again. Does it ever stop?

By the stars, my head hurts.

I'm dimly aware of being loaded into the back of a truck. There are two thugs with me, another in the driver's seat. Only three guards. Maybe I can escape. Three on one—that's better odds than I had a moment ago.

Despite my thoughts, I don't move. I'm a puddle on the floor as the truck glides down the street. I can barely lift my arms, let alone fight off three goons. Plus, I might hurl.

I roll into a ball, my stomach clenching in agony once again.

Eventually, the truck stops, and I'm unceremoniously carried out, this time into Gussart's warehouse. I'm aware of passing crates, and all I can think is: *shinver.*

There's shinver in those crates. I just need one little, tiny hit. Just a little taste.

Everything goes dark when I'm thrown into a room at the back of the warehouse and the door is shut and locked behind me. I sink into the darkness, happy to have it envelop me. Only sleep offers a reprieve from the pain, and I long for it.

I don't know how long I'm left in there. It's dark the whole time, a fact I'm genuinely grateful for since light burns my eyes. I'm given food at one point, but I ignore it. I wonder how long I'll last before my body completely shuts down. Will they one day open the door to find me completely wasted away to nothing, just a pile of bones?

This isn't how things are supposed to go. This isn't how I'm supposed to die. Pedders and I were going to get free of this life. We were supposed to join the UoW Military and protect the galaxy, like Colonel Wang did, not be on the run from them. Instead, I'm rotting in Gussart's dungeon. How did this happen? I've always been one step ahead of that mudhole, but he got the best of me this time.

Eventually, the door opens, letting in a stream of brutal light, and I'm dragged out. We don't go back through the warehouse.

Instead, I'm taken farther away from the stock of shinver and into Gussart's private entertaining rooms.

There are so many people milling around, all dressed up like it's a party. Probably because it *is* a party. There are tight clothes everywhere, bright colors, see-through fabrics, sparkles and sequins, long and short dresses, tight pants, a lot of skin, cleavage, gold, and silver.

They're drinking cocktails, chewing on finger food, dancing to music—all of them are high. Some drop shinver into their eyes; others snort the powder straight up their noses. I have no doubt the food is laced with it—lucky bastards. Even if I can't stomach any food, I wish I could get a bite of theirs.

As I'm brought in, a partygoer shies away from me, then another and another. I don't blame them. I *do* stink.

I'm barely conscious as a girl in a see-through skirt brushes past in her hurry to get away from my stench. A tattoo on her forearm catches my attention: three stars among some swirling loops. I can't remember why it's significant right now. The girl scowls as she curls into the arms of her lover, who sneers at me.

The music gets quieter, and I'm dumped on my knees in the middle of the room. Partygoers sidle apart, and then I see Gussart, sitting before me like he's the king of Keplerane.

He stares down at me with a sinister smile.

Standing beside him is his wife, looking just as lovely as ever in a long red gown. She's a petite little thing, about eighteen, with a heart-shaped face, large brown eyes, and long black hair. What she's ever seen in Gussart, I don't know. When I look at her, her gaze drops to the ground. I look back at Gussart, squinting so I can focus my blurry eyes on him.

"Ya not lookin' so hot these days, Sung," he says.

"I'll be all right," I croak, trying to find a comfortable position on my knees with my hands still cuffed behind my back.

"It's time for ya to pay ya debt," he says.

"Sure, sure, I'll get you the money. Just give me some time."

"No, ya time is up. It was up the moment ya laid eyes on my wife." She shrinks away as he frowns at her. "Ya gonna pay ya debt in flesh."

I groan. I don't know what he means by that, but it doesn't sound good.

He nods to something or someone behind me. Clumsily, I twist around to see what it is. There's a metal pole in the middle of the room, but I don't have a chance to wonder what it's for. My two guards seize me under my arms again and drag me to it. They release my hands, and I have a moment of relief as the blood returns to my shoulders. Then they yank my hands above my head and secure them to the pole.

I'm now strapped to the pole with my back to Gussart.

I've got a bad feeling about this.

A trickle of fear sends electricity down my spine, and I want to thrash and get away, but I don't have the strength. I hear Gussart rise from his chair, and I twist my neck trying to see him. One of his goons hands him something, but I can't see what it is. The crowd cheers.

"Ya know," he says as he approaches, the crowd quieting down to hear him speak, "I've heard that ya ship, the *Huxian Fox*, is named after a Chinese deity. I've heard that deity often appears as a fox with nine tails." This is when Gussart's voice takes on a sinister edge. "Do ya know what else has nine tails?"

And *this* is when I realize what he's holding: a dark plaited rope handle with nine whips extending from it.

Commonly known as the cat-o'-nine-tails.

"The cat," Gussart sneers.

He flicks the whip to the side, and it makes a series of snapping sounds. The noise is enough to liquify my guts.

If my legs weren't already shaking, they would be now.

Gussart comes closer. He's right behind me, and I turn my face back to the pole. If I were a believer, I'd be praying to God right now. Instead, I wish on the stars.

He takes his stance—I see his foot out of the corner of my eye before I close them and brace for the worst.

And *blazin' rockets* does it hurt.

Gussart grunts as he swings that whip—hard.

I feel all nine tails as they lash across my back, ripping through my shirt and my skin. It burns.

I gasp. Involuntarily, my eyes open wide again. I'm more awake than I've been in days. The crowd cheers again—sick bastards.

He swings a second time, and my back turns to fire. Blue flame licks every inch of my back.

I grit my teeth.

With the third blow, I can't feel one tail from another. It's just one big blur of pain.

On the fourth pass, I cry out uncontrollably, a lung-rending cry that bursts from me.

I lose count after that.

My whole body feels aflame, not just my back. The burn radiates out from it, bleeding into my legs and arms, right down to my little toe.

I see blood splatter onto the ground. My blood, I realize.

It goes on and on, and by the end of it, I can't think…I can barely breathe. I am only pain.

Eventually, Gussart stops. Over the roaring of my heart, I hear his labored breathing.

"Bring her down," he rasps.

There is no relief as they release my hands from the magnetic cuffs. Jolts of pain run through my back as I collapse.

Suddenly there's the whir of something mechanical moving beside me, but I'm too spent to turn and look. The revelers shuffle away, avoiding whatever it is while they whisper excitedly. After a moment, the whirring stops with a clunk, and someone asks, "Boss?"

"Feed her to the rats," he orders.

The rats?

There's applause, and then hands are on me again, pulling me toward whatever that mechanical sound was.

I manage to open my eyes in a squint in time to see a gaping hole, perfectly round and about twenty yards in diameter and thirty feet deep, imbedded in the floor of Gussart's party room—

—and then I'm thrown into it.

I fall at least ten feet, hit something soft and furry, before falling the rest of the way to the floor of the pit.

My body is bruised, bloody, torn, and I consider just lying there and letting death take me.

Then I feel the air shift. And that big furry thing I hit on my way down is moving.

My eyes blink open. I can barely focus, but through the blur, I see the massive two front teeth of a rat-like creature, so big they could cut through an arm or a leg.

Enough adrenaline blasts through me to get my limbs moving, and I crawl away even as every inch of me burns from the movement. I don't want to die—but I'm going to if I don't think of something quick because there's not only one massive rat to deal with—there are three. I see them now, all turning their noses to me.

How the stars am I gonna get out of this one?

I look around. The extra adrenaline helps a bit, but that won't last long.

My eyes land on my arm where there's a small streak of white.

White powder.

Shinver.

It must have rubbed onto me from one of the partygoers or a guard.

I don't hesitate. I lick the white powder straight off my arm.

Almost instantly, my energy increases, and after a few seconds, the pain in my back begins to ease. My muscles turn rubbery as dopamine floods my brain. I retreat farther from the rats as the raw nerves turn numb.

My vision unfogs and I see the rats clearly for the first time. They're as tall as a full-grown man, with gray fur, beady red eyes, and tails so thick and strong that they're more like a kangaroo's than a rat's.

One of them looks scruffier than the others, its fur sticking out crazily, another has extra-long whiskers, and the third has particularly beady eyes. So I nickname them Fuzzy, Whiskers, and Dave.

They all have two large teeth jutting from their jaws. Three pairs of teeth to deal with. Their throats make strange gurgling noises that are nothing like the squeak of a mouse or the hiss of a rat. More like the sound of water going down a drain. Wet and guttural.

They're edging closer, their noses twitching as they sniff. Their heads move from side to side like they can't quite figure out where I am, and I realize they can't see out of those beady red eyes—they're blind.

As I think that, Whiskers charges me, his head low and teeth bared.

Father's fist.

I duck just in time, his teeth coming within an inch of my neck.

Gasps and cries from the crowd above make me glance up. They stand around the edges of the pit, watching. Glee and malice glow in their eyes—barbarians. Gussart's there too, and he looks pretty happy with himself, watching me scramble around in this rat's nest, blood dripping from my back, my shirt in tatters, and stinking like a sewer. I've seen better days.

As Whiskers tries to turn around in the tight space of the pit, Fuzzy catches my scent too and hurtles closer. I'm squeezed between the pit wall and Whiskers' rump, with Fuzzy coming at me head on. Instead of accepting my fate, I step toward Fuzzy and, dodging his teeth, roll right over his neck, smearing my bloody back across his fur and ending up on the other side of him.

The rat is disoriented and slow to react. His head swivels as he tries to find me. That's when Whiskers finally manages to turn around. He catches the scent of my blood on his brother and strikes.

His two front teeth sink into his sibling's neck, right where my blood was smeared, sliding through flesh like it's cheese.

The crowd cries out, but none as loud as Gussart's angry "*No!*"

Fuzzy's gurgling ramps up to a new level. He tries to free himself, but Whiskers holds on tighter. His teeth sink further and further into the flesh, and I watch in horror as he tears through the muscles. Eventually, Fuzzy's thrashings lessen and then stop altogether.

However, Whiskers doesn't stop there. He continues to chomp those big damned teeth—*eating* his brother. He slurps and gnashes at his meal.

I turn away from the sight.

And come face-to-face with the third rat. Dave.

Chomp!

His teeth swing down, and I duck before he can take my head off. They dig into the wall instead.

I skirt the edge of the pit. It's a great big round hole, the walls smooth rock and unclimbable. The bottom is covered with dirt and...bones? Yes, they're bones. A tremor runs up my spine. Others have died in this pit. Were they also eaten alive?

Now that I know they're chasing the scent of my blood, I can use it to my advantage.

I reach behind and run my hands over my back. Despite the shinver, it still hurts when my fingers touch the slices in my skin. My hands come away red with blood.

Turning to the two remaining rats, I assess my next move.

Whiskers is still chomping away at Fuzzy, but his nose is twitching, and I wonder how long he'll be distracted. Dave has dislodged his teeth from the wall and maneuvered his oversized body around to face me. His beady eyes stare blindly, but his nose is about to catch my scent.

I move fast.

Running around the edge of the hole, I avoid Dave and head toward Whiskers, who's still distracted by his meal. I rush at his neck, my hands outstretched and ready to smear blood and mark my target.

His head turns at the last second—right toward me.

I screech to a stop, my legs skidding out from under me, and I land on my butt. Scuffling my feet, I push myself away as those blood-stained teeth come at me.

Chomp, chomp, chomp!

This one is quick, but somehow I get to my feet and skitter away.

He keeps coming. And now Dave has caught my scent. The blood on my hands, the blood on my back, the blood still in my veins—it's an intoxicating, attractive scent to these two monsters.

They inch closer and closer, following their noses, which twitch and tremble. Their lips snarl, their throats still making that awful gurgling noise.

With each step they take, I step back, trying to figure out what to do. I stumble on a rock but don't fall. Upon closer inspection, it's not a rock, but a human skull.

I pick it up and launch it at Whiskers, who is only a step ahead of Dave. It bounces off his forehead and rolls in the dirt, absolutely harmless. Whiskers barely flinches.

I gather up more bones and rocks and start throwing them indiscriminately, lobbing them at the rats' eyes, noses, and heads. None of it does any damage, and both rats keep coming.

My back hits the wall, and I hardly notice the pain. I'm too distracted by my predicament—I'm about to get eaten alive by freaking rats.

My eyes dart from side to side, searching for anything that can help me, anything to get out of this mess. I've never wished harder for my duster pistol.

"Whiskers, Dave," I croon. "We could be friends. Don't eat me." Stars, I'm desperate. I'm talking to a *mouse!*

Whiskers gets to me before Dave does. He sniffs so close that his long whiskers brush my arm. I shiver. Then he lifts his head high, opens his mouth wide, and brings those big chompers down.

Chapter 18

Eshan'ya

"No invite, no entry."

An angry little man blocks my way, so I stand taller, lift my chin, and turn ever so slightly so the cuff on my arm glints in the light spilling out of the party inside. King Vald was able to fight off the Quain—for now—and kept his power over Keplerane, so I'll use that to my advantage.

"I don't need an invite," I say, making sure my royal accent is pronounced. I may not be a real princess, but I've still had all the royal training, and this man won't be able to tell the difference, especially since the real princesses are never seen in public. Plus, as much as I hate to be associated with them, I still have rights as a member of the royal household. I push down the disgust that churns my stomach and continue to play my part.

The little man stops tittering and finally looks at me. He takes in my long gown made from finely spun Saturn silk in an aqua-blue hue that hangs perfectly from my curves like it was made especially for me—because it was. His eyes flutter over the jewels hanging from my neck, ears, and even in my hair, all stolen when I fled the palace. Finally, he sees the cuff with King Vald's crest engraved on it.

"My apologiesss, Your Majesssty," he hisses and bows low.

I brush my hand through the air, dismissing him. "It will be forgiven if you provide me entrance at once."

"Of courssse. Pleassse, you are mossst welcome." He stands aside, still bent double, and holds his hand wide in invitation to enter.

I step over the threshold, looking down my nose at the little man and the others that mill in the doorway. My two guards follow—Pedders, who refused to be left on the ship, and Luchlon. Both are dressed in the uniforms stolen from Vegasin, but they have removed the three stars that mark them as members of the Quain. Instead, they look like plain black military uniforms and, in a pinch, private security for a royal princess of Keplerane.

Pedders' uniform is way too tight, but we couldn't risk staying on Vegasin to steal another one, so he squeezed into one we'd already stolen. It looks ridiculous, but he wouldn't be talked out of coming.

As we enter the party, I realize there is no music playing, although there is plenty of noise from people talking, cheering, and shouting. Most people are huddled in the middle of the room, looking down at something, maybe on a sunken level, but I can't see what it might be.

I look for the shinver lord, Gussart. I've seen his face often on news bulletins when he's been in trouble with the law, but King Vald always seems to let him off for some reason—likely a big case of shinver. But I don't see him among the stragglers dotted around the room. He must be part of the crowd in the center.

Pedders breaks away to look for Gussart or Fan. Luchlon stays beside me as my guard, and the two of us approach the crowd.

My long royal gown is out of place here. Most people wear skirts and shorts that barely cover their bums. Their clothes are overly sparkly or made in bright fluorescent colors—it's all very gaudy and over the top. No style.

Some of them have the tattoo on their forearms that mark them as prostitutes. The three stars circled by interlacing loops is a cheap copy of my own. My heartstrings vibrate. Suddenly, I'm wondering how they're being treated here and if they need help. But I can't be diverted from my mission.

As I approach the crowd, some of them spot my gown and instantly move aside, recognizing my importance from its sheer elegance. Some see King Vald's crest and gasp; hands fly to their mouths as they stoop in a bow or prostrate themselves on the ground.

I keep my head high, ignoring them as I hurry past, toward whatever is entertaining them in the middle of the room.

As I get closer, I can see it's a large sunken pit. The crowd is watching and cheering at something going on at the bottom.

My skin prickles with dread the closer I get.

I smell the blood first.

One section of the pit is covered in it.

Then I see a mauled jenpritta rat, its gray hair turned red from all the blood pouring from its neck. My heart goes out to the misunderstood creature. They can be quite gentle if treated right, but it's obvious from the other two rats prowling nearby that these have been bred for fighting.

Then I see what the other two rats are hunting.

Fan.

She's also covered in blood, her clothes torn and barely hanging on. She's backed against the wall of the pit with nowhere to run, and the two rats bear down on her viciously.

The one closest to Fan lifts its head, its mouth opening wide, and swings its large teeth toward her.

Oh, no! She's got no hope.

Whomp!

A lava blast shoots out of the crowd somewhere. It's set to annihilate, so when it hits the rat, its head explodes. Blood, brains, and bone rain down on Fan.

Pedders stands on the opposite side of the pit with his smoking lava gun.

There's a roar to my left. It's Gussart, stamping his feet and yelling, "Grab that dirt grinder!"

His thugs descend on Pedders.

I'm too far away to help. I watch helplessly as they try grabbing his arms, but Pedders doesn't go quietly. He fights back with the fury of ten hungry redrynches, his face going just as red as one, too. But more guards arrive, and it's five on one, far too many for Pedders to fight off.

The scuffle brings them close to the pit's edge. Pedders hollers and pushes a thug off his back, and the man falls thirty feet or more into the pit. He lands on his back with a splat and doesn't move.

The sound attracts the attention of the last rat, saving Fan from being eaten. The rat scuffles around toward the fallen thug. But before it gets to him, Pedders and another thug tumble into the hole.

Pedders falls on top of the man, which cushions the impact, but he cries out as his head hits the pit wall.

Fan moves quicker than the rat. Avoiding it, she skirts around the edge and makes her way to Pedders.

"Where's the gun?" she cries as she reaches him. But the gun didn't fall with Pedders. It rests on the ground floor of the entertainment room among the feet of the crowd.

They have no guns. No weapons at all.

I look over my shoulder for Luchlon. He's also got a lava gun, but he's not standing behind me like he's meant to be. I glimpse him behind the crowd, not even paying attention. His head is bent over his tech point like he's making a call, but what call could be so important right now? I don't have time to figure it out. I call his name, but he doesn't hear me over the roar of the room. I turn back to the pit.

"You'll be all right, Qiqiang," Fan says, patting Pedders on the arm. "Drop a Y chromosome, suck it up, and we'll get out of here."

Pedders only shrugs in response. He's been incapacitated by the fall, and his eyes have gone glassy from the knock to his head. Fan is bleeding and hurt. The rat is getting closer, its teeth chomping in anticipation of its meal.

They're sitting graks.

My brain searches for a solution. What do I know about jenpritta rats? They're native to Keplerane, quite resilient to the wet climate, eat meat, and their jaws can slice through metal. That's not good.

What else? They're blind but have a heightened sense of smell and...*hearing*.

That's it! I put two fingers in my mouth and let out an ear-piercing whistle—completely undignified, but effective.

The rat stops in its tracks and swivels toward the noise.

And so does everyone else in the room.

Gussart's mouth hangs open as he stares at me.

I regain my composure, keeping one eye on the rat to make sure it doesn't advance again, and demand, "Call off your pet."

Gussart gapes, and then his face turns back into a scowl. "Why should I do that?"

"Because I command you." I jut my chin out and purse my lips.

"Who—?" He doesn't finish his question; he finally sees the cuff on my arm.

Just to make sure he knows how serious I am, I say, "By order of the Royal Palace of Keplerane."

The people gasp and shrink away from me, some bowing, some retreating in fear of being arrested. They're liaising with criminals, and they've *all* been engaged in illegal activities.

"Yes, yes...of course, Ya Highn...Ya Majesty," Gussart stumbles.

He pulls a whistle from his top pocket and blows one sharp note. The rat abandons its hunt and slinks to the other side of the pit, away from Pedders and Fan.

"Get those people out," I command, and I'm instantly obeyed. My heart flutters with satisfaction.

A propulsion platform descends into the pit. Fan helps Pedders onto it, then climbs on herself. It's an effort, and I see why—her back is completely torn apart. My chest squeezes tight at the sight of it. How she could battle at all is a wonder to me.

One of Gussart's thugs who survived the fall also joins them on the platform, and then it lifts them out of the pit, setting them down on the rim on the opposite side to where I'm standing.

Luchlon comes out of nowhere. I don't know what's kept him all this time, but he now approaches the platform and helps his crewmates.

Gussart says, "Excuse me, Ya Highness, but may I ask what ya require with my prisoner?"

"You would do well to mind your business," I snap. I go to leave, but turn back instead. "And return whatever you've taken from her. Weapons. Tech. Everything." Then I storm away.

Chapter 19

Fan

WHEN I COME TO, my brain feels like I've been hit by ten pulsar shots on the highest stun setting. But I'm grateful to be back on the *Huxian Fox*. I'm even in my own quarters. There's my stack of *Just Squitos* and *Ship & Pilot* that I enjoy reading, mostly for the pictures. Hanging on the wall is my medal from winning the Earth-168mk obstacle race. And pinned next to it is a picture of me and Pedders as kids at the orphanage in China, arms wrapped around each other's shoulders.

I'm lying on my stomach. My back has something resting across it, something wet and soothing. They must have given me painkillers or something because I'm a little groggy, not everything is making sense, and thoughts are coming slowly.

After a moment, the memory of being whipped by the cat-o'-nine-tails comes back, and I cringe at the pain even though my back is totally numb right now. That stupid crud dweller, Gussart. Getting pleasure from causing pain. What he doesn't realize is that I'm worth more alive, even if I steal a little shinver for myself—and a wife or two.

"She's awake."

I'm not alone. Sitting on the edge of my bed and reading a book projected from her tech point is a very pretty lady. *By the stars, she is pretty.*

Princess Eshan'ya.

Her blond hair is loose and falls softly around her shoulders and down her chest like a waterfall cascading down. Wow, where did that poetry come from?

She's not dressed in the fancy dresses she usually wears. Instead, she's got on an outfit that looks like something from Tika's wardrobe: sturdy trousers and a soft beige shirt. She looks like royalty anyway. On her left arm, she's wearing that gold cuff with King Vald's crest hidden—it covers her tattoo, I realize. She must really hate that tattoo.

Too late, I notice she's looking back at me. She's seen me watching her. Stars, my brain is working sloooowly.

She smiles. "How are you feeling?"

"Numb," I croak, wishing I could be a little more eloquent. I've got a beautiful girl in my room, but man, I sound dumb.

She reaches out as if to grab my hand. "That's goo—"

"Oh, Captain Sung"—Eshan'ya snatches her hand back at the sound of Tika's voice—"it is so good to see you awake and alive. We thought we'd lost you."

Interesting.

Tika's in the doorway, closely followed by Pedders, Luchlon, and even RAN-8, who probably doesn't care if I survive, since he has no feelings. They all hang around outside because my quarters are far too small to fit all of them inside.

Pedders grunts, his face splitting into a wide smile, relief flashing through his eyes. He's such a softy.

"Welcome back to the living," Luchlon says.

"Glad you're not dead. It would have been a real hassle finding a new captain," RAN-8 says. Such compassion.

"How did you find me?"

All of them talk at once, telling me about the heist gone wrong on Vegasin, not finding the key we went to all that trouble for, and returning to the ship to discover I was missing. Something about looking for me in a prison, some gunfight or something or other, and something to do with Shikha. I don't know. None of it makes sense. I start drifting off again.

"I think she needs her rest," I hear Eshan'ya say as the world goes black.

The headache has lessened the next time I wake up. My room is dark except for a small beacon of light that comes from the tech point on Eshan'ya's finger. She's reading a hologram, sitting in a chair that she must have pulled in from the dining hall.

Before she notices I'm awake, I get to stare at her for a moment, her face lit by the tech point. She looks up as if she feels my eyes on her, but she doesn't seem to mind. The princess gives me a smile that has my heart beating harder.

"Hey," I say in a voice that comes out huskier than normal, thick from sleep. "You're still here."

"I hope you don't mind," she says, keeping her voice low and turning off the hologram. The tech point still emits enough light that I can make out her features. "I just wanted to keep an eye on you. You were hurt pretty bad, and you don't have a medic. I thought I could help. I have some first-aid training."

She's rambling, and if I didn't know better, I'd think she's nervous.

"I put xertgo salve on your back, so it should heal your wounds within twenty-four hours. You might get some scarring, sorry."

"Don't be sorry. I'm grateful," I say.

I realize I'm no longer wearing the ripped shirt I was whipped in, and my bare breasts rest on my mattress. Was I undressed by Eshan'ya or another member of my crew?

My face starts to burn.

I try to sit, bringing my bed linen with me as cover. It's an effort—although it doesn't hurt with the salve on my back—and I do it clumsily. But when I finally get into a seated position, I see Eshan'ya has modestly turned her eyes to the floor. She looks up when I clear my throat.

"Um, actually...what I want to say is...well, thank you." Now I'm burning hotter than a blue star.

"For what?"

"Well..." I run a hand through my hair. "That's the second time you've rescued me from...well, capture."

She laughs. I don't think I've heard her laugh before. It's musical.

"Do the Gerangans truly count?" she asks, that laughter still in her voice.

I chuckle. "Those pinkies had me tied up good. I thought they were gonna eat me."

Our laughter slowly fades, replaced by an awkward silence. Eshan'ya looks away again, but I can't keep my eyes off her. She opens her mouth to say something but thinks better of it. I rub the back of my neck, waiting for her to speak.

She seems to find her resolve and, raising her eyes again, says, "So that powder you had...it's a drug, isn't it? Shinver?"

No wonder she was unsure about bringing up the topic—it's an uncomfortable one.

I nod.

"And you're addicted?"

I nod again. I hold my breath.

Her eyes lower, not in shame, not in judgment, but in pity. And I wonder if that's worse.

"Why did you start taking it?" she asks.

My breath comes out in a whoosh. "Well, I...don't know." The look she gives me says she doesn't buy that. So I try again. "It's a long story."

She shrugs. "It's a two-day journey to Farnth. We've got time."

"Farnth? Why are we going to Farnth?"

Eshan'ya huffs. "That's also a long story. Let's hear yours first." She's certainly no wilting flower.

"OK. Hand me a shirt?"

She goes to my tiny wardrobe and pulls out a brown T-shirt.

My back protests as I lift it over my head, but I get the shirt on without excessive pain. Eshan'ya has turned away again, giving what privacy she can in the small room. She now looks at the photo of me and Pedders.

"So you've known Pedders for a long time?" she asks.

"Yeah. We met at a Chinese orphanage." I get up to stand beside her, flicking on the lights to look at the picture. "He was a chubby thing, and the other kids teased him. Until I came along." I grin. "It wasn't a good idea to tease him after that."

"I can imagine." She smiles. I catch the scent of jasmine wafting off her, something I try to ignore as I continue.

"He's always had my back, and I've always had his. Except for one period of my life when I broke away from him," I admit.

I lean my shoulder against the wall while the princess sits on my bed, waiting for me to tell my story.

"It was just after I won the Earth-168mk obstacle race and I bought the *Huxian Fox*. You see, I wasn't really an orphan. I was only in an orphanage because my parents...well, let's just say they liked shinver more than me."

Eshan'ya purses her lips.

"So when I won all that money, all of a sudden, my father, who'd had nothing to do with me in six years, wanted to hang out...I guess I knew it was about the money, but I wanted to believe that he was proud of me." I huff. "What a joke." But neither of us are laughing.

"He joined me on the *Huxian Fox*, even helped me paint it. He did the orange stripes. Maybe I shouldn't be so sad they're covered in pink now." I scoff and pick up a copy of *Ship & Pilot*, flicking through the pictures of ships, squitos, and hovercars.

"He's the one who introduced me to Gussart. Said we'd make great money running for him, and we did. Pedders tried to warn me. I wouldn't listen...I accused Pedders of being jealous that I had a father and he didn't. You see, Pedders is a genuine orphan.

Both his parents died in the Union War. So it was a pretty low blow. And when he kept bringing it up, I kicked him off the crew."

I don't know why I'm talking so much. I never talk about this stuff, and only Pedders and my crappy father know the whole story. But Eshan'ya doesn't look at me with disgust or even pity. She just waits for me to continue, and that patience is somehow comforting. I keep flicking through my magazine.

"So my dad and I went into business together with Gussart, doing runs for him. What I didn't know was that my dad was using. And not the small amounts I do. No, he was taking several hits every day."

"How did you find out?" Eshan'ya asks in a hushed tone.

I flick the page to a picture of a scantily dressed woman sitting on a squito. It's the kind of thing I'd usually spend more time admiring, but as my cheeks flare, I quickly flip the page. The next page is even more embarrassing, featuring a man with his bum in the air, bending over the hood of a hovercar and looking back at the camera provocatively. I slam the magazine shut.

"Huh? Oh, it was Gussart who noticed first. It was eating into his profit, so Gussart withheld payment to cover the costs of my father's habit."

As I push the magazine aside, images of my father high on shinver flash to the forefront of my mind. He'd gotten so skinny, his teeth rotted from chewing it without any dilution in liquid. He was paranoid, aggressive, toxic. And he was high all the time.

"After a while, I saw the destruction shinver wreaks—on people, on relationships. I didn't want to smuggle it anymore. I wanted out."

Eshan'ya looks confused. She's got the cutest little dent in her brow—she's probably wondering how I ended up like this if I'd already decided to stop smuggling. I wish that had been the end of the story.

"I made the mistake of discussing it with my dad, telling him he needed to get off the drug. I told him I'd help him. Spoiler alert: that didn't go down very well. He agreed at first, to keep up appearances, and then he started lacing my food and drinks with it. I'd never had the stuff at that point, and I had no idea I was getting addicted.

"Then suddenly, he stopped. He stopped lacing my food. Made me go cold turkey. I didn't even know I was taking it, so I didn't understand this sickness that came over me. It was withdrawal. And Dad had the cure. A hit of shinver."

A flash in Eshan'ya's eyes tells me how she feels about that. It's pure hatred. I wish I hated my dad—he deserves that—but somehow, even after all he's done, I still don't. I'd like to slap him silly and make him care an inch about me, but I can't hate him.

"It still took him a while to convince me, but it was like my body *knew* that's what it needed. So when he gave me the little eye-dropper—put it right in my sweaty palms—I couldn't resist."

I can't look up from the floor of the ship and the metal panels running across it, perfectly sealed together to protect us from the void of space.

"And that's how I got addicted." I shrug and fall quiet.

When she realizes I'm not going to continue, she asks, "What happened after that? What happened to your father?"

"Well...I figured out what he did, and I sent him packing," I say, simplifying the story. "I convinced Pedders to come back—I had to do a bit of groveling—but eventually he came back to be my copilot. He's always looked out for me.

"After that, my dad disappeared and left me to work off his debt, so I couldn't stop running for Gussart. I worked out that if I combined my runs for him with runs for Shikha, I could make double the amount with only a slight detour."

"That was smart." It's a compliment I don't deserve. None of this is something I'm proud of.

"And I also worked out how to scrape a little shinver off the top of each crate for my own personal use, totally unnoticed...until a few days ago, that is. Hence this." I gesture to my back.

"I'm sorry this happened to you," she says.

I shrug. This talk is getting uncomfortable, and I've said more than I meant to. "I can handle it. I just need to find a new shinver supplier."

"That's the last thing you should do," she exclaims. "Don't you see? You've got a chance to break away now. You've only got a small amount of shinver in your system. You just need to get clean, and you're free from this life. As long as you're hooked on shinver, you'll never be free. You will always be a prisoner, no matter how much money you have. But you can get clean. I know you can."

I'd love to believe she's right, but life isn't that simple. She's coming from a place of compassion, but she doesn't understand what it's like to have an addiction, so she doesn't understand that her words aren't helpful. It's not right to tell me to 'get clean', as if I'm dirty. It's not something I can scrub away.

"What about Gussart? What about Shikha? They're still after me. I still owe them. Not only for my father's debts, but I just flushed a stars-load of Shikha's product out the airlock." I violently sweep my arms wide. "No, I'll never be free until I've paid off my debts—"

"But the money you'll get from me—"

"—even then, they'll find a way to trap me. That's how they win. That's how they always win. There's no way to ever pay off your debts." My breath is heightened; my nostrils flare. I want to scream, but it's not her fault, so I bite my tongue.

She waits while I get myself under control, then calmly says, "I don't think Shikha is going to be much of a concern anymore. Gussart was attacking her when we were on Vegasin. I believe that's called a hostile takeover. And I don't think Gussart will be keen to chase you, knowing you're under the protection of the Royal Palace." She grins, and my mouth twitches too.

"I would've loved to have seen Gussart's face when you came in." I chuckle as I imagine his stupid mouth hanging open in shock. "I was a little busy with three blind mice to notice."

"It was quite a sight." She turns serious again and says, "So you see, you can be free."

Free. No more dangerous runs for Gussart and Shikha. No more dodging the Union planets. No more craving my next fix. No more adventure and excitement.

"And then what will I be?"

She looks at me with those big blue eyes, not comprehending my question.

"This has been my whole life," I tell her. "The only thing I'm good at. What will I be if I'm not this?"

"You can be anything you want to be," she whispers.

I don't know about that.

I turn away again, looking at that picture of Pedders and me when we were so young and innocent.

I whisper, "Pedders and I had dreams of joining the military, protecting the Union. We joined the Junior Union Cadets when we were still at the orphanage. The JUC offered combat, shooting, and piloting lessons, and we took all of them. We thought we would be heroes like Colonel Wang. Respected. All those dreams were crushed when we became criminals. I'm not a hero. I'm just a shinver addict."

But Eshan'ya's eyes sparkle like she sees so much more.

I want to believe that's true, that I can recover, but I struggle to visualize that path. And her stare, her thoughts, are making me even more uncomfortable, so I change the subject. "Anyway, why are we going to Farnth?"

Chapter 20

Eshan'ya

By the way Fan avoids talking about her future, I can tell she doesn't believe she can be anything she wants to be. Her constant confidence is just a facade. Deep down, she doesn't believe in her own worth.

But she's wrong about being a hero. She might still get a chance, albeit not within the Union military, but if we get the Device before Braxt, then we'll save this galaxy, and she'll be a hero. Even if nobody knows it.

"Farnth is the location of the next key," I say, letting the subject change and allowing her to regain some composure. "Ranate retrieved the information that was found on the first key. It directed us to the solar system with three sister stars and eight planets. It highlighted the fifth planet orbiting the smallest star. Its designation is Farnth Five, as there's no modern civilization on the planet."

"Yeah, aren't all those planets too far from their stars? I hear it's a damned cold planet," Fan says.

"That's right. But it once orbited much closer to its sun and was cultivated by the Protogenoi. There have been excavations of the site, but there's still plenty to explore."

"The planet is used for shinver mining. Did you know that?"

I nod. "The crew told me."

"Then how do you know they haven't found the key?"

"I can't be sure. But the 'laxy-net says the ruins are still in good condition, which implies they haven't been touched by the miners. Of course, we won't know for sure until we get there."

"But an entire planet is a big area to search. How in the stars are we going to find it? Plus, the Quain have a massive head start on us. Surely they've already found it."

"Yes, they might have. But I hope not. There were more instructions on the key."

I turn on the tech point and display a hologram of the information RAN-8 stole from the Quain's computer. First, it shows the planet Farnth Five, then it zooms in, pointing at a city on the surface. Lastly, the location fades to words, with the three stars and three half circles of the Protogenoi sigil shining above it.

In Protogenoi, it says:

"Follow the light of the third sun
through the void of chaos
on sunrise of the winter solstice
to find Portunus awaking."

I read the passage to Fan.

"What does that mean?" she asks when I'm done.

"I'm still working on that, but I have some ideas. I'll need Ranate to help me with some research and calculations."

"OK." Fan looks sidelong at me. "You're a woman of many talents."

My pulse quickens. "What do you mean?"

"Well, you just read a paragraph in Protogenoi without blinking."

I shrug, trying to be casual. "Ranate transcribed it. I remembered it."

"But you didn't, did you?" she says, no doubt in her eyes. "You can read it, can't you?"

"Well..." What can I say? There's no point in lying, not when she's clearly worked it out. I wonder how much else she's worked out. Finally, I nod and try not to fidget.

"Does King Vald teach all his ladies how to transcribe Protogenoi? Or did you learn it somewhere else?"

My neck prickles, but I don't move. She *is* onto me.

"I learned it elsewhere," I say cautiously, taking deep breaths.

She looks at me then, square in the eyes, but with a softness I haven't seen before. A kindness.

"How old were you when he took you?"

At the thought of King Vald, my stomach cramps instantly, crushing me from the inside.

I gape at Fan.

What is she asking? Is she asking when he stole me from my home? Or when he *took* me? When he...

I set my jaw. "How did you...?"

"I saw your tattoo." Fan nods at the gold cuff. She comes over to where I sit on her bed and gently, very gently, removes it. Her fingers leave trails of fire on my skin. I don't move an inch.

The dark print is a swirling circle of several lines. None of them make a full circle individually, but many lines overlap and cross over each other, so the overall impression is one of a circle. Three stars sit in the middle of it all.

A brand.

Inspired by the Protogenoi sigil—supposedly an indication of beauty.

No two tattoos are alike, so if scanned, you can trace the tattoo back to the person's owner. Like a barcode.

"It took me a while to figure out why you hate it so much, why you always cover it up. And it looked kinda familiar, although it's much prettier than the tattoos of the prostitutes in Kep City. I suppose King Vald wanted the women of his royal harem to have the most beautiful design."

My throat feels thick. But there is some relief that she doesn't know the complete story, that it wasn't King Vald who gave me the tattoo.

"I was twelve when I was given to him," I say through my clogged throat.

"Twelve?" Fan shakes her head, her brows drawing together.

"But I was sixteen when he *took* me." I lift my chin higher, waiting for her to call me a whore, waiting for the judgment.

She surprises me by saying, "I'm so sorry, Eshan'ya." There isn't any judgment in her eyes, only pity, only sadness. And none of the jealousy I've seen in the eyes of other girls who wish to be a *princess*. I squeeze my eyes shut.

"It's not something I wanted," I say, and I'm pleased my voice doesn't quiver.

She nods, swallowing. "Of course not. I wouldn't...I didn't think that." Her face twists in anger, and she leaps across the room and punches her fist against the wall. "I'll cut his balls off," she cries.

"Not if I do it first."

She looks at me from the corner of her eye, and her mouth twitches. Maybe she's imagining me doing exactly that: slicing King Vald's most precious jewels right from between his legs.

"Do you...Do you need to talk about it?" she asks. I'm not sure if she's more scared of hurting me or getting stuck with me if I start crying. But I'm not going to cry. I don't need to cry for myself, and I've cried so many tears for the other girls, but it never did any good. They still went through what I did.

"No," I say. "There's no point, so it's best just to forget it."

Silence falls between us again.

Fan looks around the room. I suppose she's not sure what to say, and she doesn't seem to find any inspiration on the walls. She shoves her hands in her pockets and presses her lips together awkwardly.

"So...that Protogenoi passage, heh?" she asks after a time. "We need to crack that."

The atmosphere in the room breaks, and we're back on solid ground again.

I consider whether I should reveal everything to her now, but I decide not to. We've already shared so much tonight. My heart is heavy, and I don't know if I can speak more about my childhood, about Declan—and how he abandoned me.

Chapter 21

Fan

"WE'VE GOT FOUR HOURS until we reach Farnth. Princess, Ranate, have you gotten any further with the Protogenoi clue?" I stand in the doorway of the mess hall. My back has now recovered, thanks to the quick healing xertgo salve that Eshan'ya had on my back for two days. Other than a bit of tightness in my skin, I feel almost normal, even if I do have a handful of scars.

My crew sit around the large metal dining table, except for Pedders, who is at the cooktop preparing suan cai and fake pork stew, sending the scent of cabbage and spices through the room. He's got on that purple apron he always insists on wearing, which is way too small to cover his large frame, but makes me smile and feel at home. Tika was chatting away, as usual, but she quieted when I spoke and now waits with wide eyes for the answer.

Eshan'ya sits among the crew wearing another borrowed outfit—a white linen shirt that, from the way it hangs across her body, looks like it was made for her even though I know it's Tika's. I can't stop my eyes from flicking to her, no matter how many times I tell myself to look away. Despite her not being a *real* princess, she still looks regal. She holds herself with poise and class. She's sharply intelligent and resourceful. Where she came from doesn't define her.

Maybe I can take some inspiration from her.

She's been through a lot in her short lifetime. Given to King Vald at only twelve years old. Whoever did that to her is the biggest scum in this universe. Sure, she would have been taught royal traditions and given some benefits for her stature as a member of the harem, but nothing would be worth what she's been through.

It turns my stomach.

I'd take a beating from my dad over that any day.

"We know the planet and the city," Eshan'ya says, "and I've been working on the clue."

She reads it out again.

"Follow the light of the third sun
through the void of chaos
on sunrise of the winter solstice
to find Portunus awaking."

She looks up at the faces watching her from around the table. Luchlon shrugs, Pedders grunts as he stirs our dinner, RAN-8 stares straight ahead, and Tika blinks furiously.

Eshan'ya says, "It seems to me we need to calculate where the sunshine of the third sun would hit at sunrise on the winter solstice through something they call the void of chaos."

"What's the bit about Portunus awaking?" I ask.

"Portunus was the Greek god of keys and doors," she says.

"Who cares about Greek gods?" Luchlon asks.

"Many of the Protogenoi deities can be compared with Greek gods," Eshan'ya explains.

"Do you know a lot could be translated using Chinese mythology too?" I say.

"Yes, I'm aware. But I'm not familiar enough with Chinese mythology to do that. Maybe you can teach me one day." She blushes.

"The Menshen might be comparable in Chinese mythology. They were guardians of entrances," RAN-8 supplies helpfully.

"I'd be honored to teach you," I say quietly.

She looks at me for a beat too long before she continues. "As for the *awaking*, well, that refers to the second key. The Protogenoi did many things in thirds. You're all aware of the three stars and the three semicircles?"

Everyone nods or mumbles, "Yes."

"They also broke their days into thirds. Sleeping is the first. Awaking is the second. Walking is the third. The stars also represent these three states. Therefore, the clue is referring to the second state and the second key."

It makes sense, especially since we already knew it was the second key because we've been directed there by the first.

"The bit I can't work out is the void of chaos," Eshan'ya says.

"Wasn't Chaos also a Greek god?" I ask.

"Yes, that sounds familiar..." Tika chimes in.

"Sort of. It's the void state, the emptiness, which was believed to have preceded the creation of the universe. So when it says the 'void of chaos', I don't know what that means. According to legend, chaos has already passed."

"Maybe it meant something different to the Protogenoi than to the Greeks?" Luchlon asks as he inspects a dent in the table.

"Maybe." Eshan'ya frowns in concentration. "But they believed in something similar to the Greek Chaos…I don't know." She spins away in frustration.

"OK," I say, "what about the rest of it? Ranate, can you calculate the rough coordinates of where the third sun would have been in the sky on the winter solstice back in the Protogenoi days?"

"Yes, Captain." RAN-8's eyes glow brighter. "As you know, the planet's orbit has changed since the time of the Protogenoi, but through some very clever calculations—even if I do say so myself—I have figured out where each sun would have been during the winter solstice for Farnth Five fifteen thousand years ago when it was occupied by the Protogenoi.

"There's actually three different possibilities, given the orbit of the third sun is slightly out of sync with Farnth Five. So for every three rotations of Farnth Five, the third sun will be in three different locations in the sky on the solstice. After three years, it returns to the first location once again."

"Three options make sense, given the Protogenoi were obsessed with the number three," I surmise, and Eshan'ya gives me an approving nod. Did my heart just beat a little harder?

"It's possible the Chaos clue will lead us to the correct location out of the three, as long as I can figure it out," Eshan'ya says. "Ranate and I can go through the archives on the Protogenoi and see if it helps."

"You've got four hours, princess." I give her a wink of encouragement, and she smiles back. "For everyone else, let's check over the ship, make sure she's running smoothly, and check munitions and weapons. We might encounter resistance from the Quain. We'll try to avoid them, but if we can't...well, we had best be prepared."

"But we're about to have dinner," RAN-8 complains.

"You don't even eat food, Ranate. As for the rest of you, you'll get dinner after your chores are done." I sound like the minders in the orphanage.

My grumbling crew meanders to their feet. "Move!" I demand, and they notch it up a gear, racing out of the mess.

"I think I've figured it out," Eshan'ya says as she rushes into the cockpit where Pedders and I are getting ready to come out of hyperspace and enter the Farnth solar system. "I found references to Chaos in the Protogenoi archives."

She sits behind me, and I swivel my chair around to give her my attention. She turns on her tech point, and a hologram pops up: three stars surrounded by three half circles.

I can't help but see Eshan'ya's tattoo—*her brand*—in its design, and my heart feels sore for her all over again.

"The Protogenoi sigil?" I ask.

"Exactly. But if you take the stars away..." The stars fade from the hologram. "The remaining lines are the symbol for Chaos. The middle is empty, symbolizing the *void* before the creation of anything else." Her eyes shine with excitement.

"OK, but how does that help us?"

She slides the image across to a new one. The hologram now shows an ancient city. "This is a depiction of what historians believe an ancient Protogenoi city looked like." She slides through a few more pictures, all of them different cities, but all of them similar in one way.

At the grand entrance to each stand three pillars guarding the way. They're similar to an Egyptian obelisk, except these columns only have three sides and a tetrahedron pyramid at the top. These obelisks are also intricately carved. And just below where the obelisk slants into the tetrahedron, is a symbol, a different one for each obelisk.

The first is the Chaos symbol, the three semi-circles. The second is the three stars without the circles. And the third is the combination of both circles and stars.

It's the same in every city Eshan'ya shows me.

"As far as archaeologists can tell, the only outside structures that depict the symbol of Chaos are the obelisks guarding each of their cities."

Pedders grunts in question.

"Don't you see? These obelisks with the Chaos symbol are the only place the light from the third sun would hit. Every other depiction of the symbol appears indoors."

"But what about the part about the void?" I ask.

"Look closely." Her voice goes husky as she leans in, zooming the hologram in on the Chaos symbol.

I gasp when I see it.

Pedders grunts.

"There's a hole straight through the center of the obelisk, right in the middle of the Chaos symbol. A hole that a light could shine through," she says, like it's a wonderful secret. "We have the solar system, we have the planet, we have the ancient city, and now we have the tool that will show us the final resting spot of the second key."

The way she glows when she talks makes me want to kiss her. With her cheeks slightly flushed, her eyes sparkling, she looks so alive.

"You're amazing," I tell her. "OK, get Ranate to figure out the final coordinates of where that sunshine would hit. We're almost there."

Eshan'ya is beaming when she leaves.

Pedders looks at me sidelong and grunts. I know what that grunt implies, "*You'll do anything for a pretty face.*"

And yeah, Eshan'ya is drop-dead gorgeous, but I'm beginning to realize I like her for a lot more than just her looks.

A few minutes later, Pedders drops the *Fox* out of hyperspace, and the Farnth solar system is laid out in front of us.

The smallest star with its eight planets is closest, so it looks like the biggest one. Beyond it, the other two stars shine bright. I can't see all eight planets; some are just a sliver of light in the darkness, the suns only lighting up a small portion of their surfaces.

Others look as small as moons because of their distance from us. But one red gas giant takes up the entire view to the right.

I steer the *Fox* to the left, then we see Farnth Five.

Its surface is all gray and white hues, as if it's made of EconCrete. And the truth is, it's not much more exciting than that—the majority of the planet is covered in rock. There are no trees, no grass, no greenery at all. Even the oceans have turned to ice, rock hard and white cold.

"We're here, team," I call over the ship's comms.

I take the *Fox* into the atmosphere of the planet and fly to the coordinates of the city indicated on the first key.

The surface is a rocky, mountainous place. There are other long-forgotten structures built by the Protogenoi, other cities carved straight out of the mountains, though all of them now lie in ruins. Where once a building stood tall and strong, half is now rubble. What might have been a temple is now only crumbling walls and a few columns.

I don't see any signs of a shinver mine, and I'm not sure if I'm relieved or disappointed. I must admit that it's safer to keep clear of them.

We fly over some city gates that are still intact, but the obelisks standing out the front are now only short stumps rather than the towering monuments Eshan'ya displayed on her tech point. The *Fox* continues on; this isn't the city we need.

Flying around a mountain, I follow its cliff face down to the gorge below, traveling just above the frozen river at the bottom.

Despite all the gray and gloom, it's kinda pretty.

The gorge eventually opens up to a valley with one, two...yep, there're three mountains on each side. Those Protogenoi really liked the number three. It's a wonder why they didn't build this city on the third planet instead of the fifth—maybe it was uninhabitable or something.

It's a massive valley, filled with the ruins of the city that once stood here. The remaining walls and structures outline some of the streets while also giving me a sense of just how impressive the city must have been.

My blood turns as cold as the ice outside when I look out further over the city.

We're not alone.

In the distance, I see vehicles and cranes and other excavation equipment—all painted shiny black.

The Quain.

I quickly lower the *Fox* so it skims mere inches from the ground, hoping we're hidden behind the crumbling gray buildings.

"Braxt's men are here," I warn over the comms.

Turning to the right, I take the *Fox* around the city. The ship is too big to fit through the streets, so I keep to the outskirts on the other side of the outer walls. The city is set out in a circular fashion, and I follow the circumference until we reach where the front gate once stood. One obelisk still reaches several hundred feet high, but it's broken about halfway up. The two others are mere stumps, though a few triangular blocks lay nearby.

None of the Quain are in the vicinity, so I land the *Fox* right there.

I don't need to announce the landing to the crew. They're all waiting in the main hold when Pedders and I get there, all wearing layers upon layers of clothing to stay warm.

Eshan'ya has borrowed a ski mask. Only her eyes are visible, but it's still enough to get my heart beating harder. *You're such a fool, Fan!*

Pedders cycles the airlock and opens the hatch.

The cold hits me in the face like one of Gussart's men. I'm also bundled up, but blazin' rockets, it's freaking cold. I snap on some protective glasses so my eyeballs don't ice over, and the crew does the same.

"I'm already freezing up," Tika complains. "I can feel it in all my joints."

Pedders grunts with a frown, and Tika grunts back, but she refrains from whining more.

The ramp takes us down to more gray rock, but as we descend, the real view unfolds before us—I'm impressed.

The city might be in ruins, but it's still remarkable. The remaining obelisk is massive, at least two hundred feet tall and fifty feet wide, and it's only half as tall as it once was. It towers menacingly over our group.

"What's the point of this, anyway?" Luchlon grumbles, his words muffled by the cloth over his mouth. "The Quain are already here. They must have already done this. Maybe they've already found the key."

"If they'd found the key, then they wouldn't still be here," Eshan'ya reasons. "And if they interpreted the clue wrong, then they're looking in the wrong spot."

Luchlon huffs.

"Tika, grab my squito," I say. "We'll need it to hover at the height this obelisk would have been. Princess, do you have the three coordinates?"

She nods.

"Right, let's do this."

"So we don't need to wait for the solstice?" Luchlon asks as Tika prepares my squito. She starts the motors, and the sleek red machine floats down the ramp.

"No point in that," I say, taking the squito from Tika. "The planet is out of orbit, so it won't tell us anything anyway."

Eshan'ya adds, "Ranate has made all the calculations to determine the projection of the three suns fifteen thousand years ago. Even with rounding, we should be able to determine each location within a few yards."

"Right, OK," Luchlon says.

Pedders grunts behind his ski mask.

"Yeah, me too, buddy," I agree. "Gotta hope the Quain have their calcs wrong."

I swing my leg over the squito, ready to launch, and Eshan'ya gets on behind me. My body sings at her touch, even though there are thousands of layers of clothes between us.

The squito jolts as I launch it from the rocky surface. The gauge shows our height as we ascend, all the way to 456.2245 feet—the peak of the Chaos obelisk—the height at which the Chaos symbol would have been inscribed on the obelisk if it still stood whole. From this height, I can see the Quain working in the city's west a few miles away. My pulse quickens.

I hear Eshan'ya's muffled voice say, "Hold it steady."

She pulls a tech point out from under her glove and holds it at the exact height the Chaos symbol would have been. The holo-display reads the landmarks of the city below, mapping it, and with a swish of her finger, it calculates the three locations the third sun would have hit at sunrise on the winter solstice fifteen thousand years ago.

I let out a frosty breath as the three spots light up on the map—one point is where the Quain are. Eshan'ya takes a snapshot of the locations, and I lower us to the ground.

"So the Quain got at least some coordinates right," Luchlon says, looking at the results.

"Yeah, let's skip that location for now," I say and organize the crew into three groups. Pedders and RAN-8 will stay with the *Huxian Fox*, hiding her back in the gorge. Luchlon and Tika will investigate the location in the center of the city. And Eshan'ya and I will go to the location in the east.

I load my squito back into the *Fox*—the streets are narrow and the paths aren't clear, so it would be dangerous to take, not to mention the noise of the engines could alert the Quain if we get within sound range.

"Keep in contact," I command. "If you see any Quain soldiers or hear even a whisper from them, I want to know about it."

And with that, we head out.

Chapter 22

Eshan'ya

DESPITE THE COLD, I am warm after sitting behind Fan on the squito. I'm still thinking about the feel of her strong, lean form even through the layers of clothes. She has recovered well from her time with Gussart; her strength and energy have returned fully. I just wish she'd stop taking shinver.

I turn my attention to the city. It must have been beautiful—it still is. I can imagine the three obelisks standing tall in all their glory, and in my mind's eye, I can even see the stately gates, the city walls standing strong, the temples and palaces beyond the wall. Some of it still stands. Roofs and walls are missing, buildings have long since caved in, and many of the adornments have worn off in the elements, but it's still a magnificent sight, almost as resplendent as the city I grew up in.

My eyes sting behind my protective goggles.

Fan and I enter the city gates, which are made of gray stone. The right side has collapsed into a pile of rubble, but the left side still stands proudly. It's at least double the height of a person.

The map on my tech point directs us to a path running along the inside wall on the left as soon as we pass the gates. If these ruins were on Shadé, there would be moss and plants growing through the rocks. But all life on this planet died out a long time ago, so the only variation among the rock and stone is the occasional slick of ice that makes the path slippery.

It's amazing what has survived over thousands of years. I marvel at an ornate arch as we walk under it. Engraved in the rock at its crest is the Protogenoi sigil with both the stars and half circles. It looks exactly like an arch I loved from my childhood. Farther along, a bridge with portico fences lining the sides spans a river that has gone so dry that not even ice remains. The images engraved on it have long since eroded, and I'm unable to make out any details.

I look up at the three suns. Through Farnth Five's atmosphere, two of them look like large stars, still visible even though it's daylight. The star we orbit is much bigger, and although the planet's trajectory has shifted, it still looks large and yellow in the sky.

"It's bigger than Earth's sun," Fan says all of a sudden, looking up.

"But not as warm." I pull my coat closer. "That way." I point, reading the map and directing us through the winding streets. "So you're interested in Chinese mythology. Is that why you named your ship the *Huxian Fox*?" I ask.

"Kind of," Fan says. "You know the famous warrior, Colonel Wang? Her ship was named *Yü* after the legendary Chinese emperor who could shapeshift into a golden dragon. Her ship was even painted gold. I always liked that idea, but I don't consider myself a dragon."

"You see yourself more like a fox?"

"Exactly. Not to mention that Huxian was said to be very beautiful in any form—female, male, or fox. Plus, the goddess is a bit of a trickster who seduces both men and women. Now I'm not saying I'm *anything* like that, but it's a good name for a ship."

I chuckle, and we continue walking in a comfortable silence until Fan says, "You never did tell me how you learned to read Protogenoi."

I breathe deeply and take a moment to find the right words. "I was brought up by a man on Shadé."

"Not your father?"

"No, not my father. His name was Declan Axtryn." I give the map all of my attention, and Fan doesn't press. After a while, I tell her, "He knew a lot about the Protogenoi. On Shadé, there are more Protogenoi ruins, another large city like this. But the planet is habitable, so it's a good place to study the ancients."

"And that's what he did?"

"Yes." I nod, still not looking at Fan. "He taught me about it. He taught me their language, so I can read it. I'm not sure I can speak it, though." My chuckle is a little more high-pitched than normal. "You know, because it hasn't been spoken in centuries, we're just guessing what the words sound like." I try to slow my heart rate. "Anyway, he told me stories about them. He's the one who first told me about the Device."

"Oh, you didn't hear about it on Keplerane from King Vald?"

I shake my head. "Not at first. It's a legend many on Shadé know about and even believe."

When Fan stops walking, I eventually stop too, lifting my eyes to look at her. She tilts her head as if she's appraising me.

"I think you're hiding something," she says, and my breath catches. "It's OK. You don't need to tell me. I trust you anyway."

Maybe it's the ease of her stance, her dilated pupils, or the hint of a blush on her cheeks that pokes out between her ski mask and goggles, but something in the way she says it makes me believe her. She trusts me.

A wall inside me breaks, a wall that has always protected me from others, keeping me distant from anyone and everyone. It's just a crack in the wall, but for the first time in a long time, it's letting some light into my heart.

"You're right," I hear myself say. I turn and keep walking. She follows me quietly. I'm grateful she doesn't push me to keep talking, and after some time, with that light bleeding through my wall, I say, "I grew up..." I take a breath and stop walking again. She stops beside me and waits patiently. "I grew up in a community called the Protectors."

Through her goggles, I see her brow crease in confusion.

"They're an order of people who have sworn to protect the Device."

"What?" Fan's eyes grow large.

"Come on," I say. "We should keep walking."

She blinks a few times, then takes off, matching my stride.

"I know it sounds crazy," I tell her. I've never told this to anyone, and there's no slowing my heart any longer. "But I was taught all about the Device at a young age. I was one of these Protectors. We lived apart from others on the planet, a group of us all committed to preventing anyone from finding the Device."

"Like a commune?" Fan asks, and I cringe. "Sorry, I didn't mean..."

"No, it's fine." I brush off her apology with a flick of my hand. "I know what it sounds like. A crazy cult. But my childhood was happy. I had all these people who loved me. None more than Declan.

"He was so kind, always encouraging, and he always had time for me and my many questions. He taught me all about the Protogenoi and made sure I kept up with my training to become a fully fledged Protector."

My soul feels heavy thinking about him.

Is he still alive? Did Braxt kill him? He should have been there for me.

"It's not crazy," Fan says, looking into the ruins with soft eyes, like she's lost in her own memories. "It's amazing how people who aren't related by blood can become family."

Fan would know that feeling better than most. She has created her own family with Pedders as her brother, Tika her sister, and Luchlon...well, he's obviously her lover, but I'm not sure if he's family. I hope not. He's not someone I'd trust.

"That's not why I didn't tell you. I'm not embarrassed." I take another deep breath. Am I really going to admit the truth to a criminal? To someone desperate for money?

I dare to glance at her again, though I can barely see Fan under all her layers. Only her large brown eyes are visible through her glasses. But those eyes are wide and honest despite her criminal past. I realize I trust her too, and a huge chunk of my wall comes down, letting in loads of light.

"Fan, the truth as to why I didn't tell you...and the reason I was sent to King Vald's harem to hide among those women, is because Braxt has been hunting the Protectors. He wants every last one of us dead. And he'll pay handsomely to see it happen. You can't tell the others." My voice is husky, my throat clogged.

"No. *No*, I wouldn't," Fan says. She steps closer, her hand resting on my arm, telling me without words that it's important I hear her. "Princess...Eshan'ya, you can trust me. I won't betray you."

I believe her. My body loses its tightness, and my shoulders ease for the first time in a very long while.

"I know." Even though she can't see it under my ski mask, I smile. I pat her hand, which is still resting on my arm. The touch feels awkward, charged, and I'm hoping she moves while hoping she won't. The air between us thickens.

When I turn back to my tech point, the tension eases, and I realize we only have a few more turns until we reach our designated location.

"We're getting closer," I whisper.

Chapter 23

Fan

It's empty.

It was once some kind of temple—I can tell from the magnificent columns that surround the square, that are cut off halfway, and looks like a giant took a machete to it. I guess the pile of rocks, rubble, and ice to the west of the square is what's left of the roof and the tops of the columns.

But in the middle of the square, right where I'd expect to see a floor, there is none. It's been excavated. Dug through. Thoroughly.

The Quain have already been here. They've been, they've looked, and they found nothing.

Eshan'ya and I stand at the edge, looking down at the rock and dirt—turns out this planet actually has dirt, not just rock—but there is nothing to see. Only a hole.

"Maybe it's at one of the other locations," I murmur.

"Yeah, it's got to be." She blinks her icy eyelashes a few times.

"Fan, do you read?" It's Luchlon on my tech point.

"Go ahead, Luchlon."

"It's not at this location. Looks like the Quain have already come and gone from here. The whole place has been torn up."

Eshan'ya's gone stiff, listening.

"Have you had any luck?"

"It's the same here. Nothing but dirt and rocks."

The line is quiet for a moment, and then Luchlon says, "So what do we do now?"

"We return to the *Fox* and plan our next move."

"Copy that."

Eshan'ya has stepped away from me. I can tell she's disappointed. The blue fire in her eyes has dulled, and her regal poise has deflated slightly.

Despite her trepidation to tell me about her past, when she did, she lit up. She was remembering a happy time. She had a purpose—to protect the Device. Now, she must think she's failing. There's only one location left, and the Quain are already there. There's little chance we can get to the key before they do.

The two of us go back the way we came, and the *Fox* meets us at the entrance to the city. We get there a little before the others.

When Luchlon sees me, he raises his arms in the air and says with a scowl, "This was a stupid idea from the start. Of course the Quain got here before us. We already knew they would. We never had any hope."

My eyes slide to Eshan'ya, who's been quiet the whole walk back. Even now, she doesn't rise to Luchlon's jibe. She looks back into the city, frowning. I guess she's not ready to give up.

"Well, yes, of course we knew the Quain were here," Tika mutters, "but we still had to try, even though the odds were eight thousand to one."

"Eight thousand and fifty-two to one," RAN-8 corrects her from the ramp of the *Fox*.

"Why are they still here?" Eshan'ya says, her voice barely audible.

"What?" I ask.

She turns back to me, the fire in her eyes kindling again. "The Quain have had plenty of time to search for the key. If it was where they're looking, then they should have found it by now. So my question is, why are they still here?"

"You don't think...?"

"I do."

"What? What do you think?" Tika asks, eyes darting back and forth between us.

"That they're looking in the wrong spot," I say.

Eshan'ya's eyes smile.

I charge up the ramp, Eshan'ya almost skipping up behind me.

"But how can they be in the wrong spot?" Tika says. "That's the third spot. Unless Ranate's calculations were wrong. You can never trust a droid—"

I tear off my woolen hat and gloves, jerking down the cloth at my mouth as soon as everyone is back on the ship and the airlock cycles shut. I rub my hands together, bringing some warmth back to them.

Eshan'ya does the same, and it's all I can do to stop myself from reaching out and warming her hands myself. Her nose has turned pink, and her cheeks are flushed. It looks very cute on her.

"Did you remember to carry the two?" Tika is asking RAN-8 to confirm his calculations.

"Tika, Tika." I laugh, stopping her. "It's not the calcs that are wrong."

"It isn't? Then what, Captain?"

"It's the interpretation of the clue," Eshan'ya says.

She reads it aloud again.

"Follow the light of the third sun
through the void of chaos
on sunrise of the winter solstice
to find Portunus awaking."

"Follow the light of the third sun," I say, and she gives me an approving nod.

"But we did that," Luchlon grumbles.

"Yes," Eshan'ya agrees, "but we assumed the winter solstice was in relation to their primary sun—they actually have three different winter solstices, one for each sun. It doesn't translate perfectly in English because Earth only has one sun. But if we consider that the third sun has its own day, which is also considered to be a solstice, then..."

"Then the void of chaos would point to a completely different location," I finish.

"Right!" She grins.

"In that case," I say, putting more of the pieces together, "it wouldn't be the sunrise of the primary sun, either. It needs to be based on the third sun."

"That's my guess."

"Ranate, run the calculations," I say, still smiling at the princess.

"A please would be nice," he responds.

"You're a machine!" I say, breaking eye contact with Eshan'ya to frown at RAN-8. "Get on with it."

"Yeah, yeah, yeah, politeness still goes a long way," he grumbles as he clomps to the engineering point.

I run my hand through my hair, my face heating as I turn back to the princess.

Eshan'ya is glowing again, and all I want to do is gather her up in my arms and kiss her. And even though she's smiling at me so openly, I don't think it's a good idea. Not yet.

Instead, I ask, "Ready to go for another ride on the squito?"

Her eyes flash a darker shade of blue, and, if I didn't know better, I'd think desire was fueling them.

Chapter 24

Eshan'ya

With me behind her once again, Fan flies the squito back into the location where the peak of the chaos obelisk once stood.

With the new calculations RAN-8 has processed, I hold out the tech point in my shaking hand to determine where the key is hidden. Energy pulses through me—somehow I know we've got it right this time. We're going to find the key. And I can take it away before the Quain figure out they've interpreted the clue wrong—and before they use it to find the Device.

A hologram map of the city shines from the tech point once again, but this time, only one location is highlighted with a red spot. It's at the rear of the city, far to the north and right at the base of the tallest rocky mountain.

My heart skips a beat.

"Got it," I say to Fan, and she lowers us quickly.

As we descend, I steal a glance at the Quain working to the west. I pray to the stars they don't see us. We were quick, but if just one of them was looking over at the right moment...

I shove the thought down. I can't let doubt stand in the way. I'm retrieving the second key, and that's final. Nothing will stop me.

The squito lands, and I share the location on my tech point with the crew.

"Right, let's hustle," Fan says, picking up on my urgency. Does she have the same fears as I do? Or is it just the excitement of the hunt? We're about to find long-lost treasure, and if I know anything about Fan, it's that this kind of thing is sure to get her heart racing.

We leave Pedders and RAN-8 in the *Fox* again, but the rest of us set off for the key.

"It's kinda exciting, isn't it?" Tika says, and I can't help but smile. She's feeling it too.

Luchlon only huffs and looks over his shoulder in the direction of the Quain.

All four of us hurry through the ancient city, following the map projected by my tech point. The red spot flashes like a beacon, pulling me to it. My heart beats in time with it.

I lead us through the narrow winding streets, between crumbling buildings, up stone stairs that have remained intact, and around the bends of the walls. We jump the expanse of a short bridge that has broken in the middle, leaving a yard of vacant air. We travel under several arches, all marked with the Protogenoi sigil at their apex.

As we reach the flashing dot on the map, we find ourselves in a narrow corridor that curves gradually. One side hosts the sturdy rounded wall of a building still in good condition, and the other side is a sheer cliff face of solid rock. The mountainside rises hundreds of yards above us, making me feel small.

The corridor is dark and inconsequential compared to the many other grand streets and avenues we've been down. My fingers tingle with anticipation. I swallow, trying to ease my parched throat.

I reach the dot on the map first, though the other three quickly join me.

We're still wedged between the stone wall and the cliff face, and the corridor continues around a bend. There's no ornate temple, no altar, no obelisk or shrine to mark that the key is here.

The frowns on my comrades' faces show they're confused; they're wondering where the key is. Fan gives me a gentle look—pity. She must think we've failed again.

But I know we haven't. I realize now that the Protogenoi wouldn't advertise the key's location. Of course it would be hidden down an insignificant street.

My eyes roam the stone wall of the building, then the cobbled street. I inspect the cliff face.

There.

At the base of the cliff, level with the street, is a strange crack in the rock. Anyone who wasn't looking for the key probably wouldn't notice it. It looks like a natural fracture. But to my eyes, it's clear—three semicircles.

My heart soars like an Earth eagle.

They're not the smooth lines that the Protogenoi sigil boasts. They're crooked and out of shape—just like any fracture in a rock—but it's clear to me this is the chaos symbol, maybe the only one we'd ever find outside that wasn't on the obelisks guarding the Protogenoi city.

"It's here," I whisper and hunch down to look at the crag more closely.

"That's not...? It is...?" Fan stumbles on her words and then joins me in a crouch. She reaches out, her gloved fingers feeling the rock around the symbol. She tries to pry it from the wall in a couple of different places, and when that doesn't work, she presses on the rock.

When she touches the center, right in the void, we hear a soft click, and the rock moves slightly—enough that Fan's fingers can now get purchase on the edges of the cracks and pull.

My breath catches.

The rock slides out like a drawer, stone scraping across stone.

And there, sitting in the middle of a dark slit, is a deep blue jewel, its glow distinguishing it as a Shadé diamond.

I stare in wonder at the soft glow, the deep blue, the secrets it holds. My childhood was full of stories about the keys, but this is the first time I've seen one. It is completely smooth. I thought the map would be engraved on it or the next clue, but I don't see either. The exterior is glossy and untarnished, its secrets still veiled.

My friends all seem to be under the same spell, staring at the crystal. There is something captivating about it, like it's alive, enthralling and pulling me to it.

Finally, I reach out and touch it. I take it out of its home within the rock, holding it in my gloved fingers, feeling the heavy weight of it in my palm. The others watch in awe, all of us forgetting about the hurry we were in.

Shwoom!

The blast of a pulsar gun breaks the spell.

Instincts kick in, and we all drop to the ground. The blast goes over our heads, the electric charge dissipating into the cliff face.

I look up and see the Quain, their black uniforms with extra padding against the cold, their faces covered to keep warm, and the three silver stars on their shoulders.

They're racing down the corridor. They must have followed us. Luchlon spins and shoots back. His pulsar isn't set to stun. They're forced to duck around the curve of the wall.

"Run!" Fan yells, but I don't need any orders. I've already taken off with the diamond clutched in my fist.

Fan and Luchlon take defensive positions at the back of the group, allowing Tika and me to run ahead.

We're running in the opposite direction from where we came, and I don't know the way, so I lift my tech point, showing the map of the city. I lead the way; the others following as they defend me.

I skirt over rocks, slip on ice, jump through a narrow arch, and skip over a bridge, keeping my head low the whole time.

The Quain are on our heels, their shots filling the air around us. Fan and Luchlon shoot back so they have to hide behind walls, buildings, large stones, and whatever else can shelter them. The sizzling of the electric pulses fills my ears.

I clutch the jewel tightly, desperately.

They follow us under a bridge with gapped and crooked brickwork. Fan shoots it, and the bridge comes crashing down, right onto the heads of several Quain soldiers, crushing them. The remaining rubble blocks the rest from following.

We're given a small reprieve before more Quain come at us from a street on the left. Tika shoots, one, two, three times, but none of them hit the mark.

Fan catches up to us and hits a soldier on the first shot after barely glancing in their direction. Then she aims at the wall and brings it down with a few well-aimed shots of her duster, blocking the path again.

She continues to thwart the Quain's advances by bringing down the city around us and barring their way. I'd feel bad about ruining the ancient city if it wasn't so effective.

"Pedders," Fan screams into her tech point, "we need extraction! Pronto."

I barely hear Pedders grunt over the gunshots from the Quain. They're too close. I flatten myself against a wall to avoid getting shot. Fan takes four quick shots as she runs to where I'm cowering.

"Come on." Fan collects me with one arm as she returns fire, pushing me along the path.

We're nearing the edge of the city. I can see the *Huxian Fox* hovering just beyond the walls, ready to collect us.

Fan takes my hand in hers and sprints.

We're almost there. The two of us run under the final arch and out the front gates. I see the obelisk, broken in half, and the *Fox* right in front of us. Tika and Luchlon are bringing up the rear.

Bwaaamp! Bwaaamp!

The ground explodes right in front of me. Fan hauls me backward, covering my body with hers as she pushes my head down. Dirt and stone rains over us.

Those powerful shots came from the Quain vessel, from weapons capable of blowing up a ship—shooting right at us.

Pedders reacts quickly, and the *Fox* scuttles away before the Quain starts firing at it, but he's left us with nowhere to run. We duck back into the city.

Fan pushes me from behind, shooting up at the Quain ship as she does, though her little duster pistol won't do much damage. I hear the bullets ping off the metal hull, barely causing a scrape.

"We're done for," Tika gasps, catching up to us just inside the city walls and seeing the situation. Between the soldiers in the city and the ship outside, the Quain are hemming us in.

"They can't just blow us up," Fan says. "They won't risk blowing up the key."

"We can't let them have it," I say, my eyes skimming over the gray stone walls as I look for an answer.

"What if we hide it?" Fan asks. "Then even if they capture us, they won't have the key."

"*If* they capture us?" Luchlon yells. "If they capture us and we don't have the key, they're going to torture us."

"It's our only hope," I say, nodding at Fan.

"We can't hide it here." She holds out her hand. "I'll take it back into the city. I'm quick. I can hide it and get back without them killing me."

I stare at her outstretched palm.

She's Fan Sung, a smuggler, a drug addict, a criminal, asking me to give her one of the most precious jewels in the galaxy.

I grip the diamond tighter for a moment, and then I slowly reach out and put it in Fan's hand.

With grave eyes, she gives me a nod of understanding as her fingers curl around it. Her chest rises with a deep breath.

Just as she turns to run off, a massive explosion sets my ears ringing.

All of us freeze—Fan too—and our heads turn to the sky.

There's another ship, but it's not the Quain. It's not shiny or black—it's a run down brown thing. In fact, it's shooting *at* the Quain ship, and they're not being polite about it.

"Shikha." Fan's mouth is agape.

"But I thought Gussart attacked her," Tika says.

"Guess she fought back," Luchlon says.

Another ship, one that matches Shikha's, swings low and fires at the Quain ship. The enemy turns from us and engages the two vessels owned by the shinver lord. They don't have a choice; they won't be able to withstand many more direct hits.

The soldiers within the city finally catch up with us, climbing over the rubble. Fan fires at them before they can get a shot off, and the soldiers drop to the ground, right on top of all the fallen rocks.

"Here." Fan throws the blue jewel back to me and then pulls out her pulsar gun, using both hands to blast multiple shots.

"Come on!" I yell, and we all charge to the city gates again.

"Pedders! Pick us up and be quick about it," Fan yells down at her tech point.

"Roger that," comes the crackled reply.

I reach the other side of the city walls in time to see Pedders swing the *Fox* out from the gorge, staying low to keep under any rogue blasts from the battling ships. The hatch is open before he lands, and we all run up the ramp, Fan and Luchlon shooting back at the foot soldiers until the hatch bangs shut.

All four of us are inside the hold, safe.

Chapter 25

Fan

"Why the stars was Shikha's crew here?" Eshan'ya asks.

"Farnth Five is a favorite location for Shikha to mine the active chemical in shinver," Tika comments. "She must have seen the Quain as competition, especially when they started shooting."

I laugh. "Shikha will be so peeved if she ever finds out that she just saved our cute behinds."

Eshan'ya holds the dark blue jewel in her hand—the second key.

I rise from the floor, discarding my gloves and hat, and approach her. Looking closely at the Shadé diamond, I see it has that strange glow that all Shadé diamonds have, but this is the largest and most beautiful I've ever seen.

"I thought it was supposed to have the map to the next key on it," I say.

She holds it up to the light. "I thought so too." She twists it left and right, but I can't see a map or words.

"I thought you knew about this stuff," Luchlon says with his usual frown.

She shrugs. "I've never seen one before. All I know is that each key leads to the next."

"So it's just a useless artifact? A pretty one, but useless?" Tika asks.

"Not necessarily," RAN-8 says, clomping closer to Eshan'ya. "Crystals can be used to store data. My guess—and my guesses tend to be right—is that this crystal holds all the information we need. We just can't see it yet."

Eshan'ya is nodding. "That makes sense. I mean, the Quain got all that information from the first key. It must be contained within." Her eyes glow brighter than the diamond.

Luchlon scowls at the jewel. "Right. So how do we get the information out?"

"You just sit back and relax those muscles," RAN-8 says. "Let me deal with the crystal." He holds out his hand.

Eshan'ya shakes her head. "No, we don't need the information. We have the key, and Braxt can't get the Device without it." She holds the jewel close.

"Shouldn't we make sure that truly is the key?" Luchlon asks.

"What do you mean?" She blinks at him, clutching the diamond even tighter.

"I mean, what if that's just a decoy, and it's not even the second key? That would mean Braxt could still retrieve the second key and find the Device."

Eshan'ya shakes her head. "No. I *know* this is the key. I'm certain."

"But still," Luchlon continues, "isn't it risky leaving that Device out there? You said yourself that the first key was found by mistake on Keplerane. What if a random someone finds the Device by accident? We're better off finding it and destroying it."

He's got a point, but I'm surprised to hear it coming from Luchlon's mouth. He's not usually so responsible or conscientious.

"Yes, you're right," Eshan'ya says, decisive. "We need to destroy the Device."

RAN-8 holds out his hand again for the jewel. Eshan'ya hesitates for another second, then hands it to him. I know she trusts me, but after the life she's had, it must be hard to trust anyone, and my crew aren't the most honest of folks. It's understandable she'd hesitate.

RAN-8 raises the jewel up between his mechanical thumb and forefinger. His left eye gets brighter and brighter until a beam of light shines out of it, aimed at the diamond. The laser radiates out the other side, projecting three stars, three half circles, *and* a detailed map.

"Where is that?" Tika asks.

Everyone in the hold steps closer to see it better.

The first thing I notice is the asteroid belt orbiting the star. Three planets are nestled within the belt, one of which is flashing. The location looks familiar because we've recently been to this very same system. Vegasin and Shadé sit within that asteroid belt.

Eshan'ya's face has gone deathly white, her eyes bigger than I've ever seen them.

"That's Shadé." Her voice shakes.

I frown. Shadé, where Eshan'ya said she spent her childhood.

"OK, at least we know the planet. Ranate, can you access the next clue?" I say, hoping to take the focus off Eshan'ya.

"Of course," he says, and the light from his eye shifts spectrum. As soon as it does, the projected image changes, zooming in to a location on the planet's surface.

"Lyran," Eshan'ya barely whispers.

"Do you know it?" I ask.

"I should. I've spent a lot of time in that city. More than half my life."

My crew exchange glances with each other. They must be wondering what in the stars a little girl was doing in an ancient city when she was growing up.

"Ranate, the next clue, please," I say before anyone starts asking questions.

He changes the spectrum again, and the image alters to the Protogenoi sigil and four lines of text below it.

"I'll need a few minutes to translate this," RAN-8 says.

"No need." Eshan'ya steps closer to the image. "It says
"Travel down the waters of Enipeus
under the gaze of Helios.
Portunus walks here
as does Kratos. Beware."

"Hang on." Luchlon is frowning again. "You can read it, just like that?"

Ignoring his question, I ask, "What do you think it means?"

"Travel down the waters of Enipeus is easy to decipher," she says. "There's a river beside Lyran, and Enipeus is a river god in Greek mythology."

"That might be Hebo in Chinese mythology," I say.

Her brow furrows as she paces and ponders. "I'm not sure about the meaning of 'under the gaze of Helios'. Helios is the god of the sun, but that would be a large area, so it doesn't narrow things down. Then 'Portunus—or the Menshen—walks here' is obvious again."

"The third key?" I ask.

"Yes, the first was sleeping, the second is awaking, and the third is walking. But Kratos..." She trails off, putting a hand to her chin as she thinks. After a moment, she shakes her head. "Kratos is the god of strength, and that, coupled with the very obvious warning 'beware', must mean there are dangers hidden here." She shrugs, not taking her eyes off the projection. "I think we should go straight to Shadé. It'll make more sense when we get there," she says after a few moments.

"So we don't know what we're doing at all?" Luchlon complains. "We're just going to this city, Lyran, and searching the whole river?"

"No." Eshan'ya shuts him down. "I'll know more when I get there." Her fingers flick with tension, as if she's stopping herself from clenching them.

"Either way," I say pointedly to Luchlon, "we'll be heading there, so there's no point in sitting in the middle of space busting our brains trying to figure it out."

"Whatever you say," he grumbles.

"That's right," I say, "because I'm the captain." I storm to the front of the ship to set the course to Shadé.

Chapter 26

Eshan'ya

I'M IN THE COCKPIT with Fan and Pedders when the *Huxian Fox* drops out of hyperspace in the Vega system. The massive asteroid belt orbits the blue-white sun. Some rocks are as big as cities and others as small as golf balls, and there are even particles as small as a grain of sand. Among those rocks are a handful of planets.

Even though I was here only a few days ago, my heart thumps harder this time because we're not heading for Vegasin. We're going to Shadé. My home planet.

The blue light from the sun shines across the planets, highlighting their curvature, and they come into focus as we get closer. Vegasin shines green in the distance, but Shadé draws my gaze—the planet's blue oceans shimmering just beyond a cluster of asteroids.

It's been five years since I was last here.

It was once a happy place. I had a family; they might not have been blood relations, but they were home. There's no one I have missed more than Declan. My own personal Protector, or so he liked to call himself. He was like a father, he was a mentor, and he was my friend.

He always had a kind word to say, a lesson to teach, a laugh to share, and an ear to listen. I remember him wrapping his arms around me and kissing my forehead when I was sad. I remember him patching up my scraped knees when I fell. I remember him dancing with me under the starlight when I could barely reach his elbows, letting me step on his feet and twirling me around. All within the ruins of Lyran. That beautiful, wonderful city, full of mysteries and hiding places that I once played among.

Then Kriinal Braxt declared war against the Protectors. He found out about the Device, about my people protecting it, and he wanted it for himself no matter the cost. The cost was our lives.

I cringe at the memory of our rushed escape, of Declan bundling me onto a ship, telling me I had to hide among the ladies of King Vald. His face crumbled, and his voice cracked as he spoke.

"I'll come back for you. I swear, Eshan'ya, I'll come before...before anyone hurts you."

I didn't know what he meant then, but I do now. He never intended for me to stay at the palace for so long. I've always wondered what went wrong, why he never came.

Why did he let King Vald hurt me?

Declan held my hand while the tattoo was painfully stenciled onto my skin, hiding the stars I've had since birth that mark me as a Protector. I can't help but remember my arms around Declan's neck, begging him not to make me go, begging him to let me stay with him.

Shadé will be empty without him. The streets of Lyran will always be missing something without Declan and the other Protectors. They brought life to the old laneways. I dread seeing it empty.

But we edge closer anyway.

Fan easily maneuvers the *Fox* around the asteroids, big and small, just as she did when we went to Vegasin, and the blue waters of Shadé deepen as we get closer.

Fan enters the atmosphere near Lyran, avoiding the other modern cities that have been built on Shadé. It's probably wise for us to avoid them given she is a criminal and this is a UoW planet.

"Follow that river," I say, pointing. "That will lead us to Lyran."

Fan flies lower so the river is easy to see. It rushes along between lush green trees that are similar to the rainforests on Earth, only twenty-five lightyears away. The river sparkles in the midday sunlight, and as the water runs over boulders, it goes white, turning clear again a few yards on.

"It's beautiful," Fan breathes.

Pedders grunts his agreement.

My heart is torn. In one heartbeat, I want nothing more than to go down to those waters and splash in the river like I did as a child, but in the next, I'm so sorrowful for what I've lost that I can't bear to face it. I squeeze my eyes shut.

My childhood rushes back to me, thick and fast. My throat tightens as I open my eyes again and follow the river, still familiar after five years.

And then the city comes into sight.

In front stand the three obelisks that guard every major Protogenoi city. Two of them are still at full height, though the last is broken about two-thirds of the way up. All three are covered in green moss that weaves around and up from the bases.

Beyond the obelisks is a large staircase leading through the gate to the city of white stone, though it's also covered in moss and the forest is overgrown around it. Many large temples and structures remain intact, though they have long been abandoned.

The city sits beside a massive waterfall that feeds the river we followed to get here. The water trumpets down the cliff, splashing white as it falls and spraying rainbows.

It's still as stunning as I remember.

My eyes smart as I take it all in: the steps I played on, the waterfall I showered under, the grass I slept on, the bridges I skipped across.

My stars, I have missed this place.

A hope blooms—if I can destroy the Device, and with it Braxt's chances of ruling the galaxy, maybe I can return here and live out the rest of my days in peace.

"Are you all right?"

Fan is watching me.

I straighten my back and nod firmly. She gives me a lopsided smile and returns her attention to flying.

The *Fox* flies over the waterfall, then turns and comes back, looking for a place to land. There's a small clearing with bright green grass—the lawn I played nassy ball on—which is big enough for Fan to land on.

When I step out of the ship, the familiar, sweet aroma of the forest and river, and the musky smell of moss wash over me. It almost brings me to tears, but I keep my composure, biting the inside of my mouth to be sure.

Fan joins me, eyes wide as she stares up at the ancient city. She has traded her layers of winter clothing for the outfit she wore when I first met her: her gray leather jacket and trousers that hug her legs in all the right places.

I've also changed. Tika loaned me some more clothes—she might be incessantly chatty, but I can't help but be grateful for her kindness and generosity. I'm now in brown trousers like Fan's, a tan shirt, and the sturdy brown boots she gave me on Gerangan. The outfit is much more practical than the fancy dresses I brought with me from the palace.

"We'll find it," Fan assures me. "Have you had any more luck deciphering the clue?"

"Not yet," I say, putting my memories aside. "Ranate and I went through all the pictographs and writing in the 'laxy-net archives, but we couldn't find a reference to Helios or the sun. We thought it might have been like the reference to chaos, a symbol found somewhere in the city—and maybe it is—but we haven't found it in the archives. We'll need to keep our eyes open for any symbols within the city. There might even be one for Enipeus. I assumed it meant the river, but now I'm not so sure."

"OK, so we search the city for clues—or anything that might lead to the key."

I nod, swallowing down a rising ache.

"What if the river has clues?" Tika asks.

"Just stick to the city for now," Fan says.

"But what about the waterfa—"

"Right team," Fan calls to the group, "let's split up again. Pedders, you're with the ship. Tika, Ranate, and Luchlon, you're teaming up. Look for any clues about the sun and the river."

"Better if I head off alone then, Captain," Luchlon says, "and cover more ground. Tika and Ranate will be fine by themselves."

"Yeah, good call. OK, move out and keep in contact. I want to know about anything you find."

We all walk up the mossy stairs together, past the obelisks, and into the city before splitting up. Birds chirp overhead, giving us a peaceful soundtrack as we walk.

The sun is high, lighting up the streets, but it's not too hot to walk. In fact, it's that perfect temperature that's not too hot and not too cold, exactly how I remember Shadé to be—a paradise.

In the daylight, all the places I used to know and love are illuminated.

There's that niche in the wall that was a perfect hiding place whenever I played hide-and-seek with the Protectors. Vines grew over it so I'd be almost invisible—or at least that is what the Protectors would have had me believe as they called, "Where's Eshan'ya?" when they stood right in front of my hiding spot and I sat giggling at my brilliance behind the vines.

Up ahead, although the moss has grown thicker and has nearly covered it, I can still see the place I scratched my initials into the stone. I place my hand on it. It's lower than I remember, but back then, I was shorter.

"E.P.," Fan says. "Your initials?"

"Eshan'ya Primorsa," I say with a small smile.

"Eshan'ya Primorsa," she repeats quietly, and at the sound of my name on her lips, my heart knocks twice at my ribcage. Her eyes are dark, penetrating. I quickly look away.

As we keep walking, I see the archway where I had my first kiss. I was only twelve years old and so innocent. It was only a few months before I left Lyran. A girl from the city had come to the ruins on a school excursion. There was an instant attraction, but I think I was just enamored with meeting someone from the city. It wasn't love, but it was fun. Neither of us knew what we were doing at that age. I blush, and I'm glad Fan doesn't notice. She's busy looking for clues, which is what I should be doing.

I search the walls, the buildings' facades, carvings over doorways, the tops of arches, and the railings of bridges, yet nothing here seems to relate to the sun or the river.

And still, memories flood my mind. Declan singing happy birthday to me from a balcony. Swinging from the beams under a rotunda with friends. Self-defense classes in the courtyards with the other Protectors in training. Declan teaching me the Protogenoi language in the small building we used as a school. Playing chase between the columns of a temple.

It feels like I've lived in darkness for the last five years. I've stayed hidden within the palace—in the harem—and although I was given certain privileges as an *honored* lady of the harem, it was not a life I would have chosen. I found no honor in serving King Vald.

A pure anger ignites in my heart as I survey all I've lost, these beautiful, empty streets without my family and Protectors, only filled with memories. I'm angry at Kriinal Braxt and the Quain for taking it all from me. Why didn't Declan come back for me? He should be here. He should *be* here.

I can't let Braxt find the Device. But why can't I figure out this clue? What does it mean?

I stop in the middle of the street.

Fan stops too, looking back at me.

"Travel down the waters of Enipeus," I say, repeating the first line of the clue. "I'm a fool. We're looking in the wrong spot. We need to follow the water *down*."

"The waterfall," Fan surmises.

Tika was right.

Just as Fan starts to head back, I see movement behind her. A black uniform, a gun—

"Look out!" I call.

We dive in opposite directions, dodging the blasts. Birds screech as they flutter away in fright.

Chapter 27

Fan

Where in the stars did they come from?

The Quain are all around us. They're coming from the front, the left, the right—the only way open is behind us. And Eshan'ya is all the way over on the other side of the street, hiding inside a niche. She's drawn the pulsar gun I gave her and is holding her own, shooting out from behind the stone wall. I can't help but feel proud of her—she's not a natural fighter, but she isn't going down without one.

I've got both my duster and my pulsar drawn, and I'm firing without mercy. I get one Quain in the leg, another in the chest, and a third in the head. All go to the ground, but the one I got in the leg keeps shooting. I aim again, and this time, I get a headshot.

But as quick as I am, there's too many of them. And they're not holding back, either, though their pulsars are set to stun. *Curious.* Are they scared of hitting the jewel, or maybe they need our help to decipher the clue? If they know Eshan'ya is with us and they recognize her as a Protector, then maybe they know she has knowledge that can help them. But then what? They'll kill her.

Bang! Bang! Bang! Shwoom! Shwoom!

I shoot with a vengeance.

Two more go down.

Four more replace them. They've got me pinned behind the pillar of a temple.

Even if their guns are set to stun, I'll be useless to Eshan'ya if I go down.

What was a pleasant day has now turned hot and humid. The air is filled with a rainbow of electric pulses. Red, blue, and green bursts crackle through the sky next to my duster's bullets.

The ground is littered with the five soldiers I hit, plus one that Eshan'ya got. They should have taken more target practice, but the Quain's strategy is to overcome us with brute force and superior numbers, not by hiding and playing it safe.

And their strategy is working.

I call to my crew on my tech point, still shooting with my duster pistol. "We're under attack. Repeat, the Quain are here, and we're under attack."

"Same here!" comes Luchlon's shout.

"Oh, Captain," Tika's voice shrieks down the line, "they're here. They're here! Come save us. Please, Captain!"

I huff. *Well, they're going to be no help.*

"Pedders?"

He says, "I can't get to you, Fan. They're everywhere."

"Copy that."

Back pressed against the stone, I peek out from the column. The Quain have gained on my position.

Where's Eshan'ya?

I spin to the other side of the column. There she is, wedged into her crevice. But the Quain are gaining on her too, and they're way too close for my liking. I can't get to her.

"You've got to run, Eshan'ya!" I call. She looks up, fear and panic in her eyes. "I'll cover you."

She nods, ducking away as a blast sizzles near her head.

"Now!" I yell, darting out from behind the pillar and shooting with both guns.

Eshan'ya takes off, pointing her pulsar and shooting behind as she runs. I keep one eye on her as she sprints. She's fast, and she knows this city. Maybe she'll have a chance. She can save herself and get that key away from here.

She takes an alley to her right and, within seconds, disappears around a corner. Several of the Quain follow. I pray she outruns them.

Once she's out of sight, I dash backward—I also need to get away. They're getting far too close for the column to protect me much longer.

I bolt over a stone fence, trip at the top, and fall facedown onto a patch of moss on the other side. Instantly, I roll over to face my pursuers.

Shwoom! A shot burns the moss between my legs.

Fiery balls.

Breathing hard, I scramble away, guns up and shooting again. The Quain are forced to duck, but they're just behind the stone fence, which means there are only a few yards between them and me.

One lifts her head slightly above the stone. *Bang!* I take off her hat and maybe her head too. I don't stick around to see. I bolt again, running over the moss and jumping onto a bridge. Then it's up some steps, through a broken-down building, and out the other side.

The Quain chase me, the stamping of their feet setting my pulse on overdrive.

I take the next set of stairs three at a time, pushing my legs and my muscles to their limit as I ascend. I slam into the stones of an unexpected twisting stairwell. The Quain keep coming. There's nowhere for me to go but up. So I keep running with the Quain hot on my heels. I leap as a blast almost catches my boot.

Up and up and around and around the spiral staircase goes, and I realize I must be traveling up one of the towers. Defiant of the dark, moss makes the steps slippery, and the whole place smells of dirt and musk.

Abruptly, the steps end, and sunlight shines on me once again. As I climb the last step, I see there is nowhere to go. The top of the tower must have toppled off years ago, and all that is left is open space...and a long fall down.

From here, I can see the tops of the other abandoned buildings of the city, the roofs caved in on most of them. There are a few other towers and the obelisks at the front of the city, plus the cliff with the waterfall pouring off it. It all sparkles in the midday sun.

But there's nowhere to jump. Everything is too far away or too far down.

I'm stuck.

My chest heaves, and even the flywheels on my squito can't race as fast as my pulse right now. I spin around when I hear the Quain clomping up the stairs.

I'll have to make my stand here. At least the spiral stairs create a bottleneck, so they can't come at me all at once. I can pick them off one at a time as long as my pulsar has power or I don't run out of ammo for my duster.

The first sign of them is a soldier's foot and then his head. *Bang!* And he's down. Another takes his place, and I shoot again...and again...and again.

They get smart after I've dropped a few of them. They hang back, shooting first before sticking their heads out.

Shwoom! Shwoom! Their shots miss me by inches. There is no cover up here other than the curve of the stairwell that *they* are hiding in. I rely on the shots from my pistols to keep them back. I reload my duster and take aim again.

I curse as I see a Quain ship, all black and shiny with three silver stars on the side, fly over the top of the mountain.

And it's coming straight at me. I don't have a hope in hell of surviving this.

The Quain soldiers on the stairwell have disappeared now. I hear their boots rushing back down the steps. I could run, but I'd only be running to my death with those soldiers waiting for me at the bottom.

No, I'd rather die where I stand with a view to die for. I stare at the rainbow arching out from the waterfall. The sunlight glitters off the water and shines on the city of white stone and green moss.

I didn't think this would be the way I died, but it's not a bad way to go.

The Quain's gun turrets swivel toward me, and I close my eyes.

A whoosh of air blows my coif of hair across my face.

And suddenly, there's not just one ship in the air, there's two—the second one is striped orange and red with an underbelly stained an awful bright pink. I've never been so happy to see that pink underbelly as the *Fox* opens fire on the Quain.

"Sorry I'm late," comes Pedders' voice over the tech point.

"Better late than never."

The hatch is already lowered, and as Pedders continues unloading on the Quain ship, I jump onto the ramp, slamming the button to close the airlock after me. I don't have time to feel relieved as I race to the primary weapons console that Luchlon usually operates. It's got more power than the guns Pedders is using. As I throw myself in the seat, the screens slide up, and I take aim immediately, letting off a volley of high-power blasts.

Pedders has jammed their targeting systems, making it more difficult for them to aim at anything important. But at this close range, it'll be hard for them to miss the ship altogether. The *Fox* rocks as some of their shots land, the metal shuddering under my feet. But our shots are more effective. I target their engines. A few direct hits, and I get through their shields. Another shot, and one of their engines explodes.

The Quain can't take more of this without losing control and crashing. They bank away from us. We've got them on the run. The black ship speeds away before any more shots can get through their deflector shields.

"Let's get the others, quick!" I call to Pedders over the ship's comms. "They'll be back soon with reinforcements. Eshan'ya, Tika, Luchlon, report your locations. We're coming to pick you up."

"Thank you, thank you, Captain," Tika says. "Your timing is impeccable. We're trapped on the west side of the city."

"Copy that. Eshan'ya, Luchlon, report your location..."

There's only silence.

"Eshan'ya, Luchlon, report."

Still no response.

"Pedders, collect Tika and Ranate, then do a sweep of the city and search for Eshan'ya and Luchlon. They might not be able to hear me on the tech point."

I don't voice what I'm really thinking: they've been caught by the Quain...or they're already dead.

Chapter 28

Eshan'ya

I ROUND A CORNER, and there's a dead end up ahead. The Quain are right on my heels, but I don't stop. It might look like a blank wall of white bricks, but I know there are some little recesses in the stone, and with some well-placed steps, I hoist myself over the top.

I flash back to a time when I was half as tall, running from Declan and the other Protectors, giggling as I did. But a glance over my shoulder as I clear the wall sends a spike of fear down my spine, slicing the memory away.

The Quain don't stop. It doesn't take them long to figure out how to jump the wall, and their black-clad bodies roll over the top.

My chest is heaving, and my feet pound the stone as I run for my life.

The second key is in one of the many pockets of my trousers, and I feel it bounce against my leg. It's reassuring to feel it against me, but it also reminds me of how much I have to lose.

And the Quain are gaining on me.

I duck under a doorway and run through the crumbling room beyond, lichen falling from the eaves above. Then I'm through another doorway and back out into the sun.

I slide to a standstill.

I'm in a town square lined by buildings decorated with white columns that are covered in velvety green patches. It would be beautiful if it weren't for the large black Quain ship sitting in the middle and the dozens of soldiers aiming their guns at me.

The thud of footsteps from behind prevents any thought of retreating the way I came.

I'm trapped.

I lift my arms above my head in surrender, panting for breath.

They're a plague. There's twenty or thirty of them in their black uniforms, like flies spoiling the gloss of this pretty city.

I should have known there were more of them. I should have anticipated they'd be in this square. If only I'd stayed in the tight alleys and buildings, the secret paths through the city that I know. I should have gone through the sanctum instead of the square.

Urgh, I should have thought.

They edge nearer, the crowd of them stepping closer and closer while my chest heaves. I lift my head. There's no place to run, so I don't bother looking for an escape. I don't bother aiming my pulsar. I just hope Fan and her crew keep looking for the third key and get to it before Braxt does. Maybe I can distract the Quain or misdirect them somehow. While I'm still alive, I won't give up.

From among the black uniforms steps a familiar figure.

The lieutenant.

I admit there certainly are similarities between us. We're both white, blond-haired, and young. Yet her firm chin and the sharp edges of her face are a contrast to my rounder features. Her eyes are a darker shade of blue, and she's shorter than me. But I can see why the Quain soldiers were easily tricked into believing I was her.

Of course, I had already noticed our similarities when we met in the palace before I escaped. Madame Aphelion had retrieved me from the ladies' parlor, dragging me to King Vald's chambers. I thought *he* had requested me, and my stomach was full of lead-winged butterflies. I was surprised to find the lieutenant waiting for me instead. King Vald was also there, but he merely stood by while the lieutenant scrutinized me, coming so close I felt her breath on my face. Although I knew King Vald was capable of awful things, the lieutenant chilled my blood. I knew she was a threat, not just to me, but to the entire galaxy.

Now she's walking toward me full of self-assurance, and though that confidence scares me, I don't show it.

"Nice to see you again, Eshan'ya," she says, her voice like a rottweiler's growl.

"Enchanted, I'm sure," I say, clipping my words.

She chuckles, unperturbed by my sarcasm. She takes my pulsar, and I lower my hands.

"You are bold, aren't you?" She doesn't wait for a response. "You genuinely thought you could beat Kriinal Braxt to the Device. Kriinal Braxt! You were never going to win, but you tried anyway. It's so cute."

"He can't get that Device. We're all doomed if he does."

"On the contrary, he *will* get the Device. And the galaxy *will* be better off for it. He's going to rid this world of the murderers, the rapists, and the thieves. There will be order. There will be peace."

"But he's a murderer. He's killed so many already, and he's going to kill more. He's a tyrant. He only wants peace on *his* terms. He doesn't care about free will or the wishes of others."

"Look where free will has gotten us," she snaps, bringing her face close to mine. Anger burns in those dark blue eyes. "Wars, death, pain...so much pain. Kriinal Braxt is going to eliminate all that. And you can't stop him."

She truly believes that Kriinal Braxt can make the galaxy a better place. She doesn't see he'll take away love, friendship, spontaneity, fun—everything that makes life worth living.

"I want to see peace in the galaxy too," I say, "but ruling with fear is not the way to do it. He'll kill humanity."

"You don't understand," the lieutenant says. "He'll make humanity whole again. It's a shame you won't be around to see it."

Her hand reaches into my pocket and pulls out the dark glowing jewel. The second key. Then she nods, and some nearby soldiers immediately grab my arms. I keep my head held high as they lead me to their ship. I need to keep my cool if I'm going to find a way to stop them.

As we reach the Quain ship, I glimpse someone across the square who's not a soldier. Is it Fan? No, it's Luchlon, standing there talking to the Quain soldiers.

Traitor.

In my mind's eye, I see him at the back of Gussart's party talking on his tech point when he should have been protecting Fan. Is that when he betrayed us? Has he been working against us all this time?

He disappears from view as I'm taken up the ramp and into the Quain's ship. They don't bother cuffing my hands, but they do confiscate my tech point, then seat me against the side of the cargo hold.

I seethe. I paid him off, promised him even more riches, and he still betrayed us. The Quain must be paying handsomely for him to give up the jewels I promised. The ones I already gave him are enough to buy his own ship and crew. With the rest, he could have bought several ships. The Quain must be giving him enough for a whole fleet.

Fan might now be dead, as well as Pedders and Tika. My heart aches at the thought. But worse is the reality that the Quain now have the first and second keys, and there is nothing stopping them from getting the Device. They just need the third key.

"I've got the second key and the girl," the lieutenant says into her tech point.

"Copy that," comes the reply. I wonder if it's Kriinal Braxt.

For years, he's been hunting me and the other Protectors. Because of him, I lost my home, my family, my innocence. I was branded, hurt, and shamed. I lost Declan. I almost lost myself.

A surge of hate builds within me. I boil and bristle as I sit quietly in the hold. Neither the lieutenant nor the other Quain soldiers speak to me. They don't see me burning with hatred, plotting ways to escape and ways to make Braxt pay.

They've got the second key, and they are consumed by it. They bend over the jewel, and I assume they're working out the clue. They must figure it out a lot quicker than I did because I hear the clunk of the landing gear, and soon the hatch opens. We're at the top of the waterfall...and somewhere below is the third key.

Chapter 29

Fan

"How did they find us?" I ask the remainder of my crew as I pace across the cockpit. The space is only big enough for me to take two steps before I reach the wall, turn around, take two more steps, and repeat.

Pedders sits in his usual spot in the copilot's chair while Tika and RAN-8 stand in the doorway, all of them watching me pace.

"It was like they were lying in wait, like they knew we would be here," I say. My stomach churns like the turbines on a plane. I don't like what my instincts are telling me.

"Maybe there was a clue on the first key that led them here?" Tika supposes. "What if they followed us? What if there's a tracker on the ship?"

"No," says RAN-8, shutting down this line of thinking. "I checked the database for all information on the first key. They had no more information than we had, and there are no trackers on this ship—I would know if there were."

"So they followed us?" Tika asks.

"Or there's a mole in the crew," I say, finally saying out loud what my gut is telling me.

Pedders grunts.

"Oh, there couldn't be," Tika jumps in. "Who would do such a thing? Pedders is your oldest friend. He would never betray you. RAN-8 is programmed to follow your instructions, so not him. And me...oh, you don't think *I* had anything to do with this, do you?"

"The thought *had* crossed my mind," I grumble, and Tika's eyes go wide, flashing with indignation. "But I don't think so."

"Yes, well. I should hope not." Tika blinks hard, like she's blinking away the insult.

"So...Luchlon?" Pedders' gruff voice interjects.

"Maybe." It makes sense. He's not here, but would he really betray the crew? Would he betray me?

I pace a little more.

Would he sell us out for the right price? And if so, was he offered the right price? Does it matter if we've been sleeping together?

"Try radioing both of them again," I command and plonk down in the pilot's chair.

RAN-8 calls to both Luchlon and Eshan'ya over his tech point, but there's still no response, no matter how many times he tries. I let him keep radioing while I think.

"But why would he betray us? And where is the princess? Will we ever find them?" Tika asks.

I try to drown out Tika's fussing as well as RAN-8's robotic voice calling over the comms. Pedders finally grunts loudly.

I interpret that grunt to mean, "*What are we gonna do?*"

"They're probably dead," I say, and everyone goes quiet. I ignore the ache in my heart as I think of Eshan'ya's stern expression, the tilt of her head when she stands tall. "And that means the Quain have the second key."

Tika gasps.

"And they'll soon have the third key *and* the Device." I spin in my seat to face them. "Which means we need to get to the third key before they do."

"Even though the princess is gone? You're still going to go through with the mis—"

"Yes." I nod decisively, cutting Tika off. "Yes, despite the princess being captured or killed, we still have a mission. We can't let Kriinal Braxt take over the galaxy. And if the legend is true, there will be no stopping him if he gets that Device. We will all be enslaved."

"But we don't know where the third key is," Tika points out.

I give her a crooked grin. "That might not be true."

I keep the *Huxian Fox* low to stay under the radar and land her at the base of the waterfall. The crew hurry down the ramp with me.

"Pedders, you're staying here," I say. "I need you with the ship."

"*Dǎ sǐ yě bù qù,*" he grumbles in protest, his brows so low I can barely see his eyes. That's his stubborn face. He doesn't wear it often, but when he does, there's no chance in the 'laxy that I can change it. I turn to RAN-8 instead.

"Ranate, stay with the ship. Make sure she's ready to fly when we are."

RAN-8 flexes his mechanical fingers. "Yes, boss. I'll treat the lady well. There won't be so much as a scratch on her with me as the pilot."

Pedders rumbles in indignation at RAN-8's insinuation.

"No scratches," is all I say. My mouth is a firm line as I look at my beautiful ship. She's not looking the prettiest right now with her pink underbelly, but I don't want any additional damage. Even though RAN-8 isn't the best pilot—he has no instincts to drive him—he's the best I've got right now.

While RAN-8 clunks up the ramp and closes the hatch, Pedders, Tika, and I stare up at the waterfall.

"Look," Pedders says a few moments later, pointing at the base of the cliff. It's almost hidden behind a boulder, but once I look right at it, I realize there's a slim walkway leading upward.

"Let's see where it goes," I say, and start walking.

It's a squeeze to get around the boulder. Being double the size of me or Tika, Pedders struggles with it, but he lifts his belly and somehow slides through. Water sprays out onto the rock path, making it impossibly slippery, but we hurry as much as we can.

Soon the path becomes steps, distinctly man-made—or Protogenoi-made. The steps twist back and forth behind ferns and lichen growing from the side of the cliff, occasionally taking us behind the waterfall. Up and up and up we go. I'm soon covered in sweat and grateful for the gentle spray misting off the waterfall.

The path finally winds to an end behind the waterfall. It opens wide into a cave, and I know we've found what we're looking for.

Like a veil pulled across the entrance, the waterfall completely hides the cave. I use my tech point to light it up.

"By the stars..." The words escape my lips as I gaze in awe. Pedders' eyes are wide, and Tika is speechless for a change.

It looks like a natural grotto that reaches deep into the mountain. Its unpolished walls and ceiling are slick with moisture, and stalagmites and stalactites spike every which way. But in the center stand three short obelisks. When I say 'short', I mean they're shorter than the ones that guard the cities; however, these three are still taller than a five-story building. The cave is enormous, and the obelisks reach right to the top. My nostrils are filled with the musky scent of wet moss.

Behind the obelisks are three more waterfalls, though they're much smaller than the one roaring outside. One barely trickles down the cave wall, another splashes from rock to rock in great white bursts, and the third arches out in a steady stream. At the base of each lies a deep pool.

Only a sliver of sunlight filters into the cave through a small gap in the ceiling. It glitters on the third waterfall, painting the dark walls with a rainbow. The sunlight only reaches *one* waterfall. The other two remain in darkness and can only be seen by the light of the tech point.

"Under the gaze of Helios," I say.

"What?" Tika asks.

"It's a line from the clue," I explain. "Helios is a sun god. The clue says:

Travel down the waters of Enipeus

under the gaze of Helios.
Portunus walks here
as does Kratos. Beware.

We have to follow the waters that are under the gaze of Helios. The one that is lit by sunlight. It's the third waterfall."

"How do you know it's not either of the other waterfalls?" Tika asks.

"Because the light will never reach them," I say, pointing to the high ceiling. "See the angle of that gap? It points away from the other two waterfalls, so the light will never shine on them."

Pedders grunts, a grin spreading across his face as he rocks on his heels.

"OK." Tika shrugs. "So where is the key? And what does the bit about Portunus and Kratos mean?"

"Remember, Portunus is another name for the key, so my guess is that the key is at the base of that waterfall. I still don't know what Kratos means. Eshan'ya said he was the god of strength. We need to be careful there aren't some other dangers here."

I walk to the pool at the bottom of the third waterfall and shine my tech point into it. The pool is deep enough that the light fades before it reaches the bottom. I gulp. I can swim, but I'll never win any competitions for it.

"Be careful," Pedders says.

"I know it's dangerous," I say, "but I have to try. The Quain will be here soon, and we can't let Braxt get the third key *or* the Device."

Pedders grunts, and I know he agrees with me. I also know he's not getting into that pool. He was never a great swimmer.

I shrug off my gray leather jacket and remove my boots. Then I unlatch my holster from my waist, removing both my duster and pulsar gun. I feel naked without them, but those old duster pistols aren't great when they're wet, and the pulsar will get in the way while I swim.

Pedders turns on his tech point to provide more light, and I keep mine lit on my finger as my toes edge toward the water. I look into that endless pool and glance over my shoulder at Pedders. I swallow, turn back to the water, take a deep breath, and dive in.

The water is cool and refreshing after our hike up the waterfall, but I don't take the time to enjoy it—I'm not here for a bath. I kick my legs hard, descending into the pool as I shine my tech point at the sides. The waterfall has pounded most of the rock smooth, and where it hasn't, vegetation grows like green hair, moving and flowing with the water.

The deeper I swim, the colder the water gets. I swim so deep that the pressure clutches my head, and my lungs are burning. I need to surface. I kick my feet furiously, and I'm straining for air by the time I finally burst out of the water.

"Did you find it?" Tika asks before I have my breath back. I shake my head, take a few gulps of air, and dive back down.

I do this a few times, unwilling to give up. It has to be here. It makes sense. The clue said to follow Enipeus under the gaze of Helios—that has to mean this waterfall, where the sunlight hits. It *has* to be here.

It's my fourth dive when I finally see something scratched into the rock. I swim closer, but my lungs are screaming. I need air.

"I think I've found it," I gasp as I break the surface.

Tika claps her hands and yelps. "What does it look like? Is it as pretty as the second key? How big is it?"

Pedders grunts, and she shuts up.

My chest is heaving as I gulp enough air to go back down. "I don't know. I think I've found the compartment, but I need to get inside."

I wish Eshan'ya was here. She should be here to witness this discovery. It would be appropriate for her to discover the key, not only because of everything she's been through but also because it's her birthright as Protector of the Device.

When I dive in again, I go directly to that scratch in the rock, shining my tech point on it.

Blazin' rockets, this is it. The rock is scratched with the symbol of chaos, just like on Farnth Five. I swim closer, holding onto the rock to keep from floating upward. I press the indentation in the middle of the symbol, and I feel a shift in the rock. My fingers claw at the edge. I slide the little cavity out and shine my tech point into it.

It's empty.

I point the light all around the edges of the drawer.

But it's still empty.

The third key isn't inside.

Is it a trick? Did we get the clues wrong? My gut says no. This is the only chaos symbol I'm going to find in this cave. I won't find it under any of the other waterfalls. I found the location of the third key, but it's empty. The key has already been taken.

I swim back up, but my sorrow weighs me down, making it harder to rise. Now I'm glad Eshan'ya isn't here; I don't think I could stand seeing her disappointment.

How did the Quain get here before us? Did Luchlon give them the clue, as well as our location? Did they work it out quicker than Eshan'ya? But I didn't see them when we flew over Lyran. It doesn't make sense. They couldn't have arrived here quicker than we did.

I break the surface, saying, "It's not there." No one answers. I fling my hair out of my face and look up.

A man stands at the edge of the pool. Two Quain soldiers are nearby holding guns to Pedders' and Tika's heads. Both of my crew have been disarmed and stand helpless.

I go for my duster, then remember I took it off when I got into the water. I see it now, sitting on a stone, along with my pulsar gun and my jacket, all out of reach.

"Who...?" I ask the man standing by the pool.

"Kriinal Braxt," he says. "Pleased to meet your acquaintance, Fan Sung."

Kriinal Braxt. In the flesh. He's more handsome than I expected, even with his lethal stare.

"How...?"

"How did I get the key before you?" Braxt finishes my question. "I'm sorry to tell you, but it hasn't been there for years. It's now in my possession, and my lieutenant is bringing it to me."

"Then why are you here? What do you want with us?"

He laughs. "You've done well to get this far when you apparently know nothing about the legend. I'll let you in on a little secret." He lowers his voice. "The Device is here."

What? The Device is here as well? Realization dawns. "Kratos," I whisper. The last lines of the clue: *Portunus walks here, as does Kratos. Beware.*

"You are clever, I'll give you that." Braxt grins.

There's a commotion behind him, scuffling, like more of his soldiers are coming into the cave. While Braxt is distracted by the noise, I remove the tech point from my finger and slip it into my shirt pocket, securing it tightly with the button.

"Sir?" a gravelly female voice asks.

"Do you have the key?" Braxt asks.

"Yes."

"Come forward."

The lieutenant comes into view. She's nowhere near as pretty as Eshan'ya. Those Quain fools are idiots for confusing Eshan'ya with this woman. The lieutenant's eyes are hard and cold, whereas Eshan'ya's are clear, intelligent, and kind—beautiful. The lieutenant doesn't compare.

Her hands are empty. She's not holding the key, but two more Quain soldiers march in behind her, and between them is—

—Eshan'ya.

She's *alive*.

Her back is ramrod straight, making her look as if she's the queen of a procession, not a prisoner.

But as Kriinal Braxt turns to her, she falters. Her mouth drops open, her eyes flutter, and she takes a step back, gasping.

"Declan?"

Chapter 30

Eshan'ya

He's standing right in front of me. Declan. My old Protector. The man who raised me, who was like a father to me. He was my best friend. His dark brown eyes, his lightly tanned skin, those long, agile fingers, that strong chin. How I've missed him.

But he can't be here now. This can't be real. I've wished every day for *years* to be with him again. And here he is. Just like a dream.

My eyes search for the truth. They flicker to Fan. She's treading water under a waterfall, looking as confused as I feel. Tika and Pedders stand by the edge, held at gunpoint. They both stare at me blankly. There are several stone-faced Quain soldiers, but none of them say a word. I press my eyes shut for several seconds. Miraculously, Declan is still there when I open them.

This must be a dream. But if it was, I wouldn't feel the stone beneath my shoes, the slight breeze on my cheek, the hands of the Quain soldiers harshly gripping my arms. This is real.

I try to remain composed. With all the effort and steel in my bones, I try. But I can't. My face crumbles.

"Declan." I choke out his name. "Where have you been?" Tears run down my cheeks, unhindered, unchecked. I'm beyond stopping them.

Where *has* he been? Where was he while I was trapped in the palace? Where was he while I did what I could to survive? He's alive, but he wasn't there for me when I crushed myself into the tightest ball, wishing and praying he would return for me, when I wanted to curl up and stay there, wasting away.

He said he would come back for me. He told me he was protecting me. He branded me with King Vald's seal and left me there.

He left me there.

"Where were you?" This time, the words burst out of me. They burn from my throat.

Declan just stands there, watching me break down. He makes no move to comfort me, to hold me in his arms, wipe the tears from my eyes. The corners of his mouth curve in the slightest smile. It's not the wide smile I always expected him to give me when we reunited. It's almost like he's laughing at me.

He probably thinks I'm acting undignified. He always told me to keep calm, to stay focused. And now I'm falling apart. He finds it humorous, like I'm a child again, just a girl throwing a tantrum, not wanting to go to bed. Back then, he would watch me with this smile, waiting for me to calm down. Any second now, he's going to start lecturing me.

But he doesn't. Instead, he looks down on me like I'm an insect, a pawn in his games, worthless. As if he doesn't care what

I've been through. What *he* put me through. Anger swells in my heart.

"You left me there," I say hoarsely. "How could you?" Tears run into my mouth, and I choke on them. I feel sick. The grungy hair below King Vald's navel flashes through my mind. I'm left in fragments. "I trusted you."

I'm struggling to regain control. My composure is shredded—just like my heart. I gulp, trying to settle myself, trying to catch my breath. I need to pull myself together. Breathe in and out, in and out. After a few moments and deep breaths, I glare at him, waiting for an explanation. Waiting for some reason why he didn't return sooner.

"Are you done?" Declan asks. My eyes lock on his. My cheeks are wet, but I can hold my head up once again. When I stay silent, he continues. "Well, that breakdown was entertaining. You obviously think I'm Declan."

The words slap me in the face. They don't make sense. None of this makes any sense.

"You're not Declan?" I whisper.

Looking closer, I realize there are differences. Of course, he's older, with more gray in his hair, but it has been five years since I've seen Declan. This man has a scar that runs from his temple under his left eye, but that could have happened at any time since I last saw my Protector. No, it's something else. The way he tilts his head slightly, the way his nose is pointed up, like he's looking down on me in more ways than one. His jaw is a little too square.

And he's standing among the Quain, unbound, not a prisoner. He's working with them.

My eyes widen.

There will be no hugs, no lectures, no kisses on my forehead. My dreams are shattered. Because no matter how angry I am with Declan, I still wish he was here. With me. But this man is definitely *not* Declan.

He laughs as though he can see the moment realization hits me. "No, I'm not Declan. I have more spine than my brother. You can call me Uncle if you'd like."

Brother?

"Let me introduce myself," he says, giving me a small bow. "Kriinal Braxt, formerly known among the Protectors as Brandon Kriinal Axtryn, brother of Declan Kriital Axtryn."

He's not Declan. He's Declan's brother, and he's still the man who forced me into a life of horrors. My head spins. Emotions crash over and under each other: anger, hurt, hope, despair, bitterness. It's hard to concentrate.

"I didn't know Declan had a brother." What other secrets did Declan keep from me?

Braxt scoffs, "Of course he wouldn't talk about me. He's ashamed. Ashamed that I could do what he couldn't."

"And what's that?"

"Bring peace to the galaxy."

"All you've brought the galaxy is pain and suffering. You're a monster."

"You're just as shortsighted as Declan." He rolls his eyes. "Don't you see that I can eradicate all evil with the Device? There'll be no crime, no murders, no thievery."

I shake my head. "At what cost? What does the Device do?"

"Provides power."

It's the only response he gives, and that's all I know about the Device too. It makes me think he doesn't even know what it does.

And that makes me even more afraid.

I turn to the pool where Fan is treading water. "Whatever you do, Fan, don't give him the key. Get away somehow. Just don't let him have that key."

Fan's mouth drops open, her head shaking slowly. "Even if I wanted to, it's not here."

My heart clenches.

Braxt laughs again, and it's nothing like Declan's laugh. There's no joy in it. "The key hasn't been hidden in this cave since Declan and I were boys."

"What?" I gape at him.

"The Protectors took it."

He doesn't seem concerned by that and my skin starts to crawl. What has he done with the other Protectors? "Don't look so worried, Eshan'ya." My name sounds like poison on his lips. "I'm no longer pursuing the Protectors. They've scattered across the galaxy. Declan is hiding, just like the coward he is."

Declan's in hiding?

If that's true, then Braxt is right: Declan is a coward who hid away while I suffered.

"But I did catch up with one Protector. Her name was Reeola."

Was.

I remember Reeola. She was a kind woman with rough hands and a powerful hug. She would make me chocolate chip cookies when she wasn't busy growing cocoa beans.

"What did you do to her?" My fingers clench.

"She's not worth your worries, child. She sold you out trying to save herself. She told me your little secret."

He raises one eyebrow at me, the same way Declan used to when he knew I was hiding something from him. The tightness in my chest increases, and I think I might implode.

But what does he think I'm hiding? He already knows all my secrets. He knows I was hidden among the royal harem. He knows I'm a Protector. I don't have any other secrets.

Braxt chuckles as he stares into my wide eyes. "So…Declan didn't even tell *you* the truth?"

He steps closer, and I flinch as his fingers deftly unclip the cuff from my arm to reveal my tattoo. I look down at it, then back at him. Braxt's grin widens. He's enjoying my confusion.

He's still standing closer than I'd like, but I hold my ground, resisting my instinct to get as far away from him as possible. He says, "You thought it was just to hide you among the royal harem, didn't you?"

I'm speechless. I don't know where he's going with this.

"But you already had those three stars."

"It's the symbol of the Protectors. So what?"

He steps back—allowing me to take a breath—then pulls the first key from the inside pocket of his jacket. His lieutenant hands him the second key, the one she took from me. Braxt holds both of them in the palm of one hand, lifting them so the light that filters through the cave shines upon them. One glows red, the other a deep blue. He then lifts his tech point to project a beam through them both, and the two clues appear in hologram form.

"Look closely," Braxt says.

I squint at the holograms, reading the lines of the clues over and over again, trying to work out what Braxt already has. Nobody speaks or even moves while I stare at the holograms. I can't figure it out. They're just the clues to the next key. We've already followed them, and the third key is missing, so why is Braxt showing me this?

"Look at the sigils." Braxt's voice isn't much more than a whisper. He steps forward again so I can examine the images even closer. I'm only a foot from his outstretched hand, but I lean in even further—my heart a windmill in a hurricane—staring at the sigils.

I look back and forth between the two sigils shining out of the crystals. Finally, I realize they're not quite matching; the stars are not aligned the same way. The points of the stars are tilted in different directions, and the way they're pointed doesn't match from the red jewel to the blue jewel.

"The stars aren't aligned," I whisper.

"That's right. Well done." Braxt's voice sounds exactly like Declan's whenever I got the answer right in my lessons. "The stars on your arm don't quite align either. It's a combination. All three keys are needed to work out the combination, and the stars on your arm are the exact replica of the stars in the third key. You are the substitute for the third key."

I take four steps backward. If it weren't for a guard's hand landing in the middle of my back, I probably would have kept going.

I'm the third key.

I blink at Braxt. My palms are sweating. My mind is going a million miles a second. How could I have missed that the stars in my tattoo weren't aligned the same way as the standard Protogenoi sigil? How can I get away so Kriinal Braxt can't get the combination? Why did the Protectors make me the third key? Why didn't Declan tell me? How can I save Fan and my friends? Why didn't the Protectors destroy the key and never replicate it so the Device could never fall into the wrong hands?

"Why?" is all I can manage.

Kriinal Braxt might be a coldhearted monster, but he *is* intelligent. He knows exactly what I'm asking. "For all their righteousness, the Protectors could never bring themselves to destroy the path to the Device. They say the Device is evil, that it should never be wielded, but they couldn't destroy it in case they ever wanted to use it themselves one day. Such hypocrites. They're so spineless. Afraid to destroy it and afraid to use it. So they sat frozen, immobile, doing nothing while the galaxy fell into chaos.

"They knew someone would come looking for the key one day. So they removed it. To where? I don't know. But they couldn't bear to lose the knowledge, so they imprinted it on a little girl. And they imprinted themselves with the Protogenoi sigil in the hope the combination would be lost within a sea of symbols. Sort of how Declan hid you among the royal harem—hiding in plain sight."

Braxt chuckles that humorless laugh again. "I have to admit, it's kind of clever. But luckily for me, Reeola couldn't keep her mouth shut under duress."

I wince at the thought of Reeola being tortured. A flash of anger sparks again. Declan should have told me I was the key. The

Protectors should have destroyed the Device. They've put us all in danger, and it could all have been avoided.

"Now it's time to recover the Device and clean up the galaxy." He stands taller, ready to take action. I'm still trying to think of ways to stop him when Braxt nods at Fan. "Captain, if you would please exit the pool and follow us."

Fan scowls for a moment, then swims to the edge and lifts herself out of the pool, rivulets of water streaming from her body. She flicks her hair out of her eyes but ignores the wet clothes clinging to her. She glances across the cave to her jacket, boots, and two guns, but she'd never be able to reach them before Braxt's soldiers shot Pedders and Tika. Or me. It's clear she knows that when she glances away. She swaggers up to us with as much dignity as she can muster in bare feet and dripping clothes.

"Braxt." She nods as if they're meeting in a restaurant and she's not being held at gunpoint. "I recommend a dip in the pool. It's quite refreshing. You should stick your head under for an hour or two while you're at it. It'd do wonders for your complexion."

"Once I have the Device, my complexion will be the least of your problems," he retorts. Braxt turns back to me, politely gesturing for me to walk ahead. "Eshan'ya."

I don't see any other choice but to do as he wishes. So I lift my head high and follow the lieutenant.

Chapter 31

Fan

THE LIEUTENANT LEADS THE grisly procession of soldiers, followed by Eshan'ya and Kriinal Braxt, and then me, Pedders, and Tika—all of us at gunpoint. We're led deeper into the cave, past the three obelisks and the three waterfalls, and further into the darkness beyond.

The lieutenant throws flash plates from her belt that stick to the walls of the cave and light up the space. As we go deeper, the space gets narrower, but it's still so big I could park the *Huxian Fox* in here if I could get it past the obelisks at the front of the cave.

As the passage tapers, it changes from the natural rough rock with speleothem formations spiking from it to polished rock molded by the ancient Protogenoi. A stream follows us down the left side of the smooth cave.

Voices up ahead echo back to us, and eventually I can see the glow of flash plates already set by the several Quain soldiers waiting by a large manufactured lake.

Standing between them is Luchlon, the scoundrel who sold us out. My veins sizzle like overheated circuitry at the sight of him.

"*Pàn tú*," Pedders mutters. *Traitor.*

Luchlon doesn't look happy, though. He's arguing with a soldier, gesturing at us.

Snippets of what he says echoes back. "Not part...deal...I don't...reward...leave."

He makes to walk away, but a soldier holds him back, and another points her lava gun at his head. Luchlon freezes.

He must finally be realizing he should never have trusted the Quain. They're unpredictable. But why should I care about him after what he's done?

Luchlon and the Quain turn to us as we approach. When his eyes lock with mine, he quickly looks down at his feet, guilt crossing his handsome features. If only I had my duster, I'd shoot him right in the gut where it'd hurt the most. Once we're only a few steps away, he looks up again. This time, his gaze holds mine.

"Sung," he says, shaking his head. "This isn't what you think...I didn't...I didn't betray you."

"Save it," I snap.

I hear Braxt chuckling behind me. "Lovers' quarrel."

Eshan'ya's red-rimmed eyes snap to mine with a question. But why would she care? I run a hand through my hair and turn away with a huff.

Our congregation gathers by the edge of the lake.

Now that we're closer, I can see three flat stepping stones—all a little further than a natural footstep away from each other—leading to a larger one in the center of the lake. Then three more lead to the other side of the pool. There's no way to get to the other side without traversing the stepping stones.

The back of my neck prickles, and I rub at it as I study the dark waters.

Stars above, I feel uneasy.

Eshan'ya must also have a bad feeling because she says, "Let the others go, Kriinal. You've got me. You don't need them."

"On the contrary," he says in a politely lethal tone, "I'll probably need each one of them before we reach the chamber holding the Device. You see, the Device is protected by three challenges. Those Protogenoi loved their challenges and clues, everything grouped in threes. And there are three more challenges to get through before the Device will be revealed. Those challenges are most likely deadly."

Eshan'ya inhales sharply. I straighten my back.

"And I don't want to waste the lives of my loyal soldiers, so I'll use your friends instead."

"We're not doing anything for you," I say.

"Oh, I think you will." Braxt smiles, and fear sizzles down my spine. He nods at the two soldiers standing behind. On command, they both viciously pound the butts of their guns against Pedders' and Tika's heads.

Pedders grunts in pain, then falls to his knees.

Tika shrieks and clutches her head as she wails, "Ow! My head! You didn't need to hit me so hard, you brutal oafs." Her guard threatens to hit her again, and Tika shuts up, joining Pedders on her knees.

Braxt smiles. "You see, if you don't participate in the challenges, then I'll have no reason to keep your group of drug-smuggling criminals alive. So how about you try your luck and maybe you'll survive?"

"We'd rather die than help you, Braxt," Eshan'ya spits.

He laughs. "Speak for yourself. I think you'll find your friends have a far better sense of self-preservation than you do."

I avoid Eshan'ya's eyes when she glances at me, and I notice the others avoiding her as well. I don't want to help Braxt, but I don't want my friends to die, either. Surely there's another option. I just need the right opportunity.

"See?" Braxt continues to chuckle. "Now, who wants to go first?" He looks around at each of us. "How about the best friend, Qiqiang, a-k-a Pedders? Or the smart little mechanic, Tika? Or yourself, Captain Sung?" He turns his back on me, and I'm tempted to pounce on him, but I know it'll do no good. "All right, I'll make it easy on you. Let's make your backstabbing lover, Luchlon, go first."

Luchlon's face twists in anger. "No way. You owe me. I got you the girl."

I knew he'd betrayed us, but the confirmation still boils my blood.

"You let me and the crew go right now," Luchlon demands. "This was never part of the—"

"You're in no position to make demands." Braxt cuts him off. "You called us, let us know Eshan'ya's location, and you received your reward. Deal complete. By the way, the transfer was very considerate of me, given we already knew she would end up on Shadé. I never made a promise to preserve your life. And as far as I can see, you deserve what's coming to you after betraying your friends. You're no better than the scum locked in my basement."

Luchlon's face goes white.

Eshan'ya told me about the criminals that she and Luchlon found in the Quain's dungeon. Even if Luchlon is a redrynch's turd, he's not as bad as those lowlifes.

"Now get a move on before I shoot you where you stand."

The soldiers around Luchlon take a step away from him. Luchlon stares daggers at Braxt, but the lieutenant only has to lift her gun to make him face the lake. I see his shoulders rise and fall as he takes a deep breath. He looks like he's about to step out, but before he does, he looks around at me, Braxt, the lieutenant, and the princess.

I press my lips together, and everyone else stays silent as well. No one is going to save him; there's no escape other than surviving whatever this challenge is. He must get to the other side of the lake or die trying.

His shoulders slump.

He focuses on his task and braces for the leap. Then he jumps and lands on the first stepping stone. A click echoes menacingly around the cave as a mechanism beneath the step is activated.

A whir of noise fills my ears. Suddenly, the lake is no longer placid; the water churns. Several whirlpools begin swirling, and all the stepping stones start to drop below the surface. If Luchlon falls into the water, the whirlpools will suck him under and drown him. With his steps disappearing by the second, he doesn't have much time.

Luchlon realizes the risk and speedily leaps across the stepping stones, heedless of what other dangers might await him. And that's a mistake.

When he steps on the largest platform in the middle of the lake, metal bars shoot up from the dark waters, clanging together at the top and trapping Luchlon—

—on the sinking stepping stone.

Tika shrieks. Eshan'ya gasps.

Luchlon spins to face us. His hands clutch the bars as he sinks into the water. His eyes meet mine, and I see something I've never seen in them before: fear.

On impulse, I take a step closer. But what can I do? The whirlpools will suck me under, and he's in a cage that looks impenetrable. I won't be able to get him out of there before he drowns. And he betrayed me. He called the Quain, gave them our position, and sold us out. He's a traitor.

"Help me, Fan," Luchlon calls. "I...I never meant for this to happen." The water is already up to his waist. He rattles the cage, but the bars don't budge. "Braxt, you Urfarian snake. Get me out of here."

Nobody moves. He rages against the cage, moving frantically, helplessly to each side and shaking the bars, but none of them shift. He's stuck.

The water rises to his chest, then his neck. He's sinking fast.

The water has reached his chin. He starts to tread water, but the cage is dropping further and further; soon it will push his head under. Luchlon tilts his face up and screeches, "Fan! I'm sorry! I didn't mean to betray you! It was only meant to be the girl. And she lied. I didn't betray you!" His hands grip the bars at the top of the cage that's bearing down on him. He pulls his head a little further out of the water to yell one last time, "Please, Fan!"

He takes his final breath before the bars push down on his face, forcing him under the water. His fingers reach out of the cage—the only part of him that's still visible—until they disappear too.

My chest feels tight. Luchlon might be a money-hungry traitor, but he doesn't deserve this. And he's part of my crew.

Something like stupidity comes over me, and I find myself darting toward the lake at an alarming speed. The water is less tumultuous in the center where the stepping stones once were, so I aim my dive there, jumping out as far as I can before arcing into the water.

My head goes under, and the water snaps me up, swirling me around until I don't know which way I'm facing. There's a pull at my leg, and I'm dragged in one direction before my arm is caught in the churn, and I'm hauled another way.

Through the bubbles, I glimpse the metal bars of the cage. I thrash my legs to propel myself toward it. I can't tell if Luchlon is still alive. He must be; he can't drown that quickly. I'm pulled backward by the swell of the water, losing the distance I've just gained. I surge forward, using all my strength, and my fingers brush the bars. Another kick of my legs and I've got a hold.

Luchlon's still alive. His eyes are wide, watching me, pleading with me. His fingers are white from gripping the bars.

My lungs burn. I'm almost out of air, and Luchlon must be too.

There's got to be some way to get him out. I dive lower, using the bars as a guide and a handhold against being sucked into a whirlpool.

I lower myself to the bottom of the cage, though the light from the flash plates barely reaches me now. Searching blindly, I try to find something to reset the challenge or raise the cage. There must be some way to complete the trial. The Protogenoi couldn't have wanted everyone seeking the Device to die in the first challenge. Surely not.

My vision is darkening, and it's not just because the flash plates don't reach this far down. I need oxygen. I need oxygen now, or I'm going to pass out.

Chapter 32

Eshan'ya

FAN HAS BEEN UNDERWATER for too long.

I stare at the turbulent waters, willing her to resurface. The cage has sunk so deep that not an inch of the top is visible.

Suddenly, the bubbles give way to Fan's mop of hair. She bursts from the water, her mouth gulping in air.

"Fan!" I shout.

But she doesn't hear me or doesn't listen. She immediately dives back down into the bubbling lake. Her stubbornness is going to get her killed. She has to be a hero and *save* the guy who betrayed her.

Is this because they're lovers? My heart twists. Doesn't she realize he's toxic? I wouldn't have wished this death on him, but she shouldn't throw her life away for his. She's such an obstinate, hot-headed fool.

Although my pulse pounds with anger at her stupidity, I stare at that spot in the lake where she disappeared, my body tense. I'm barely breathing.

No one in the cavern speaks. There's only the swish of the artificial rapids. It swirls white and blue and black, the bubbles tumbling over and under each other, churning as if the god Poseidon himself has caused a storm to claim his victims.

My own lungs ache from holding my breath as I wait for Fan to resurface. Something must have happened; the whirlpools must have sucked her in. It's been too long.

I breathe slowly through my nose, allowing the air to finally fill my lungs. Although, air seems like a luxury while Fan is still submerged.

My eyes squeeze closed.

The thunder of crashing water diminishes as the lake slowly settles, the whirlpools disappearing.

Only a few serene ripples mar the calm surface of the lake. I struggle to comprehend that Fan is gone. Why in the stars did she do that? Why did she sacrifice herself? She was a pain in my neck, a shinver slave, not to mention a stubborn, stupid fool, a scoundrel, a complete bum-smear on this galaxy—

Bubbles break the surface of the lake. Fan's head pops up. Flinging her hair out of her eyes, she turns to Braxt and grins. *She grins!*

Relief floods my muscles, turning them to jelly. If it weren't for the anger in my veins, I'd probably fall to the ground.

Fan, you stupid fool.

She takes a big breath and dives again.

"Fan!" I call. *What the stars...?*

Pedders grunts in protest, but she's already gone.

Slowly, the cage comes back into view above the water, and eventually, so does Luchlon. My eyes sting with rage when I see him. His lips are locked with Fan's. She holds onto the bars, letting the cage lift her out of the water with it. I look away.

It's stupid; I know she must be breathing air into his lungs, but still, the sight of them with their lips together...the image of them kissing...well, it disappoints me more than anything. Fan deserves better.

As the water drips off them, they pull away from each other. Luchlon looks spent, his eyes drawn, his chest heaving, his hair flat against his face. But he's alive.

The stepping stones rise again, and the bars shrink back into the dark water, freeing Luchlon. He sits there while he regains his breath.

Fan calls to Braxt, "If you want to get across, I'd suggest avoiding the stepping stones, and swimming instead." Then she swims to the other side.

Luchlon slides off the big stone and goes after her, crawling out on the other side on his hands and knees and flopping onto his back.

"Lieutenant," Braxt commands, and immediately the woman dives into the water with two of her soldiers. Then he turns to me. "Eshan'ya."

I scowl at him but approach the lake. Luckily, I'm not wearing one of my long gowns; they'd weigh me down. I dive in without taking off any clothes. The water is cold, but not cold enough to quench my fury at Fan's lunacy.

As I pull myself out of the lake, I give the lieutenant and Luchlon a dirty look. Then I walk straight up to Fan and slap the grin off her face.

She jumps back. "What was that for?"

"Of all the stupid, ludicrous, foolish, moronic, reckless things to do, you had to try to kill yourself!" I rage.

Fan rubs her cheek, but her lips curl upward in a smirk. "Were you worried about me, princess?"

I huff. "Don't flatter yourself," I say. "I just can't stand idiocy." I turn my back on her to watch the others as they swim across.

Tika stands at the edge, shaking her head while she wails, "Oh, no, no, no, I'm not getting in there." Her heels dig in, but her protests do no good when Braxt takes matters into his own hands and shoves her in. Her cry is cut short when she goes under. A moment later, she resurfaces, coughing and gurgling. She faffs around in the water, sloshing and slapping like a dying fish, and it looks like she's going to drown before a soldier grabs her by the collar and drags her across the lake.

Surprisingly, Pedders is just as reluctant as Tika. The big guy looks absolutely petrified, his eyes wide and darting left and right. When he's pushed in, he sinks. My blood turns cold when he doesn't immediately surface again.

"For stars' sake," Braxt exclaims. "Go get him."

A soldier dives in, and after a few moments, he resurfaces with Pedders' arms around his neck. Pedders grips him so tight it's a wonder the soldier can breathe, but somehow they manage to get to our side of the lake.

Fan and Tika each grab one of Pedders' hands and haul him from the water. He sits at the edge, gasping for air.

Once he's recovered, Pedders pats Fan on the back and grunts. It's a question and a reprimand—and somehow it has more grace than my response to Fan's actions.

"I knew there must have been a release lever," Fan explains. "It took me a while to find it, but I knew I could."

She acts so nonchalant, like it's no big deal. Like she didn't almost die. The bullheaded, arrogant fool. Risking her life for...what? Luchlon? Like he's worth it.

The rest of the Quain soldiers come across, including Braxt. I can't help but get a sense of satisfaction watching his perfectly arranged appearance come undone in the water. His hair and suit flatten against his body, but his eyes stay calm. I wish his overly large ego would pull him under or that I could reactivate the challenge so a whirlpool would finish him off. But at least one of my friends would be dead before I make one move. So I stay where I am, watching Braxt climb from the lake, soaked and dripping like the rest of us. Just a man. He's not a monster or a lord; he's just a man. I can take down a man. I just need to figure out how.

The Quain soldiers fling more flash plates onto the walls of the cave, lighting up the space beyond the lake. Stairs the width of the cave lead the way down and further into the mountain. Braxt nods, and we all begin walking, our clothes squelching with each step.

"Urgh, my toes are cold and wet now," Tika grumbles.

As we descend, the stairs curve in a wide spiral. The little river still runs along on the left, splashing down each step as if it's following us. Further below, echoing up to us, I can hear the distant sound of even more water.

Fan has been a few steps behind, but now she comes up beside me. She briefly catches my hand and squeezes. With a huff, I snatch my hand back. But my gaze flicks to her for a moment, and she gives me a quick encouraging smile that seems to say, "*We'll find a way out of this.*" Then I return my attention to not slipping and falling.

It's been several silent minutes with only the rumble of the water filling the quiet when we finally reach what I suspect is the next challenge.

Water thunders down from the ceiling *across* our path.

What's worse is that there's a gaping hole in the floor. Our way becomes a series of stepping stones over the void. Two- to three-foot squares, hovering over a black chasm we'll have to leap across. I can't see any way of getting around it. We have to go *through* the downpour, but it's pelting down so hard that surely we'll be knocked off our feet and into the void.

There must be a safe path through. The challenge is to find it.

Braxt and his soldiers stop a few yards from the waterfall. The man's eyes are lowered in thought as he assesses the challenge.

"Who...is next?" he asks, not taking his gaze off the challenge.

"I am." Fan steps forward.

I protest along with the rest of Fan's crew, but she just shakes her head.

"I'm doing the challenge, and that's final." She turns her steely gaze on her crew, and although Pedders grunts, neither Tika nor Luchlon object again.

Pedders steps toward her, risking getting shot, but his guard lets him. He clasps her shoulders tightly and pulls her in for a bear hug. She pats him on the back in return.

"Don't stress, Qiqiang," she says, running her hand through her hair. "I've got this."

"Don't be stupid, Fan," I say, rolling my eyes at her. She always wants to look so brave. "You've already proven how courageous you are. There's no need to be a big hero."

"There is every need, princess." She takes my hands in hers, and she holds on tighter when I try to pull away again. I glance at Luchlon, but if there's any jealousy in his eyes, I can't tell.

"I need to protect the people I care about."

She's not just being sentimental; she's slipped something into my hands. I close my fist around it. Her multitool.

She winks at me. "Besides, I'm not a hero. I'm just trying my best." I almost smile back at her lopsided grin.

"Hurry up," Braxt barks.

The lieutenant waves her gun at Fan, who backs away.

Her spine straightens as she approaches the wall of water. Just as she reaches it, there's an audible click. She's stepped on another pressure plate; the challenge is activated.

There's a shift in the air, a clunk above us, and the waterfall lessens in its ferocity. Instead of tons of water that would instantly knock us down, there's a steady stream, much like the palace showers, which had good pressure. Stone beams cross the ceiling, water cascading between them, but it's too dark above to see what is blocking most of the waterfall.

A blinding flash of light makes my eyes burn. When it dissipates, I see colors reflecting off the droplets: red, blue, and yellow. The colors shine up from the stepping stones—each square glowing as the water runs over them.

Fan has to choose the right path, but which is it?

She looks back over her shoulder and nods briefly at me—I'm not sure if that's further encouragement or a goodbye.

I nod back. Mine isn't a goodbye.

Chapter 33

Fan

THIS IS SOME SERIOUS redrynch turd.

I know as soon as I step through this downpour that something bad is going to happen. Just like in the last challenge. Another cage will drop, or lava bursts will shoot from the sides, or a boulder will chase me into the void.

There are three routes to choose from, each with hovering three-foot square platforms glowing red, blue, or yellow, and picking the wrong one is going to be lethal. I can't rely on anyone to save me the way I rescued Luchlon, who'd better be grateful, the lying bastard. Pedders will probably try to help—he's always been loyal—but I don't want him in any more danger than we already have with Braxt, so I'll just need to survive this without him.

I look through the waterfall, trying to see to the end of the course.

What's that?

Several yards in, the blue isn't flickering in the water. It's stagnant—frozen. I peer closer, careful not to stick my nose in.

It's hard to make out what it is through the blur of water, but there's definitely something in there.

I stare a moment longer.

Fingers.

That's what I can see. Fingers. Human fingers.

Someone is frozen in the middle of the waterfall.

Unlucky dirt grinder.

But it's lucky for me because now I know the blue way isn't right. My choices are down to two. Red or yellow?

Maybe there's a way I can work it out without sticking my neck out.

I unbuckle my belt and pull it from my waist.

Getting a good grip on the buckle, I flick the length of it at the water raining over the first yellow stepping stone. Hidden sensors pick up the movement and—with a whoosh—the water turns to ice—a *massive* block of ice—on top of the yellow platform, almost catching the tip of my belt.

Everywhere else, the water continues to fall. I turn to the red path.

But I don't trust this grand hurrah Protogenoi obstacle course, so I flick my belt at the shimmering red water too. I'm satisfied when it continues to flow over the step. Only then do I buckle my belt again, take a deep breath, and leap onto the first red square, right under the waterfall.

With water raining down my back, I look at the glowing red platform I stand on. Emptiness surrounds it. Tentatively, I peer over the edge, watching the water flow into the void. The bottom still isn't visible; the downpour disappears into blackness before it reaches whatever is down there.

Above, the water doesn't travel down over natural rock like I expected; it's all Protogenoi-made. Long beams of polished stone travel from left to right over all three paths. The water bounces off and down between each of them to create the shower I'm walking through.

It's a slow journey, jumping from one red stone to the next. The ground is slippery as hell, and the gaps between the stones are wide. I jump to the right twice to continue along the red path, then jump to the left once. After that, I lose track. H_2O runs down my face, soaking my clothes, and dripping off my bare feet. I have to be extra careful each time I leap. I can see how that popsicle crud dweller got partway through before he got himself frozen.

The route takes me closer to the frozen treasure hunter. As I approach, I can make out more of his appearance. From where I stand, he looks completely blue. Of course, that's because the platform he's on is glowing blue, not just because he's cold. Still, I shiver at the sight of him.

His mouth is open as if he screamed when he was consumed by the ice. He's quite well-preserved, like he was only frozen yesterday, but his clothes and hair are way out of style, so he's been stuck for a few decades at least. His upper lip sports a bushy mustache that I'm sure was all the rage once upon a time, along with his weird high-neck collar. It looks damned uncomfortable to me, but so does getting frozen in ice.

Once I'm next to Mr. Icebergman, I realize he didn't slip and fall into the wrong path. He got trapped because the red platforms stop and then restart on the other side of the blue ones. I look ahead and see that all three routes cross over each other, never staying in a straight line. The Protogenoi couldn't make it *that* easy for us.

I groan.

How am I going to get across the blue track to the safe red one?

I glance back at my crew, at Eshan'ya. They're hardly visible through the shower between us. I can't let them down. If I just get through these challenges, maybe I can find a way to overcome Kriinal Braxt too. Maybe Eshan'ya can do something with that multitool I gave her.

Now that I'm right behind Mr. Icebergman, he has his back to me, facing the direction he jumped. I shiver again.

I remove my belt and flick it at the ice block.

Nothing happens.

I do it again, harder this time.

Still, nothing happens.

"Hi, Mr. Icebergman. I'm Fan," I say to the popsicle while threading my belt. I think I better introduce myself since I'm going to have to get very close to him. "I'd love to leave you in peace, but you see, I'm gonna need to...kinda...well, I'm going to have to climb on top of you..."

My gaze is drawn to the chasm between my step and Mr. Icebergman. The water falls endlessly down it, fading from sight before it reaches the bottom. *If* there's a bottom.

Father's fist, I'm going to die.

My hair is soaking wet, and I flick it off my forehead. Then, taking a big breath, I leap off the red square, aiming for the ice block. My arms and legs wrap around it, hugging Mr. Icebergman near his head. The cold penetrates my clothing, and I immediately start to slide down the slippery ice.

Stars above, I'm going to slip off!

I hurry to swivel around the ice so I'm closer to the red path. By the time I'm in a position to leap across, I've slipped so far down that I'm face-to-face with Mr. Icebergman's icy crotch—glad I already introduced myself.

Sending up a prayer to the stars, I fling myself across the gap, and my stomach painfully collides with the hovering red platform.

My fingers clutch at the slippery surface. I get a purchase on the ledge and hurl myself onto it. I lay on the stone, breathing heavily, letting the red highlighted droplets rain down on my face.

That was close.

After lying there for a while, catching my breath, I hear Braxt call, "Get on with it, Captain Sung." He has no respect for what I just went through.

I drag myself to my feet. My legs feel a little less stable than they were before, but I push the fear aside, ignore my wobbles, and carry on along the red squares.

"Thanks for the good time." I wave to Mr. Icebergman.

My toes are so cold they're going numb. That's one more thing I have to worry about. If I can't feel the stone beneath my feet, there's a higher chance I'm going to slip right off the rock.

I avert my eyes from the abyss and concentrate on the path right in front of me. As I work through the challenge, it dawns on me that even if I get through, it isn't necessarily going to keep my crew safe. Braxt will send them in after me. But...

I think of the latch I found at the bottom of the lake underneath Luchlon's cage. This challenge must have something similar. It has to. Otherwise, all my friends will be dead at the bottom of this black hole.

I assess the challenge ahead. The yellow route has somehow come up beside the red, and I have to leap over it without being turned into a popsicle.

But my focus is now split. I'm searching for a way over the gap to the next red block, but I'm also looking for whatever mechanism controls this challenge. And time isn't on my side. If I take too long, Braxt might push forward anyway. My eyes dart up and down, across the walls, and even below the stepping stones. I don't find anything useful—yet. My eyes drift forward once again.

This time, I don't have Mr. Icebergman's help across the wrong path. Water flows freely over the yellow square, and if I leap onto it, I'm going to get iced. So I use my belt again, flinging it at the yellow path. Sensors react to the movement, and the water turns to ice. But this time, I'm not quick enough, and the belt tip gets trapped.

Crap.

A tug doesn't budge it. I yank harder. It still doesn't move. I consider leaving it, but I think I'm going to need it.

Planting my feet wide and shifting my weight backward, I heave on the belt with more force. My feet slip forward,

and then there's an audible *plop*,

and the belt suddenly flies free,

and I'm flung backward.

"Whoa!" I yell. My feet skate out from under me. And then I'm falling.

Broken hearts, I'm falling.

My butt hits the edge.

I twist around and fling my arms out. Stretching. Grappling. One hand lands flat on the square, slowing my descent. But the path is too wet. My fingers turn to claws, my nails digging in. Finally, they catch at the edge of the stone.

My fall stops abruptly.

I dangle from the block with one hand, my legs swinging over the abyss.

Sung, you idiot! You almost died.

"Fan?" I hear Eshan'ya scream.

My chest heaves as I hang there, my eyes bulging at the darkness below.

"Yeah." It's barely a whisper. I gather more air and try again. "Yeah! Still here."

I can't be certain, but I think Pedders grunts in relief.

I reach my other arm up and get a better grip on the platform. With water running down my face, I pull myself back onto the path. *Stupid belt,* I think as I pick it up from where it fell on the platform.

Glancing at the stone beams again, and the water falling down between them, I realize the sensors and the mechanism that turns the water to ice must be somewhere up there. If that's true, it makes sense that a way to stop the water from freezing is up there too.

Hanging the belt over my shoulder, I leap onto the yellow ice block. It's too perilous to climb with my bare fingers. So as I slip slowly down, I reach for the belt and stab the buckle into the ice. I hack at the block until my fingers have something to hold on to. I repeat the process for my other hand, just a little higher, and pull myself up. This would've been much easier if I had kept my multitool.

I keep going, hacking at the ice with the buckle of my belt and hauling my body up higher and higher.

Despite the ice, I am sweating. It's damned hard work. I get some relief after I get high enough to use the first dents for my toes. But my poor little digits are so cold I can barely feel them pressing into the ice.

How the stars did I get myself into this mess?

Oh, yeah. Eshan'ya.

It's probably worth it then.

Finally, I've climbed high enough that I can touch the stone beams. I loop my belt over the top of one and use it to drag myself up and over.

Water still beats down on my head, but I'm grateful it's not turning icy. I must be above the sensors now.

I pull my tech point from my shirt pocket and flick it on. "Ranate, do you read?" I call into it, hoping my voice doesn't echo below. "Ranate?" There's no response. Maybe the mountain is blocking the signal. I return the tech point to my pocket and look around.

The beams are much closer together than the stepping stones are, so it's easier for me to skip from one to another, searching for a lever.

In the first challenge, I'd found the lever under the cage in a small indentation that I figured would fit into a matching one on the floor of the lake. If I hadn't intervened, when the cage hit the bottom, the two indentations would have lined up and automatically reset the challenge—but only after the person in the cage had drowned. I just reset it early.

When I activated this ice course, part of the waterfall was diverted. Resetting the challenge will put the waterfall back at full power and push people off the paths. But if I can divert the waterfall completely—yes, that should work—then there will be no water to freeze.

There must be something...

I move deeper into the cave, away from my crew and the Quain. And when I see it, I know it's exactly what I'm looking for. It's a large trough sitting at an angle, and judging by the way it's collecting water, it's going to tip over. My guess is, when it does, the action will trigger a lever and the waterfall will return to the way it was. That means the ice course has a time limit and anyone still on the course will be flushed into the abyss.

It also means that all I need to do to dismantle the course, is tip the trough the other way. I grin.

Chapter 34

Eshan'ya

I SHIVER WHILE WATCHING the obstacle course, my heart in my throat. I can't see Fan anymore. She's hidden behind a veil of water and ice. She's been gone for so long now.

How long will Braxt wait until he sends someone else? Or will we all need to go through this treacherous course? I glance at Pedders and Tika. Will they make it out of this alive? It's my fault they're here. I wish I hadn't brought them into this, but it was necessary. I had to try to stop Braxt. I still have to stop him.

My fingers press into the multitool. It's exactly like the one I used to stab Madame Aphelion when I escaped the palace. I've done it once. I can do it again.

Kriinal Braxt is only two feet from me. My eyes travel to his neck. Some dark stubble appears where his neck meets his jaw, like it's been a couple of days since he's shaved. I imagine blood matting in it after I stab him.

He glances at me as if he hears my thoughts.

By the stars, he looks like Declan.

His hair even curls slightly at the back of his neck the same way Declan's does on a humid day.

I drop my eyes to the floor, trying to push the image from my mind. He isn't Declan. Declan left me.

And he kept secrets from me.

This is Kriinal Braxt. The Quain Lord. The man who has killed and enslaved millions. The man who will enslave the whole galaxy if he gets the Device. The man who hunted me and my family—the Protectors.

I grip the multitool harder.

I inch closer, ready to leap.

With a deafening roar, a million tons of water come crashing down over the course.

"Fan!" Pedders shouts.

The waterfall slows and slows until it's only a few drips.

And finally, there's Fan, standing on the other side of the course. She looks triumphant, with her hands resting on her hips. She tilts her head quizzically and calls, "What's taking you guys so long? Get over here."

Pedders chuckles, and I find myself smiling too.

"Thank the stars." Tika claps her hands together.

The muscles in Luchlon's neck relax.

Braxt nods, and the lieutenant leads us across the course. Now that the downpour has stopped, we don't have to worry about whether we take the red, yellow, or blue squares. We each take different routes to get across as quickly as possible. The paths are still slippery, and it's a long drop down, so I'm relieved when I reach the other side. It must have been an icy hell for Fan.

When Pedders reaches her, he wraps her in a hug with another one of his grunts.

Fan pats his back. "It'll take more than a bit of ice to end me."

"How'd you do it, Fan? How'd you stop the water?" Tika asks in her usual excitement.

Fan taps her nose and doesn't answer. She glances at the Quain, and it's clear she doesn't want them to know. It's smart—it could give us an advantage in an escape.

"You're quite incredible, Captain," Tika gushes. "I thought you died, and I was so scared that Mr. Braxt would make me go next. That would have been awful."

"Glad you were concerned about me." Fan laughs, playfully grabbing Tika's shoulder.

"Aww, what a happy reunion," Braxt says sarcastically as he joins us on safer ground. "Let's get a move on." He storms past, and I grip the multitool a little harder, looking for the right moment.

Fan grins at me as she follows. She seems confident that we'll get out of this somehow. I take courage from her.

The path winds down again, and the lieutenant continues to throw flash plates so we can see where we're going. Water now runs down the walls on either side and into a cavity below the path. It's probably where those millions of tons of water were diverted when Fan solved the challenge. The lively water makes a musical tinkling all around us as we walk, and it would be beautiful if it weren't for the fact that we're under threat of death.

The path opens up into an enormous cavern, another one that's been carved out and polished by the Protogenoi. It's stunning.

Chiseled artwork depicting flowers, plants, the Protogenoi symbol, and other images that I recognize from Lyran cover the walls. Directly in front of us, the water flows into a wide pool. On the other side, more steps lead upward to what looks like an altar. Three fifty-foot Protogenoi obelisks stand on the dais, and though they're much smaller than the obelisks at the gates of Lyran, they're still massive. An arched door rises behind them.

The home of the Device.

The lieutenant doesn't need to set any flash plates here. The place is already lit softly by some artificial glow radiating from the ceiling, and the light on the water reflects little lines that swirl and dance over the door and obelisks.

The path splits and runs around the pool on both sides. Little bridges cross the water where it flows from the walls and into the pool.

"Wow," Tika says, and her voice reverberates around the cavern.

The lieutenant ignores the beauty of this place, taking the path to the left in her businesslike manner, and we all follow her. Like everyone else, my mouth hangs open as we cross the bridge and climb the handful of steps up to the dais.

The obelisks tower over us like guardians. I tilt my head back to see the tops reaching high into the cavity of the mountain where the chaos symbol, the three stars, and the combined symbol—the Protogenoi sigil—are carved.

My eyes are drawn to the stars of my tattoo. Why didn't Declan ever tell me those stars were a combination? Why did the Protectors ever imprint them on me? If they hadn't, I would never have had to go into hiding in the royal harem. I feel betrayed. But one glance at Braxt brings back memories of Declan. He always looked at me with love; he cared for me. He never meant for me to get hurt.

"The final challenge," Braxt says, breaking into my thoughts.

The image of Declan dissipates, and all I see is Kriinal Braxt. My eyes glower.

He grabs my arm roughly and pulls me over to a stone slab that sits directly in front of the arched doorway. Several knobs and levers appear on the waist-high slab, but the sole button on the console has the Protogenoi sigil engraved on it. It's the third challenge—the combination to open the doors.

Braxt swivels one of the knobs, and light shines up from within the slab, fanning into a hologram, but the image is so crisp it looks solid. I stare at a star floating in the air, convinced I could reach out, grab it, put it in my pocket, and take it home with me. But it's just an image.

As Braxt swivels the lever further, the star turns, the points revolving. He stops and pulls the two keys from his pocket. He hands the first—the red one—to his lieutenant and the second—the blue one—to another Quain soldier.

"Align the stars to match the combination in the keys. They must match exactly to open the doors," Braxt says, then pulls me even closer so he can study my tattoo. His fingers dig into the flesh of my arm, burning my skin, and sending angry sparks throughout my body.

The lieutenant and the Quain soldier shine their tech points through the Shadé diamonds to see the star combinations while Braxt concentrates on my tattoo, turning the knobs until the three floating stars match the alignment.

I grip the multitool. Is this my chance? Braxt is so close, and two of his soldiers are busy. But he finishes aligning the stars too quickly, and I miss my chance. Once he's done, he looks over at his soldiers.

"Done," they say.

There's a gleam in Braxt's eye as he reaches across and presses the button engraved with the Protogenoi sigil.

Instantly, a loud screeching echoes around the cavern, piercing my eardrums. The glowing lights turn black. I can just make out the shape of the doors—and they remain closed.

Then a white-hot light, like the beam of electricity, shoots out from behind me. I look up. The top of the central obelisk is blazing.

It all happens in a flash. The light streaks out and hits the forehead of the Quain soldier who entered the combination from the second key.

Boom!

His head is gone.

I jump back. Tika shrieks. Blood is splattered across Braxt, the lieutenant, and me. Gasps burst from everyone, though I can barely hear anything over the wailing, which I now realize is an alarm.

What is left of the Quain soldier slumps to the ground, the alarm stops, and the slight glow of light returns to the cave. The doorway remains closed. My heart is so high in my throat now, it's hard to breathe.

"What went wrong?" Braxt scowls, leveling a deadly stare at his lieutenant. He tries to wipe the blood from his shirt, but it just smears.

The lieutenant collects the second key out of the dead soldier's hand and shines her tech point through it. "The combination was off," she says. "He wasn't precise enough."

"Fix it," Braxt demands.

She waves to two of the other soldiers. They hesitate before stepping forward, wary of the obelisk's power, but then they drag the body away while the lieutenant steps up to the slab.

Taking a deep breath and extra time to study the combination, she twists two levers, moving the floating stars only slightly until they appear to be in perfect alignment with the stars in the key. When she's done, she looks back at Braxt. I see a hint of fear in her eyes for the first time.

Braxt shows no such fear. He hits the central button again.

Light bursts from the cracks around the doors, almost blinding, but it's impossible to look away.

There's a clunk, and the doors start to swing open.

Braxt steps away from the stone bench and toward the arch. His eyes reflect the light, making him look like he's in a trance. But he's not. He's just eager to get his hands on the Device.

He's so eager he isn't paying attention to what's going on around him.

The lieutenant and the soldiers are also distracted; everyone wants to see what's behind those doors. Everyone inches forward.

I slip in behind Braxt as the doors fully open with a clunk. The brightness of the light lessens so we can see into the chamber beyond.

Unlike the cave, the chamber isn't made from stone. The walls gleam, and while they might simply be made from some kind of highly polished alloy, I think they're probably genuine silver. The chamber is so beautiful. Every inch is carved with stars and planets, constellations, and galaxies, like it's a map of the universe.

The room is completely empty except for something levitating in the middle of the chamber. Some kind of firearm. It's bigger than a lava gun but shorter and stockier than a rifle. I've never seen anything like it before.

The barrel is transparent and has two Shadé diamonds within it, one purple and one blue. The grip and handguard are both a silvery material, but there's no cartridge like a rifle would have. It looks more like a pulsar gun in that sense, which makes me wonder what it shoots. Shadé diamonds are said to hold a lot of power that humans haven't been able to harness. But if the Protogenoi have included them in this Device...

It must be as powerful as I feared.

Braxt makes a guttural sound as he approaches it—a sound a man might make gazing upon a naked mate. The sound of desire.

He's still staring. He hasn't noticed that I'm now only a foot behind him. My hands tremble. As he stares at the Device, slowly reaching out his hand, I'm staring at that vulnerable spot on his neck.

He's almost got the Device, and I can't wait any longer. I clench the multitool in my fist—

—and swing.

Chapter 35

Fan

FINALLY!

Eshan'ya throws a blow at Kriinal Braxt.

She's been inching closer and closer to him, and I've been holding my breath, waiting for her to make her move.

Braxt dodges at the last second, but she still manages to stab him in the shoulder.

I take advantage of the situation and dive for the nearest soldier's lava gun. He was staring wide-eyed at the Device just like everyone else, the dumbass. He never saw me creeping up on him.

I steal the gun out of his hand before Eshan'ya's blade even hits Braxt. The next second, I've shot the soldier, and he slumps to the ground. No more waiting. No more cowering. I'm back, baby. I hold the gun firmly, gaining confidence and strength from it.

Neither Pedders nor Luchlon waste time either. Both of them leap at their guards, punches are thrown, and there's an inordinate amount of grunting and groaning going on. Tika has the good sense to dive to the floor when I spin around and shoot her captor.

I turn back to the Device in time to see Eshan'ya make a grab for it, but Braxt rips the multitool from his shoulder and lunges at Eshan'ya before she reaches the Device.

"You little—"

I aim my lava gun at him.

Before I pull the trigger, a blast from the lieutenant almost takes my nose off, missing me by a miurtle's hair. I dive out the chamber door before she can try again.

Tika follows me, cowering in my shadow.

I shoot around the door to give Eshan'ya some cover. She runs for the Device again. This time, she snatches it up while Braxt takes cover from my lava gun, huddling on the other side of the door.

"Get that Device!" Braxt screams at his soldiers.

The lieutenant shoots back at me, and I'm forced to duck.

"They're going to kill us!" Tika shrieks in my ear.

"Stay calm, and we'll get out of this alive," I say. She's so close I can feel her shivering. "Here." I take a pulsar gun from a dead soldier lying nearby and hand it to her. "Shoot something."

She gulps and takes the gun with trembling fingers.

"You can do it," I say, trying to encourage her.

"I can do it." I see resolve settle in her eyes as they grow darker, and then she swings the pulsar and shoots at Braxt. She misses, but at least it provides some cover.

By now, Luchlon has knocked out his guard, stolen his pulsar gun, and is trudging over to where Pedders is locked in battle.

"I'm coming, Pedders!" Luchlon shouts.

When Pedders throws a right hook, spinning his guard away from him, Luchlon opens fire, and the soldier falls backward. The pulsar is not set to stun.

Pedders grunts his thanks, and they both turn and flee while I cover them, raining lava shots on the remaining soldiers and Braxt.

Eshan'ya is bent double as she runs out of the chamber, clutching the Device to her chest.

"She's getting away!" Braxt shouts, desperation increasing his pitch. But we've got him and his soldiers pinned down. They can't follow her.

"Keep running!" I yell, and she flees right past, flicking terrified eyes at me. In seconds, she's back down the stairs, across the little bridge, and into the cave.

Luchlon, Pedders, Tika, and I all have guns now, and we return fire as we retreat. But it's hard to hit anything when the enemy is hiding behind whatever they can. Cowards.

I hide behind an obelisk.

After the obelisks, there isn't much cover before the cavern entrance and the ascent back up the mountain. We're going to have to make a run for it.

I poke my head out.

Braxt is bleeding from his shoulder, but it's not slowing him down. His face contorts in rage and pain as he lifts his lava gun and shoots again. There are three more Quain soldiers. Their aim isn't that good, and I can probably pick one or two of them off, no problem. But the lieutenant is well trained.

The obelisk explodes just above my head. A chunk of stone breaks off and smacks me in the face. Yeah, the lieutenant has pretty good aim. She almost killed me that time.

"Pedders?" I scream as I shoot again.

He grunts.

"Take Tika and run. Luchlon and I will hold 'em off," I command.

"We can't leave you," Tika gasps.

I quickly turn back to look her in the eyes. "It's OK, Tika. Have I ever lost a fight?"

She shakes her head. "No, Captain."

"And don't I always come out on top?"

"Yes, Captain."

I pat her on the shoulder, flashing her a grin. Then I scream, "Pedders!" and keep shooting.

Pedders springs out from behind his obelisk, swoops by to collect Tika by the hand, and sprints away—chasing after Eshan'ya.

It's now two against five.

No matter what happens to me and Luchlon, at least Pedders and Tika will be safe, and Eshan'ya will escape with the Device.

Chapter 36

Eshan'ya

THE SOUND OF LAVA and pulsar shots follows me up the path, echoing off the stone walls. It sounds like a full-scale war rather than a handful of fighters.

This *is* war, I remind myself as I sprint.

I clutch the Device against my body. It's a little heavier than a football, but it's awkward to run with.

The purple and blue Shadé diamonds glow within the transparent barrel. I wonder how it works, but I have no time to stop and inspect it. I keep racing up the path past the walls streaming with water. Thinking of the void below, I pause.

Maybe I should throw the Device away.

But what's down there? I look at where the water disappears, but I can't see anything. I have no idea how far down it goes. If I drop the Device here, will it wash up somewhere else on the planet? Will Braxt be able to retrieve it somehow? What if he scours this cave?

I can't risk it. No, the only way I can be sure that the Device is lost is if I destroy it myself.

I take off again, running hard as I clutch the Device tighter than I need to.

Soon, I reach the ice obstacle course. The water is still diverted, so I hurry across. I'm slower than I'd like to be, but if I go any faster, I'll slip into the abyss.

My blood runs cold, but it's got nothing to do with the icy course. I hear footsteps running up the path behind me. They're coming for me.

I have to hurry. It's not safe, but I pick up my pace. Taking the most direct route across the course, I leap from the red path onto the yellow.

As I land, my boot hits a wet spot and slides forward.

No.

My feet come out from under me, and my butt crashes down. The Device bounces from my hands, hits the stone, and goes tumbling over the edge and down into the void.

I lunge for it.

Oh, holy stars—I've caught it.

Somehow, I've grabbed the Device with one hand as I sprawl across the platform on my stomach. I stare at the darkness below and take a breath to regain my nerve. My hips scream in pain from hitting the ground so hard. I take another breath.

I can't stay here. My pursuers are getting closer.

Careful to avoid toppling off, I reach down with my other hand, firmly grasp the Device, and haul it back up.

As I swivel into a sitting position, I hear the footsteps stop at the edge of the course.

"Princess Eshan'ya!"

It's Tika and Pedders. They got away. They're not Quain soldiers.

I'm almost sobbing with relief.

"What are you doing, princess?" Tika asks. "There's no time to rest. We need to get out of here."

A strange laugh bubbles from my lips. "I don't intend to stay here," I assure her.

Pedders does his signature grunt, and the two of them start crossing the course. I slowly and cautiously go the last few yards to safety and wait for them on the other side.

They reach me without slipping. Tika might seem fragile at times, but she sure has courage—and outstanding balance to get over the ice course so quickly.

"Run," Pedders grunts as he bounds past.

"No. No, stop," I say, and he slides to a halt.

His eyebrows pop up.

"Use your lava gun to destroy the Device," I say.

"Your Highness, surely that can wait until we get back on the *Huxian Fox*?" Tika asks.

"We can't risk waiting," I say. Using my most authoritative tone, I say, "Pedders." I won't make the mistake the other Protectors made. This Device needs to be destroyed now.

Pedders nods and lifts his stolen lava gun. I drop the Device on the ground and step back.

Pedders shoots the Device straight on three times.

Any other firearm would be reduced to burned and melted metal, but the Device looks no different than it did a moment ago. Not even a scratch.

"That's strange," Pedders says.

"Try again," I demand.

Pedders lets the lava gun rip, sending six shots right at the Device.

When the air clears, the Device is still whole and perfect even though the ground beneath is black and charred.

"Very strange," Pedders mumbles.

"Try again," I say again, but my voice has lost its conviction. And even though I see the doubt etched on Pedders' face, he follows my order and shoots the Device ten times.

Nothing.

No dents, no scratches. There's not even a smudge on the barrel. It looks like it's just been polished. This exercise is fruitless. There's no point trying again.

Gingerly, I pick it up, expecting it to be hot from the lava shots, but it's not. It's like the heat has already dissipated, reflected off the metals and diamonds. If it deflects heat, how are we going to destroy it? My legs turn to water, burbling like the rapids of the Lyran River.

I clutch it to my chest again, and the three of us run up the dimly lit stairs, my legs quivering the whole way.

Chapter 37

Fan

THAT LIEUTENANT IS A fine shot, the little redrynch turd. She has almost shot my head off at least four times now, and she's definitely got it in for me.

What did I ever do to her?

Just because she follows the commands of an evil lord and I'm not insane like her doesn't mean we can't be friends.

Another shot aimed at my head makes me duck back behind the obelisk.

OK, maybe friendship is not in the cards.

I let loose four shots. She hides behind the door again, but she's not quite quick enough this time, and I clip her shoulder. She yelps.

I grin. *Got her.*

Then a torrent of shots hit the other side of my obelisk with a vengeance. My grin gets wider. I *really* pissed her off.

"We gotta get out of here," Luchlon calls.

He's not wrong, even if he is stating the obvious. But I'm not sure how we're going to manage that. Once we're down the stairs, there isn't much cover. Between the lieutenant's keen shooting, the three other soldiers, and Kriinal Braxt, we're going to be sitting graks.

Graks—yes, that's the answer. Graks love water. An idea quickly blooms.

"Luchlon." My voice is deep with command. "If we're going to get out of here, you're going to have to follow me...no questions asked. No hesitation."

He stops shooting for a moment to look at me. He's not going to like my idea. So I won't give him a chance to complain.

I jump out from my hiding place and shoot up a storm. All the soldiers shirk away behind the doors. Then I turn and run down the stairs. Luchlon is right behind me, shooting backward to keep the Quain down.

Then I dive into the water.

It's cold. I can't see a thing in front of me and the lava gun weighs me down. But I just keep swimming.

After a moment, although my ears are muffled by the water, I hear a splash as Luchlon joins me.

My eyes are open, but I might as well be in a black hole it's so dark. No light seems to penetrate below the surface. I can't even see my own limbs stretching out in front of me. Swimming in the direction I think we need to go, I hope Luchlon is doing the same.

I swim underwater until my lungs are screaming and I can't go on any further without them bursting. After all my practice saving Luchlon earlier, I thought I'd be better at this by now, but my lungs can only hold so much oxygen.

I break the surface, bringing my lava gun up with me and shooting into the air.

The Quain have come out of their hiding spots, standing at the edge of the pool. They spot me as soon as my head pops up and start shooting. I'm already shooting back, making them dive for cover.

Where's Luchlon?

His pulsar gun breaches the surface before the rest of him, and he's shooting as well. He's only a few yards from my left. He glances at me, and then we both take a large gulp of air and drop into the dark.

This time, the pool is lit by the shots from the Quain. The energy bursts from their lava and pulsar guns slice into the water, making it glow red, blue, or green before they dissipate. But they're just guessing where I am. I take advantage of this and vary my direction before I rise for another breath.

I glimpse Luchlon's head bobbing back under just as I rise. He's only a little behind me. My eyes snap to the Quain. Kriinal Braxt is still at the base of the stairs, staring out across the pool, but the lieutenant and her soldiers are running on either side, still shooting into the water. The lieutenant is on the left path, the other two on the right. They've crossed the little bridges and are running for the entrance to the cavern.

Luchlon and I need to get there before they do or they'll cut off our escape.

I dive and swim as fast as I can, pushing my limbs and lungs harder than I ever have before. My whole body aches as I push it to its limits. I only have a few yards to go, but the Quain can move much faster on land.

My feet thrash, my arms stretch forward, my lungs strain desperately for air. I hear shots still breaking the water and the sound of my own beating heart, but otherwise, the underwater world is silent. It's eerie. Just the *thump thump* of my heart, and the *swoosh* of the lava shots, but everything is muffled like I'm already dying.

Suddenly, my fingers hit the edge of the pool. I get a purchase on the ledge and haul myself up. I roll onto the path—dripping wet, shivering, and gasping for air—and lift my lava gun as I do.

I'm too late. A Quain soldier is already there.

He kicks the gun from my hand, and it flies back into the pool with a splash. Before he can shoot me, I lunge for the soldier's legs. I tackle him around the knees, and he goes sprawling to the ground. I jump on top, punching him in the face several times to keep him down.

I've surfaced on the right side of the pool. The lieutenant is still running toward me from the left path, and another soldier is closing in on me.

I punch the soldier under me again. But he's much bigger, and I can't pin him down before he bucks me, and we're rolling.

He gets on top and pulls his arm back for a punch.

I'm staring at his fist bearing down when Luchlon rears out of the water and grabs him by the neck. Luchlon falls backward, using his momentum to pull the soldier off me. The soldier flops onto his back, but Luchlon doesn't let up, making the man's back arch as he pulls the soldier's head under water and holds it there. The soldier thrashes and flops while I sit on his chest to keep him from escaping. Then I collect his fallen lava gun and shoot it at the other oncoming soldier.

A shot from the lieutenant narrowly misses my head. She's still on the other side of the pool, but her aim is too good to ignore. Luchlon has lost his pulsar somewhere, and I only have the one lava gun to defend us with.

I jump up. Luchlon abandons the soldier, leaping out of the water, and we take off out of the cavern.

"I'm sorry, Fan," Luchlon shouts as we run.

I glance back at him, but I don't stop.

"I'm sorry I betrayed the crew," he explains between harried breaths.

"Yeah, yeah, don't do it again!" I shout over my shoulder. I can barely breathe. Every muscle is burning.

"How can I make it up to you?"

"We'll talk about it later," I wheeze. "We're kinda busy now."

My legs keep pumping up the stairs.

Chapter 38

Eshan'ya

I'M DRIPPING WET FROM swimming through the lake where we faced the first challenge. Pedders hasn't taken the plunge yet, his toes clutching the edge. He's hyperventilating.

Tika stands beside him, her hand resting on his back.

"You'll be fine," she says encouragingly. "I'll be right here with you."

Pedders doesn't respond. He clutches his lava gun tightly, and his free hand clenches and unclenches repeatedly.

"I'll take that for you." Tika gently takes the gun and slips it beside the pulsar on her belt even though it'll weigh her down more. Then she takes his hand in hers. "We'll do it together."

Pedders allows Tika to lead him into the water and while he splashes frantically, she tugs him across. The whites of Pedders' eyes are visible the whole way, Tika crooning reassurances. When they reach my side, I help Tika haul him out. He sits on the edge, struggling to catch his breath.

"Breathe, Pedders," Tika says soothingly. "You're safe now. You didn't drown."

His big hand thumps onto her shoulder. "*Xièxiè*, Tika."

"I'm sorry, but we have to keep moving." I reach to help him, but he stands with a grunt that tells me he can manage. Tika hands him his lava gun, and we take off at a fast pace.

We've gone several hundred yards and have heard no sounds of pursuit, which I should be happy about, but I'm worried for Fan. We haven't heard anything from her either. She could be dead.

Tika catches me looking over my shoulder and asks, "Should we go back and check on them?" Her eyes swim in unshed tears.

I shake my head and say between heavy breaths, "I want to, but we can't. We have to get this thing away from here." I raise the Device.

Pedders stops running. Tika and I stop a few steps later, turning back.

"You keep going," he says. "I'll go back."

He turns without waiting for an answer. I know there's no stopping him—not even the thought of that lake. I've already figured out he won't leave Fan to die. So I just keep going, and Tika tags along behind me. Pedders' footsteps fade away down the corridor.

"We'll get out of this mountain, and Ranate will bring the *Huxian Fox* to collect us and the others," I say, hoping to reassure both Tika and myself. It doesn't work. I don't even know how we can contact RAN-8. All our tech points were confiscated.

Finally, the path widens again, opening into the cave behind the waterfall. It appears darker than the man-made corridor because its vastness keeps the light of the flash plates from reaching the walls.

"Come on, Tika," I say as I charge through the opening.

The roar of the water seems deafening now. There are the three small waterfalls within the cave and the one massive one veiling the entrance outside. I edge forward, a bad feeling suddenly prickling the back of my neck. It's dark in here, and I can't hear anything over the water.

It's giving me the creeps.

I might be paranoid. The last time I was in this cave, I came face-to-face with Kriinal Braxt and found out he's Declan's brother. No wonder I'm creeped out.

But I trust my instincts and walk slowly past the waterfalls and the three half-sized obelisks.

Soon, the opening to the cave comes into view, the whiteness of the waterfall luminous behind it. This section of the cave is brighter, with daylight seeping through the water.

But I kind of wish it wasn't. I don't like what I see.

There are dozens of Quain soldiers. Dozens! And they're all pointing guns at us. I clutch the Device even tighter to my chest.

Tika is glued to my side. She raises her pulsar, but her body is trembling so much I doubt she can hit anything. I look everywhere for a means of escape. But there are too many of them; even if Pedders, Luchlon, and Fan were here, there's no way we could get through. Tika and I have no chance at all.

Or do we?

The weight of the Device feels heavy in my fingers. The blue and purple Shadé diamonds glow from within the barrel. I don't want to use it, but—

—one of the Quain soldiers steps toward us, her gun trained at my head.

I lift the Device and aim it at her.

She freezes.
And so do all the other Quain soldiers.

Chapter 39

Fan

THE ICICLE COURSE IS just ahead. The waterfall is still diverted, so it's safe to pass through on any of the paths as long as we don't slip into the void between them.

I can already hear the Quain racing after us. "Go ahead," I call to Luchlon. "I'm going to see if I can slow them down."

He does as I tell him while I find the ice block with my notches in it. I tuck my stolen lava gun into my pulsar holster. It's too big for it, and I have to squeeze it in, but it'd never fit into my duster's holster.

I climb the ice block, and just as I reach the stone beam and go to swing over the course, the lava gun slides out of the holster. I'm not quick enough, and it bounces off the ice block before disappearing in the blackness below. *At least it wasn't my duster.*

I go to the trough and wait. I don't need it to fill; I'm just waiting until the Quain have arrived, and then I'll tip it in the opposite direction and activate the course.

The wait isn't long. Kriinal Braxt and his remaining soldiers sprint around the bend in the corridor.

Damn, that soldier didn't drown.

"Stick to red, Luchlon!" I shout, just before smashing my foot against the trough. It groans as it slides back into the active position.

I see Luchlon leap to the red path just as the waterfall starts coming down again. He's almost out of the course, so he shouldn't have any problem going the rest of the way.

A scream from below gets cut off. The soldier didn't drown, but he's now frozen in solid ice—yellow light illuminates his face, forever trapped in a scream. I guess he was meant to die after all.

I hurry over the course, safe above it all. The lieutenant looks up and takes a shot, but it's nowhere near me, so I don't think she has the slightest idea where I am. Once I reach the other side, I swing down, landing on the first square of the red path, and leave the course without any problems.

The three Quain left are careful to keep to the red path, going slowly. They're halfway across, and they don't know how I stopped the challenge. If they don't figure it out, they'll have to keep dodging the blue and yellow platforms to stay alive. I've significantly slowed them down. Now we have a chance to get away.

And if we're really lucky, maybe Kriinal Braxt will make a deadly mistake and become a popsicle like Mr. Icebergman. They can be icy pals.

"See ya, buddy. Stay cool," I call to Mr. Icebergman as I follow Luchlon up the stairs to the first challenge. By the time I reach it, I still can't hear any pursuit from Braxt or the lieutenant. Maybe we've pulled it off after all. Hope surges through me.

Luchlon is standing at the edge of the lake, looking ill. After what he went through the first time around, I don't blame him.

"You'll be OK," I say. "We'll just swim across, and the course won't be activated."

He gulps visibly and nods after a pause. I pat him on the back and then dive in.

Geez, I'm pretty sick of water. How many waterfalls have I been under? How many pools and lakes have I swum? I've lost count. So much time in the water has made my fingertips pruney! I can't wait to dry out properly. In fact, I'll happily go sunbathing in the pink desert of Gerangan for a week after everything I've been through today.

I drag my wet, soggy body out the other side and turn to help Luchlon out. Just as he grabs my hand, the lieutenant arrives at the other side of the lake. Urgh, just our luck that she survived the icicle course.

She sees us and aims.

Bam! Bam!

I hit the ground before she takes off my head, Luchlon landing next to me with a squelch. *Blazin' rockets*, she must seriously have a problem with my face, based on the way she keeps trying to shoot it off.

"We have to stop meeting like this!" I shout across the lake.

The lieutenant replies with a guttural roar and a fresh volley of shots that keep Luchlon and me pinned to the ground. I cower, unable to move if I want to keep my head—which I do.

So much for getting out of this.

I crawl on my stomach with Luchlon beside me, trying to escape any way we can. A shot sizzles so close that I can feel the heat. I'm sure the next one will get me, and I throw my arms over my head.

That's when I hear yelling echoing down the corridor from the direction of the exit. A deep rumble, like thunder booming, resounds throughout the cave, sounding like a thousand men.

I would probably wet myself if I didn't recognize the voice.

I look up just in time to see Pedders careening around the corner, shouting menacingly as he does.

The lieutenant is stunned. Her eyes go wide with fear and, before she registers that it's only one guy, Pedders has let off a barrage of shots.

She flings herself to the floor but not before Pedders clips her shoulder—the same spot I got earlier. That's gotta hurt.

"Yeah!" I shout, jumping up. I pat Pedders on the back as I take off with Luchlon, leaving Pedders to bring up the rear. He runs backward, still wailing his battle cry and shooting as he does until the lake and the lieutenant are out of sight.

The three of us charge up the corridor toward the exit. I squint into the dimness as we pass the three internal waterfalls and the stumpy obelisks, then head toward the entrance of the cave. I hope RAN-8 is already there waiting for us with the *Huxian Fox*.

The sunlight spilling through the external waterfall brightens the cave and reveals a highly unexpected scene.

"What in the galaxy?" I mutter.

Scattered around the cave on ledges, steps, and rocks are several dozen Quain soldiers. Those damned soldiers from the ancient city. I should have known they were still around.

What is more unexpected is that none of them are moving. They're all stock still and staring. I follow their line of sight to find Eshan'ya, standing tall and threatening, regal even—she is unquestionably a princess—as she aims the Device at them.

At my words, she glances my way, then returns her stare to the Quain. "Glad you're OK," she says.

"You too," I respond. "Looks like you've got this handled, so let's get out of here, all right?"

She nods and then calls to the soldiers, "Clear a path."

They look at each other briefly, as if wondering whether or not they should obey, but when Eshan'ya aggressively shakes the Device, they move. They're slow about it, cautiously stepping backward or to the side, but they allow us to pass.

We inch forward as the silent sea of Quain soldiers parts. The only sound is the shuffling of boots as they back away. All of us are together again: Eshan'ya in the lead with the Device, Tika close on her heels, then me and Luchlon with nothing but our fists, and Pedders bringing up the rear with a lava gun.

"Hang on a second," I say as I run back to the waterfall, where the third key was supposed to be. Despite the fact I don't have a weapon, the Quain back out of my way.

"What are you doing?" Luchlon calls.

I skid to a stop in front of my pile of discarded clothes and weapons. "I need my stuff," I call back.

"Just leave it," Eshan'ya says. "I'll replace them later."

I shrug on my jacket, slide on my boots, and holster my pulsar gun. I snatch up my duster, give it a quick kiss, then polish the lip marks off the steel barrel.

"This duster is my favorite," I yell. "And this jacket is cool." I tug the hem of the jacket as proof.

"Don't let them leave!" Kriinal Braxt's voice booms out through the cave, interrupting my fashion show.

Seriously, he has to show up *just* when we were about to make our escape?

A few of the soldiers start to move, but Eshan'ya yells, "Don't you dare," in a voice so unnerving that even *I'm* scared. It kinda turns me on. They all freeze again, except for Braxt and the lieutenant, who appear out the dark side of the cave.

"Get her!" he yells, pointing up at Eshan'ya, Quain all around her. When no one moves, he continues to shout, "If she was going to use it, she would have already."

"Oh, I'll use it." Eshan'ya swings the Device around and points it straight at Kriinal Braxt.

His eyes are black with rage as he stares at her, but he doesn't stop. He and I are the only ones moving now, and we're both moving toward Eshan'ya. If she doesn't shoot him, he's going to get to her first.

"Don't tempt me, Braxt," she says. "You won't survive this. You know you won't."

He's not perturbed by her threats. He keeps walking, slow and casual, like he's out for a leisurely stroll. But his stare is hard and locked on Eshan'ya.

"Last chance," she says.

When he doesn't stop, her demeanor changes. Her eyes narrow, a searing blue flame burning in her stare. Her fingers shift to the trigger. There's a look of determination on her face that wasn't there before.

Finally, Braxt realizes his error. He hesitates midstride, his leg in the air. His face drains of color, but it's too late. His foot hits the ground, and as the sound rings out through the cave, Eshan'ya pulls the trigger.

Chapter 40

Eshan'ya

Nothing happens.

Nothing.

Not a whir of noise, not even the click of the trigger. No lights, no energy, no powerful stream of electricity to kill Kriinal Braxt.

No one moves as I glance hopelessly down at the Device. Then I pull the trigger a second time.

Nothing. Still.

What the stars?

Braxt's mouth twists in a cruel smile.

No.

Chapter 41

Fan

Eshan'ya actually had the guts to pull the trigger, which is more shocking than what happens next. The stupid Device we've chased across the galaxy and almost died for, the Device that is supposed to give ultimate power to the person who possesses it—yeah, that Device—doesn't frickin' work.

I lift my duster and shoot. A soldier falls. And suddenly, everyone is moving at once.

"Go, go, go!" I scream. I reach Eshan'ya and tug at her arm to make her move. She's still staring at the defective Device, but at my touch she comes to life.

I draw my pulsar with my left, hold my duster in the right, and shoot with both guns. We only have a few yards to go to get out of this cave, and only a handful of Quain soldiers stand between us and freedom. The rest moved out of the way when they thought the Device was going to annihilate them.

The problem is now the rest are closing in on us.

This part of the cave has stalagmites growing upward—the only shelter from the shooting. I vault behind one, and Eshan'ya follows with the Device. I peek out around it to see that the rest of my crew has done the same, finding their own cover.

As I shoot, Eshan'ya snarls, "You had to get that stupid jacket, didn't you?"

"What?" I frown as I flatten myself against the stalagmite so I don't lose my head—it's not just the lieutenant aiming for it now.

"You realize we wouldn't be in this position if you didn't *have* to go back and get that damned jacket?"

"I like this jacket," I say, rising and shooting. A Quain soldier goes down.

"We could have gotten you a new one."

"But this one's worn in. It's comfortable," I protest, indignant. "And besides, my duster isn't replaceable. It's one of a kind from ancient Earth. Vintage." I glance back when she doesn't say anything else, but she doesn't look impressed. "Come on, *Your Highness*, you know it wouldn't have made a difference."

Her snort sounds like one of Pedders' grunts. They've been hanging out together a little too much.

"The only thing that would have made a difference is if that Device worked." Another Quain soldier drops. Only fifty million to go, or at least that's how it feels.

She looks down at the Device cradled in her hands. "I don't understand," she says. "It should have worked."

"Well, if it's broken, at least Kriinal Braxt won't be able to use it to take over the galaxy." I shrug.

"You can't be that naive. He'll find a way to operate it; I must be missing something. Mark my words, if Kriinal Braxt gets a hold of this Device, I know he'll find a way to use it. We need to destroy it."

Another Quain soldier falls.

"OK, so we still need to keep it away from him?"

"That's right," she says as she peers over my shoulder, "and we need a plan quick. Those soldiers are getting awfully close."

She's right. They're closing in. There's just too many of them and too much firepower. I shoot one down, and another steps into place.

"Take my pulsar and give me the Device." I hold out the gun.

We perform the exchange, Eshan'ya giving me a raised eyebrow.

"I'll draw them away."

Chapter 42

Eshan'ya

With a wink, Fan is gone before I can stop her. She's going to get herself killed.

I stomp my foot in frustration, not just because we're going to fail, but because I don't want Fan to die. I wasn't supposed to have feelings for her. It's not supposed to matter if she dies, or if I die, as long as we stop Kriinal Braxt—that's what is important. I should be able to trade one life for the billions of those we'd save.

But my heart is already cracking at the thought of a universe without her vibrant, brave soul in it.

"Don't die." I send a prayer to the stars with a quick squeeze of my eyes.

She's running pretty fast with the Device under her arm; maybe I shouldn't write her off just yet.

Just as hope blossoms, it's thwarted by two Quain soldiers who leap out and tackle Fan to the ground.

"No!" I scream. I pull up the pulsar gun and start shooting. I'm a terrible shot, but I just keep shooting, hoping to hit anything, and with so many Quain soldiers, it's not hard to injure one or two of them.

Fan isn't finished, though. She twists under the soldiers and—with a bang—one of them dies. Blood smears across the stone as the soldier slips off her. Then she raises the Device and, with a shout at Pedders, she lobs it to him.

Pedders is surrounded by soldiers, but he leaps into the air, using one soldier as leverage to get more height, his feet running up their back and pushing off their shoulder. He catches the Device one-handed and comes crashing back down before anyone can shoot him. His weight flattens a soldier, who groans in pain.

He does it so quickly the soldiers are disoriented. Before they get it together, Pedders has already jumped to his feet, shooting as he does, and hightails it out of there. He's like a raging bull. The Device looks half its size squeezed under Pedders' elbow. He lowers his head and charges, knocking the Quain out of the way like they're virtual bowling pins.

I keep shooting as I back toward the exit. But, just as Fan predicted, the Quain are drawn away, most of them chasing Pedders and the Device.

He's forced to take a circuitous route to avoid being shot or overrun by Quain soldiers, so when I reach the cave exit, Pedders is still several yards away.

Tika is already at the exit, hiding just beyond the veil of water in the sunlight.

"Your Majesty!" she cries when she sees me. "You're still alive. You don't know how happy that makes me."

"You too, Tika." I give her a tight smile as we both shoot into the crowd of Quain soldiers.

"You'll be pleased to know I've contacted Ranate on the *Huxian Fox*. He's on his way."

"How? Your tech point was confiscated," I ask.

"I'm a mechanic." She shrugs. "I always have spare stuff on me. I have couplings and bolts in this pocket."

"Well done, Tika," I say over my shoulder, glimpsing her grin.

Inside the cave, Pedders is being overrun by the soldiers. He hurls the Device over their heads and shoots a handful of them while they watch the weapon fly.

Across the cave, Luchlon catches the Device, and the chase continues. Quain soldiers fling themselves at him as he runs, dodging left and right to avoid being caught or shot. Given that he originally tried helping the Quain, he's doing a great job at hindering them.

That's until the lieutenant pops up right in front of him, holding her gun in his face. He skids to a stop as he stares down the barrel. She holds out her hand, a triumphant smile on her face. He lifts it out from under his armpit—the coward is going to save his own hide and give her the Device.

But just as my hatred flares, he holds the Device out to his right instead.

Fan swoops in and snatches it out of his hand.

Luchlon ducks just in time to avoid the blast the lieutenant lets off, and then he runs toward me and the exit. His lips curled in a smirk.

Fan isn't running to the exit, though—she's running straight at the waterfall that hides the entrance to the cave. And she's not stopping.

Her legs take lengthy strides. No one is going to catch her. She's running too fast for them. Her mop of hair is flattened against her head she's going so fast.

She takes three long strides to the lip of the cave and leaps.

Chapter 43

Fan

"FAN!" I HEAR ESHAN'YA'S desperate scream just as I leap. She *does* care about me, after all.

I grin as I fall.

But I don't fall far.

Chapter 44

Eshan'ya

Just as she leaps from the lip of the cave, Braxt steps out from behind a tall stalagmite and grabs the Device. Now Fan hangs suspended from it, her knuckles white. Her heels dangle over the edge of the cliff.

"Let go," Braxt growls.

"Never," she says. I'm sure she's just trying to look brave or she's being stubborn. Surely she can't think she still has a chance.

"Fine," Braxt says with a sneer.

He bends his knees, dropping into a fighting stance on his toes, and then his leg shoots out to deliver a roundhouse kick. His form and the power behind his kick show he's had plenty of training. There's an unexpected grace in his movement, and it hides the sheer strength that propels his foot forward until it hits Fan square in the chest. The force is so great that she's flung back, her arms and legs stretched wide, suspended for a moment in the air, before she vanishes into the waterfall.

She had no chance; there's no way she could hold on after that blow.

All that remains is Braxt, standing at the edge of the waterfall with the Device. He holds it close like it's a treasured infant. His eyes widened in awe.

I move toward him, lifting my pulsar.

But an arm blocks me. It's Pedders.

"We've lost," he says, his eyes drooping in sadness and resignation. "Our only chance for survival is if we leave now."

Still, I hesitate. Every nerve in my body is pulling me to Kriinal Braxt. I want to kill him. I *need* to kill him. He has the Device. But what's worse is that he killed Fan.

"Eshan'ya." It's Luchlon who breaks into my vengeful trance. "We have to go."

I look around. The Quain are all watching Kriinal Braxt. Even the lieutenant. This is our only chance to escape before he figures out how to use the Device and executes us.

"Right," I say, letting them drag me out of the cave.

The brightness of the day blinds me, and I almost fall down the stairs that run alongside the waterfall. Luchlon catches me, keeping me steady until I find my feet.

We don't need to run very far. Abruptly, the bright pink underbelly of the *Huxian Fox* cuts into the light, and I see the hatch opening just below me. Tika leaps onto the ramp, then it's my turn, then Pedders and Luchlon.

I glance up at the cave entrance before the hatch closes.

Kriinal Braxt stands at the cave opening, watching us. His black uniform makes him a deadly silhouette against the waterfall. He holds the Device in both his hands. He doesn't aim it or pull the trigger. He just holds it like a trophy as he watches us go.

I shiver. This is the image of my failure. Until the day I die, I'll never forget that evil satisfied grin on Kriinal Braxt's face, the face that looks so much like Declan's, except that Declan would never smile like that.

Chapter 45

Fan

Booming assaults my ears. Pounding thunders all around me. Water rushes up my nose, clogs my throat, fills my mouth. I breathe in, but my lungs fill with water instead of air.

My limbs are pulled left and right.

Light bursts across my vision, briefly there and then gone.

Bubbles. So many bubbles.

I'm in water *again*! Really?

Hasn't the universe thrown enough water at me today? Obviously not, because here I am drowning, being pushed further and further under by the large waterfall. My whole body aches with each ton of water punching into me. It hurts to move. So I don't. I just let the water move me, shoving me into its darker depths. I let it engulf me—the darkness, the water, the cold.

I sink.

My waterlogged lungs burn, my vision darkens, and my limbs become water itself—elastic and flowing.

Eshan'ya's face floats into my mind with the bubbles. Her bright blue eyes, the jut of her chin, her jaw set. She's judging me. She's judging me for allowing myself to drown.

Leave me alone, I'm tired.

She continues to stare, disappointment clear on her face. I have given up, and she never expected me to do that. Yeah, she always believed I was reckless...foolhardy...a no-good scoundrel. But she never thought I would quit.

My fingers twitch in the water like a jolt of electricity has shot through them. I blink, squinting through the bubbles. I'm facing upward, and the light of the day seems a very long way away. My arms jump into action.

I draw myself out from beneath the pounding waterfall and into the current of the river. Without the pressure beating me down, I can swim up toward that distant light.

I push with my legs, kicking furiously, and pull down with my arms. My energy wanes. The light seems further away than ever. I'm starting to black out.

With the last of my strength—*father's fist*—I thrash my legs.

Warmth hits my skin as I burst through the surface. I gasp for air, spluttering and coughing up water.

I'm sucked back under, drawn down the river by the current. I hurtle over rocks, getting bashed and bruised as I go. Once more, I lurch upward, gasping for air. Despite swallowing more water, somehow air enters my lungs. Sweet, glorious air.

I roll onto my back, spreading my arms and legs like a starfish and allowing the water to drag me along while I take breath after breath. Water burbles in my ears and bubbles across my skin as I float along. I slowly regain some strength, even if most of it has seeped from me and into the river.

My eyes slit against the sun. I can just make out the silhouette of trees leaning over the river. When they disappear, my eyes open wider to see where I am. Lyran.

The three obelisks stand a few dozen yards inland, the city beyond them. And at the river's edge are long wide steps that lead right into the water. I paddle across to them and drag my sore, battered body onto dry land.

Images of the warm pink sands of Gerangan flash through my memory, and I long for them now even more than I had earlier. Get me far from any more waterfalls. At least I'm out of the water for now.

I lay across the steps, stretched out like a lizard, soaking up the sun and drying in the warmth of the day. My chest heaves up and down as my lungs gratefully take in as much air as possible.

It's several minutes before my strength has returned enough for my brain to access basic functions. I take in my surroundings properly.

I'm at the entrance to Lyran. Moss grows in the corners of the steps, and wildflowers pop up through the white stone that paves the way to the obelisks and the front gate of the city. Birds chirp in the nearby trees, and the river gurgles at my feet. It sounds peaceful now that I'm not drowning in it.

There's not a soul around.

It's a relief not to see the black uniforms of the Quain, looking like roaches crawling everywhere. But it's a bit of a problem that I'm stuck in a deserted ancient city miles from the nearest civilization and no way to get there.

There's no tech point on my finger. I pat myself down, taking stock of my injuries and possessions. The small canister of shinver is no longer in my pocket—I suspect there's going to be some nasty withdrawals in my future. Luckily, my duster is still holstered to my leg.

Fiery balls, I've got no way to call for help, and that's assuming anyone is still alive to help me.

My thoughts turn to Eshan'ya, Pedders, and the rest of my crew as I pull myself into a sitting position and lounge on the stairs, staring out at the river and the forest beyond.

Pedders was incredible, charging through all those Quain soldiers, knocking them away as if they were flies. Eshan'ya wasn't too bad of a shot in the end. I saw her wipe out a few of the Quain. And Luchlon certainly pulled through. I'm glad I saved him—hopefully it wasn't so he'd just die a few hours later. He's still got a lot of groveling to do. Even Tika impressed me during the fight. OK, so she didn't shoot anyone, but she tried her best.

I look up at the sky, hoping to see RAN-8 and the *Huxian Fox*—my beautiful ship. She's always been so trustworthy. I even miss her pink underbelly, although I can't wait to paint over it if I ever see her again.

With a huff, I flop backward to contemplate living the life of a hermit within the streets of Lyran, hunting for food in the surrounding forest and figuring out how to build a fire without a multitool to light it. My jacket flops open when I fling my arms out, and I hear a soft clunk as something plastic hits the stone. I glance over and see my tech point laying there. My shirt pocket has torn, and the tech point rolled out of it. I forgot I hid it there.

It rolls on the stone until my brain catches up with what it means. I can call RAN-8.

I snatch it up, blowing the water off its face and shaking it dry. Then I press the button and talk into it. "Ranate. Ranate, do you copy?"

There's silence on the other end. Maybe it was beaten up too much in the fight.

I try again, "Ranate, Rana—"

I'm interrupted by an excited, high-pitched squeal coming through the line. "Captain. Captain, you're alive? We all thought you were dead. How did you survive that fall down the waterfall? You can't be alive, you can't be."

I chuckle at Tika's shrill voice. "I can assure you, I'm alive."

"She's alive, she's alive!" I hear her yell to the others, and cheering follows. There's some scuffling and a gruff, "Give me that," before Pedders comes on the line.

"Where are you?" he asks, his familiar deep voice even deeper with emotion.

"I washed up at the entrance to Lyran."

"Stay put." The line goes dead.

I lay back again, soaking up the sun and letting it dry me out as a smile spreads across my face. My crew is alive, and I don't have to become a savage.

Chapter 46

Eshan'ya

PEDDERS LOWERS THE HATCH as we descend upon Lyran. There she is, leaning casually against an obelisk like she's having a normal day. Cool and collected. She grins as the *Fox* settles.

My pulse stutters when our eyes meet. She's not dead. *Fan is not dead.* No, she's very much alive. She has that confident—*arrogant*—smile. Those strong legs that her trousers cling to in all the right places. That stupid gray jacket that she went back to get in the cave, which, I hate to admit, *does* look good on her.

She runs a hand through her coif of short hair and then hooks her fingers into her belt as she saunters over.

"Nice of you to stop your joyride in my ship." She smirks. "Did you forget you have a captain?"

Pedders snorts.

"We kinda thought you were dead," Luchlon says with a smiling lilt, jokingly defensive.

"We would never forget you," Tika says seriously. "I'm so sorry, Captain."

"Tika, Tika." Fan waves her hands, trying to calm her down. "I'm only joking."

"Oh? Oh!" Tika's hand flies to her heart like it's failing, while Fan keeps talking.

"Thanks for coming back for me, though."

By now, Fan has reached the top of the ramp. She pats Tika on the back and tips an imaginary cap to RAN-8 in greeting as she ambles into the hold. She gives Pedders a brief hug and then shakes hands with Luchlon, though she gives him a scowl and says, "You still owe me." She looks at home, relaxed, despite the day she's had. It's admirable and frustrating at the same time. How can she be so nonchalant when we've just lost to the worst person in the galaxy?

"Just so you know, while you went for a swim, we lost the Device," I snap.

Fan spins around, her eyebrows raised. "Went for a swim? A swim? And I guess falling down a sixty-foot waterfall is just a leisurely dive?" Her mouth twists into what could be a smile or a grimace, I'm not sure, but she certainly seems to get some enjoyment out of annoying me. "Look here, princess, you're the one who got us into this mess in the first place. If you had only known *you* were the third key instead of making us run around all of that crumbling city—"

"Crumbling city! Lyran is a beautiful ancient metropolis."

"Yes, crumbling. I'm sure it was nice for you to run around your old home, but it wasn't much fun for us. Especially once the Quain showed up." She gestures to her crew, who all look at their feet. "What a hoot that was."

"How was I supposed to know I was the key?" I scowl at her.

"Uh, maybe because you grew up here? Why didn't your Protectors tell you? If that Declan loved you so much, why didn't he tell you?"

I step back like she slapped me. It was a shot below the belt, and Fan knows it. Her eyes drop to the ground along with her crew's. I don't know why Declan never told me. Did he think he was protecting me? Or did he not think he could trust me?

I take a deep breath to answer, but Fan speaks before I get the chance. "I'm sorry Braxt got the Device," she says in the smallest voice I've ever heard her use.

"It's not your fault." I sigh.

"What do we do now?" Tika asks.

All eyes turn to me. But I don't have an answer for them. My mouth opens and closes without words.

"We regroup and then figure out how to get the Device back," Fan says. She shrugs when I look at her, my eyes wide and questioning. "We've broken into Quain headquarters before..."

She lets us fill in the rest with our own thoughts. Yes, we've broken in before, but can we do it again? We almost died the last time, and I can no longer pretend I'm the lieutenant. They won't fall for that again. The Device will be more heavily guarded than anything else in Kriinal Braxt's collection, and he might just use the Device on us.

But there's a wild determination in Fan's eyes, like she'll never be beaten. It fills me with a strange hope that almost has me believing she's invincible. Hope surges.

The others mumble their agreement, but Fan's eyes are only on me, waiting.

Slowly, I nod.

"Alrighty then." Fan's face splits into a grin. "Let's get back to work, people."

Help Fan and the Huxian Fox crew

Did you enjoy The Huxian Fox? Please consider leaving a review.

Reviews help books reach more readers. By the stars, please help keep the *Huxian Fox* crew alive by leaving a review on Goodreads, Amazon, or the digital storefront of your choosing. Fan throws you a fist bump in thanks.

Note: Reviews are incredibly important for indie authors, helping them reach new readers and sustain their livelihoods. What's cool is that writing a review is a simple and free way to support the authors you enjoy. Every review counts and it doesn't need to be long; one sentence is enough unless you feel the urge to write more. It can be as simple as, "I loved this book." So if you have the time to leave a review, I will forever be grateful.

Acknowledgements

The grand hurrah of thanks goes to my sister Krystie. This dirt grinder continues to be my alpha reader, amateur editor, cheerleader, sounding board, counsellor (on several occasions), the first person I call with good news (or bad news), and my bestfriend.

Big thanks to my editors at Intrepid Literary, Ariane Peveto, Brian Palmer, Jackie Peveto, and Lauren Taylor Shute. You made sure this manuscript isn't an enormous pile of redrynch dung.

I thank the stars for space scum Justin Ho, for his insights on Chinese characters and culture, and Emily Wang for her help with Chinese words. Any errors are my own.

To the biggest dirt grinder on Earth, Matthew Lin, who somehow pulled together the most galactically incredible cover in record time. You are a legend!

Forever grateful for my amazing Life Coach and NLP practitioner Dr. Kim Brown, who told me to drop a Y chromosome, suck it up, and write! Just not in those words.

Big thanks to Fan Yang for letting me use her given name—who is not a drug smuggler or addict (as far as I know), but is a kick-ass woman.

Thanks to these supportive crud dwellers, Shaz, Jill, Alice, Monique, Petula, Katherine, Carina, Sarah, Jimmy, the "It's 5 O'clock somewhere" crew, Elise, Alexandra, & Patrick, and the #NoJudgement girls, Nicole, Susan, & Michelle. My work colleagues at my day job. My family, especially my Mum and Dad (Gill & Rick), my brother, Trent, and my sister-in-law, Kosoma. All have supported me in many ways, whether it was reading my book, boosting my confidence, or being an ear when I needed to vent.

Osiris and Apollo, my little mythological gods and complete bum smears, thank you for being my writing companions, making me laugh with your crazy antics, and always being available for pats.

My blazin' rockets beta readers who were among the first to read the book, Bree, Michelle, Tracey C, Tracey M, Eliana, Dom, Iman, Chioma, Nicolle, Lucy, Marie-Louise, Natasha, Sisinyana, Gano, Garnet, Elvida, Shané, Ashisha, Amanda, Lucy-Sarah, and Jessica: Thank you! Fiery balls, you had to put up with typos and poor character arcs to help shape this into something great.

Thank you to the supportive community on bookstagram, booktok, and other platforms. For all the mudholes who has shared, liked, and commented on my posts to show their support. I am so very grateful.

Stars above, the biggest thanks goes to you, my reader. By broken hearts, you're the reason I do any of this. Thank you for taking a chance on me and the *Huxian Fox* crew.

About the author

Nikki Brooke is an Aussie sci-fi and fantasy author, scriptwriter, and champion of bisexual representation—because the world needs more bi heroes! She believes stories are better with a little chaos, a lot of heart, and characters who aren't afraid to break the mould (or the universe). She writes the kind of books she always wanted to read growing up—where queerness is celebrated, the stakes are high, and the adventure is anything but ordinary.

Her debut novel Plagued Lands (2024) made a splash, becoming an Aurealis Awards finalist for Best Young Adult Novel, winning first place in The BookFest's Dystopian and YA Dystopian categories, snagging a Golden Wizard Book Prize, and earning five shiny stars from Readers' Favorite. The Huxian Fox (2025) is already racking up its own credentials as a finalist in the Launch Pad Prose Competition, a semi-finalist in the ScreenCraft Cinematic Book Writing Competition, shortlisted for Adaptable by Queensland Writers Centre, and was #1 Sci-Fi Book/Manuscript on Coverfly's Red List.

Nikki grew up in Melbourne but has lived in London (UK) and Austin TX (USA), before boomeranging back home, where she now lives with two dogs named Osiris and Apollo. Yes, like the gods. Yes, they know it. Yes, they act accordingly. When she's not writing or refereeing divine dog drama, Nikki enjoys swimming, dancing, drawing, and having grand travel adventures—all of which eventually end up in her stories.

Follow @nikkibrookeauthor on facebook, instagram or tiktok for regular updates. Subscribe to Nikki's newsletter so you don't miss any news. Join at nikkibrooke.com/newsletter

FREE Short Story

Get your FREE
story here:

Get a free short story here:
https://mailchi.mp/nikkibrooke.com/the-snow-globe

We're looking for dirt grinders to join the *Huxian Fox!!*
Are you a mechanic? A weapons expert? Can you kick butt? Have some other skill? Then we want you!!
Sign up to the newsletter for more news!

nikkibrooke.com/newsletter

@nikkibrookeauthor

Get updates about the sequels to The Huxian Fox, behind-the-scenes content, competitions, and games.

www.ingramcontent.com/pod-product-compliance
Lightning Source LLC
Chambersburg PA
CBHW030556170726
48283CB00002B/352